W9-ARY-116

"You are so soft."

He shook his head. "So incredibly soft." His eyes were half-closed, but his touch was warm and intimate as his fingers explored the front of her throat.

He didn't open his eyes until he felt her nervous swallow, and when he did, he was smiling dreamily. "Katepalmer," he said, savoring the syllables of her name in that unique way of his. "I'm afraid I've totally forgotten what we were talking about."

"So have I," she whispered.

She felt strangely separated from herself or from the usual person who was Kate Palmer. That Kate Palmer was watching in disbelief as this one sat next to Nick Capstein, bathed in golden firelight....

Dear Reader,

Spellbinders! That's what we're striving for. The editors at Silhouette are determined to capture your imagination and win your heart with every single book we publish. Each month, six Special Editions are chosen with *you* in mind.

Our authors are our inspiration. Writers such as Nora Roberts, Tracy Sinclair, Kathleen Eagle, Carole Halston and Linda Howard—to name but a few—are masters at creating endearing characters and heartrending love stories. Their characters are everyday people—just like you and me—whose lives have been touched by love, whose dreams and desires suddenly come true!

So find a cozy, quiet place to read, and create your own special moment with a Silhouette Special Edition.

Sincerely,

The Editors
SILHOUETTE BOOKS

JILLIAN BLAKE
A Vision to Share

Silhouette Special Edition

Published by Silhouette Books New York

America's Publisher of Contemporary Romance

SILHOUETTE BOOKS
300 East 42nd St., New York, N.Y. 10017

Copyright © 1987 by Jillian Blake

All rights reserved, including the right to reproduce
this book or portions thereof in any form whatsoever.
For information address Silhouette Books,
300 East 42nd St., New York, N.Y. 10017

ISBN: 0-373-09399-3

First Silhouette Books printing August 1987

All the characters in this book are fictitious. Any
resemblance to actual persons, living or dead, is
purely coincidental.

SILHOUETTE, SILHOUETTE SPECIAL EDITION and colophon
are registered trademarks of the publisher.

America's Publisher of Contemporary Romance

Printed in the U.S.A.

Books by Jillian Blake

Silhouette Intimate Moments

Diana's Folly #27
East Side, West Side #67

Silhouette Special Edition

Water Dancer #256
Heatstroke #299
Sullivan vs. Sullivan #323
A Vision to Share #399

JILLIAN BLAKE

is a voracious consumer of all types of fiction from the ridiculous to the sublime. Lately, it seems she's been finding something to write about in everything she sees and does. An ex-dancer with a five-year-old daughter and a husband who is a dedicated jazz musician, Jillian leads a busy and happy life in Cambridge, Massachusetts.

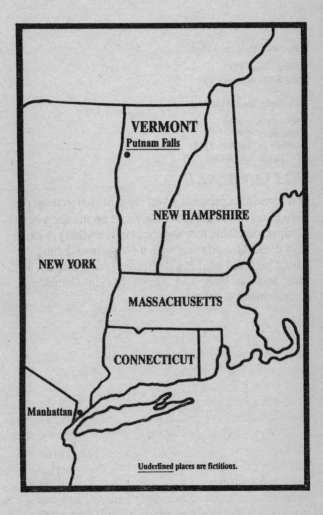

VERMONT
Putnam Falls

NEW HAMPSHIRE

NEW YORK

MASSACHUSETTS

CONNECTICUT

Manhattan

Underlined places are fictitious.

Chapter One

Kate Palmer could barely stay awake. The sunlight played a coy game of hide-and-seek with the bare tree branches, creating an intricate lacy pattern of light and shadow that dazzled her eyes, making them feel heavy, overloaded. The early-April sun was weak, but it pressed against the tinted blue glass of the Greyhound bus and infused her with a drowsy warmth. Even the drone of the engine conspired to rob her of consciousness.

But Kate had already been on the bus for four hours without succumbing to the urge to nap, and she didn't want to fall asleep now. Less than an hour remained before her scheduled arrival in Putnam Falls, Vermont, and she knew she would be sluggish and disoriented if she slept now. Business trips were hard enough without having to operate at such a disadvantage. Kate was a woman who enjoyed her daily routine, and having to settle herself into a new place, even if just a few days, required a lot of effort. She needed to be alert in order to cope with all the little details that were bound to come up, such as finding the inn where she had booked a room, getting around town without a car and making the necessary contacts to get her work done.

So, in order to pass the time and stay alert, she played a little game with herself. She memorized every road-side sign for ten miles and then, shutting her eyes, repeated each one back to herself verbatim, in the order in which they had appeared. It was a habit she frequently indulged in when she had time to pass and wanted to avoid the enervating effects of daydreaming.

Kate had a photographic memory. By looking at an object without blinking for a moment or two, she could imprint it on some mysterious portion of her brain that seemed to work with all the precision of a fine camera. Then, when she had collected all the images she wanted, she had only to close her eyes for those images to be played back before her as if they had been carefully edited onto a single clear piece of film. It was exactly like a silent movie, except that she could slow down the action or move at will from one image to another and back again.

Friends told her her ability to reproduce images so perfectly was eerie. Her old boyfriend, Carl Masters, with whom she had pursued an on-again, off-again relationship for nearly four years, had actively disliked it about her, declaring it made him uncomfortable. As a matter of fact, Kate's frequent state of dreamy distraction had been one of the reasons for her recent final break with Carl, and one of the reasons she blamed herself for the failure of their relationship.

But she could no more have changed her photographic eye than she could have changed the shape of her longish nose: both had been constants in her life ever since she could remember. She had always been a dreamy child, given to staring out the window in class and quietly cataloging things such as the cars driving by or the tiles on the ceiling rather than paying attention to her work. Fortunately, she'd been able to put her special talent to use when the teacher called on her, reciting lines perfectly from her textbook without thinking about what they meant.

Not until she was older had Kate been able to turn her incredible eye for pattern and detail into a talent for design and illustration, but again, she tended to think of her ability as quite natural and, as such, unworthy of special attention. It was simply what she did, and she counted herself lucky that she could do it well enough to make a living at it. Simmond's, the large New York auction house where Kate had worked as catalog illustrator for the past four years, seemed to agree with this humble assessment of her professional worth, which was why she was in a Greyhound bus on their behalf instead of on an Air New England flight to her destination.

Simmond's was sending her to Putnam Falls to do the illustrations on a group of Early American furniture they were in the process of acquiring from a large estate sale in the area. A public auction was to be held the following day, and Kate's assignment was to sit on the sidelines and sketch the pieces while Simmond's agents did the bidding. She rarely fraternized with the sale agents, whose extraordinary energy she found distracting to her work. For their part, the agents tended to ignore Kate unless there was a dispute about a particular object, at which point she would be summoned in like Blind Justice to settle the debate with her camera eye.

Rapid Shave, Ken's Pancake House, Valvoline Motor Oil...the wooden signs flipped before her closed eyes with rhythmic precision. She could almost feel the rough grain of the wood on which they had been written, and the peeling paint was so real that she felt she could reach out and pull off a faded swatch. No fancy papered billboards out here, just as there were no glitzy shopping centers or skyscrapers. Kate was enough of a New Yorker to notice their absence, and enough of an artist to appreciate what stood in their place. Weathered houses, faded to an indeterminate off-white, stood tall and angular like the bony silhouettes of the trees that surrounded them. An occasional trailer, surrounded by old cars up on concrete blocks, and the infrequent A-frame vacation house only added to the quirky charm of the central Vermont countryside.

Kate opened her eyes again. What she should really be doing was sketching what she saw. Landscapes always held a special fascination for her, with all the depth and life they seemed to encompass within their physical boundaries. Kate loved to conjure an image of a house and then fill it with imaginary people, giving them personalities that seemed to fit the building she saw so clearly and knew so well. She often thought of painting what she saw but was wary of putting fictional layers over her clear-as-glass perspective. Illustration, she knew, was a far cry from the creation of an imaginary reality. One was craft, the other art. And, as Carl had often reminded her, she was a craftsman, not an artist. Kate repressed a bitter welling in her throat at the memory of Carl, a classical violinist who had left New York to take a job with the Berlin Symphony. There was no reason to blame him for her attitude about her drawing. After all, he was probably right.

Still, Kate's conjuring trick was a pleasant adjunct to the seeing game, and it gave her a nice cozy feeling to play it as the bus sped through the deepening lavender dusk. That lumbering old farmhouse, for example, with the tall windows that seemed to list to one side and the yellow light filtering out through what had to be the kitchen window—who lived in that house? What were they doing right now? Did they look up as the Greyhound thundered past and wonder, even briefly, who was riding on it and where they were going?

Kate closed her eyes and found herself mentally sketching the inhabitants, seeing them as clearly as she saw the house itself printed on the reflective screen of her brain. A family sat at the oilcloth-covered table, and they were laughing gently at some joke while they ladled food from heaping platters. The father was tall and revealed remarkable warm brown eyes as he nodded at his wife to pass the mashed potatoes. He had smile lines around his generous mouth and looked as if he were a good father as well as a loving husband....

Kate chided herself scornfully. Who was she kidding? The image she had conjured was a fake, a Norman Rockwell reproduction—it came full-blown from someone else's imagination, not her own. Men were much more likely to resemble Carl or her own father, who never seemed to have time to even nod in her direction, much less smile lovingly. She had better stick to illustrating what she saw and stop trying to imagine what she wished she saw. Creating realities from illusion was not her forte.

Kate realized with a start that they had entered a town. It came up quite suddenly—first there was just one house, then there was a cluster of homes, all slightly rundown but looking warm and hospitable. Then the bus slowed down and turned, and Kate saw a neat row of houses, all newly painted in quaint color combinations and obviously in good shape. A few had storefronts at street level. Up ahead, a large dark oval signified the town green, and the bus pulled around this and came to a halt in front of a small general store.

Kate roused herself, having fallen into a daydream state somewhere between sleep and wakefulness. She blinked, ran her hand absently through her straight dark hair to pull it back off her high forehead and tugged at the plaid wool skirt so that it fell in neat pleats to her calves. Then she gathered up her pocketbook, her duffel and her large bag of drawing supplies and made her way to the front of the bus.

As soon as she got to the door she realized, from the blast of chill air that greeted her, that she had left her coat folded up in the rack over her seat. She went back to retrieve it and then made her way down the aisle again, feeling awkwardly encumbered. She was the only person getting off in Putnam Falls, and she sensed the eyes of the few other passengers as they watched her struggle. No one made a move to help, and she would have refused it if they had. This was one of those coping situations Kate disliked but forced herself to handle because it was expected of her. She expected it of herself.

At last she was clear of the bus, which started up impatiently at her back and pulled away in a cloud of dirty exhaust. She stood on the porch of the general store to get her bearings. She saw no sign of the Stonecroft Inn, the evening's final destination. There was, in fact, no sign of any other inhabited place besides the general store and a tavern a few doors down. Dusk was not even a memory; pitch-black night had fallen with the abruptness of a heavy curtain.

Kate took a deep breath and entered the store, reminding herself that she was hardly stranded in the wilderness. This was simply a small town in Vermont, and at worst she would have to walk a ways to get to the inn. After all, every place in the world wasn't as compactly navigable as New York, and New York was probably just as intimidating to Vermonters as Vermont was to Kate, a lifelong Manhattanite. With this vaguely encouraging thought in mind, she approached the woman who sat behind the counter.

"Good evening!" she said, smiling brightly.

The woman, who did not appear to have taken notice of Kate's arrival, nodded briefly and went back to perusing the newspaper spread out before her on the wooden counter. Kate could not help cataloging the dizzying array of bottles, jars and tins that were ranged around the old brass cash register and on the shelves behind it like the sentinels of someone's colorful, ragtag army. She resisted the impulse to close her eyes and imprint the scene for a future sketch.

"I wonder if you could help me?" she inquired a shade less confidently.

"Maybe I can," the woman said noncommittally, but she did not look up.

Kate sighed. This was what was difficult for her—this reaching out to strangers when in need of help. In New York, she was utterly self-sufficient, and her routine was varied but constant. In New York she could cope, because she knew what to expect, and Kate liked knowing what to expect out of life. In a strange place, she was beset by insecurities about her abilities, and uncooperative strangers didn't help. "I...I'm looking for the Stonecroft Inn."

The woman made an elaborate gesture out of snapping her newspaper to fold it up and laying it on the worn counter with precise care before raising her eyes slowly to face Kate. Her gaze was so pointedly appraising that it made Kate quail, as if she had just been judged and found wanting. "Yep. You came to the right place," she said at last.

"Here?" Kate resisted the urge to bite her lower lip. *This* was the Stonecroft Inn? "Right here?" She indicated the floor with one hand, and the gesture sent her duffel bag sliding off her shoulder to land at her feet with a thump.

Kate was sure she saw the woman struggling not to smile at her clumsiness and her apparently stupid question. But the thought that she might have to spend three days partaking of the distinctly cool brand of hospitality offered by this taciturn woman was enough to make her forget her embarrassment. "I...it doesn't look like the picture in the brochure." She tried to hide her dismay as she scanned the rows of stock reaching from the sawdusty floor to the dimly lit ceiling. Perhaps out back, or on the next floor.... Neither possibility was particularly comforting.

Now the woman did smile. "I don't mean here, in the store," she said, warming up to the entertainment the evening had just presented her in the form of this obvious city slicker. "I meant you came to the right town: Putnam Falls."

Kate blinked, unable to think of a profitable reply to this comment. Of course she had come to the right town! Even *she* would have had a hard time getting that wrong.

"Lots of folks do," the woman went on as if reading her mind. "They drive around on Route 100, and it gets dark and they can't tell one little Vermont town from another." This struck her as even more humorous, and she actually chuckled. The effect was to soften the hard blue of her eyes and make her gray curls bob jauntily across her forehead.

"I took the bus," Kate offered weakly, wondering how the woman could possibly have failed to notice her arrival in that manner.

"Well, now, that's different. The bus. The bus driver usually knows which town is which, doesn't he?" The woman nodded, satisfied that Kate had passed her secret muster, then leaned across the counter to point out the window. "You want the Stonecroft Inn, you have to take a left outside and go all the way down to the end of the green. Then take a right and go down to the end of the block. About a quarter mile. The Stonecroft's right there on the corner. Big old thing with stone pillars. You can't miss it."

Kate was still trying to assimilate the fact that she would need to walk over a quarter of a mile in the dark, with her luggage, before she reached her final destination. It seemed an impossibly long distance, and she was sure she would get the directions wrong, simple as they were. But the woman was clearly not about to offer any clarification, much less assistance. She was on her own. "Left and then right?" she inquired hopefully, but the woman had picked up her paper and was laboriously unfolding it once again.

"Thank you," Kate murmured, and reached down to arm herself with her various pieces of luggage. Trying not to appear clumsy, she managed to get the door open with a minimum of rearranging. Just before she went through it, she heard the woman speak.

"You a friend of Nina's?"

"Pardon me?" Stopping and turning around in the doorway was a chore.

"I said, are you a friend of Nina's?"

Kate shook her head. "I don't know any Nina. Who's Nina?"

The woman shrugged. "I just thought you might be," she replied unhelpfully. "You being from New York City and all." She went back to her reading with a finality that brooked no further interruption.

Kate went out to the street, wondering who Nina was and how in the world the woman had known she was from New York City. Her luggage was heavy and it was getting really cold. She felt hungry and tired and disgruntled—as much by her own inefficiency as by the woman's lack of support. "I should have asked her if there was a taxi available," she grumbled to herself as she trudged along. "I should have told her I can't carry all this, and it's late and dark and cold and I have a lousy sense of direction and no idea where I'm going...."

But in fact she had already reached the edge of the green, and by peering right, she could clearly make out the lights at the end of the road, which illuminated four large, white stone pillars.

"A quarter of a mile, my foot!" she huffed, although she was aware that she had no idea how far a quarter of a mile really was.

In fact, it took her the better part of fifteen minutes to reach the inn, although the lights seemed to beckon her on, making the distance seem short and safe. It wasn't until she was standing in front of the building—or buildings, since the inn seemed to go on forever in a succession of small, angled additions—that she realized how large it was. The path that led up to the front porch was short and bordered by low evergreen bushes interspersed with tiny white Christmas lights that gave the place a festive air. The front porch was lined with French windows—three on each side—and through these, more lights could be seen behind the parted chintz curtains. Kate breathed a sigh of relief. Now *that* was a hospitable sight.

As she made her way up the flagstone path, the front door, painted a bright-red enamel, suddenly flew open. For a moment Kate thought it might be someone coming out to welcome her, and her face lit up. In fact, the woman who appeared at the door was grinning broadly, but it was apparent that Kate was not the object of her amusement. A man stood behind her, and both turned so that they were silhouetted in the doorway, attractively framed in a pool of amber light cast by the golden glass globe that hung over the door.

"It's not that cold out, Nicky," the woman protested with a low chuckle. "Stop acting like a mother hen." She lifted up her palms to push away the putty-colored down coat the man was trying to tighten around her shoulders. Her auburn hair, cut stylishly short, seemed to gleam like a copper bowl around her oval face.

"I wouldn't act like a mother hen if you didn't run around like a baby chicken without a head," the man replied, pulling the coat closer around her and giving her a playful shake. "I know what you've got in mind, young lady. You're going to get into that little toy car and do a hundred and twenty all the way down to the city, and the wind is going to roar in through the rip in the convertible top, but you'll have your stereo going too loud to hear it. You could freeze to death and not even know it.''

The woman opened her eyes wide in mock horror. "Oooh, it all sounds so deliciously dangerous! The speed and the stereo, that is. The freezing I could do without.'' She shivered prettily.

"It is dangerously delicious.'' He grinned. "So wear the coat. That way at least you'll be warm when you wipe out on the highway.''

"No coat.'' She shrugged it off, revealing a petite figure swathed in deep-plum wool that seemed to envelop her in its soft warmth while still managing to fall into perfect lines around her curves. She looked at the down coat lying in a heap around her dark pumps, then looked back up and shrugged gaily. "I hate that ugly thing, anyway. If I'm going to die on the highway, I might as well die in style, don't you agree?''

Kate looked down. She was wearing an almost identical coat, except that hers was rust colored. Her plaid skirt stuck out from beneath the hem, and her saddle-colored boots, she noticed, were covered with a pale dust that mottled them to an ugly shade of grayish-brown. She looked back at the woman, small and vibrant with red lips that seemed to glow beneath the light of the lamp. Well, she sighed to herself, I would probably trip over myself in a getup like that, anyway.

The man stooped and picked up the coat but said nothing further about it. "I won't bother telling you to drive carefully,'' he told the woman tenderly. "But will you please try to behave yourself down there? You know how much trouble you can get into in this kind of situation, sweetie. If Jared wants something, he's got to be up to no good.'' He gave a dry chuckle. "Believe me, I should know.''

"Nicky, please!" Kate couldn't see the woman's eyes, but she was sure they were sparkling with fond petulance. "I know what I'm doing. I know how to handle Jared—and he's not like you think he is, darling. He's really just an old softie."

"Yeah? As in soft in the head." He scowled, and Kate became aware of the fullness of his lower lip. "He must be, or he wouldn't be calling you in a panic to bail him out again. Of course, maybe you're just soft in the head for doing it."

"Oh, Nicky, stop pouting!" The woman reached up and chucked him under the chin, which made him grin immediately. "And I suggest you stop trying to take care of me, darling, because you've got plenty to take care of here."

"You're right. I do, don't I?" He slumped against the door frame, suddenly dejected. His mercurial moods were dazzling. But the woman did not seem the least bit fazed. She reached out and pulled him upright, even though he was a good six inches taller than she, and a lot bulkier. "Now come on, don't start that again. You promised me, and you know you can do it. Besides, what else are you going to do while I'm gone?" The question held a definite challenge.

Kate knew she shouldn't be eavesdropping, but she could think of no successful way to get past the couple without feeling even more awkward than she already did. Besides, their conversation, with its clever mixture of concern and banter, was fascinating to her. Kate had a good sense of humor, but she was often too shy to say the funny things that popped into her mind. This man and woman seemed to have no trouble at all, and they spoke in the kind of intimate shorthand she had never been able to manage. She just stood there watching the farewell scene, her bags dangling from her shoulders and elbows, well aware that they knew nothing of her presence—and would probably not care about her if they did.

In a way, this couple was familiar to her. She had seen others like them in New York many times—men and women who moved through the city like elegant bookends, complementing one another—and themselves—by their self-confidence, style and panache. They spoke a special brand of rapid patois that made them seem members of some stylish secret society. They frequented chic night spots, shopped in fashionable stores and reeked of glamour—even if the glamour was something they manufactured themselves. Kate had never been able to manufacture the smallest shred of glamour about herself, which was why she had always watched couples like this one with a faint air of incomprehension, trying to decipher what it was that made them seem so finished, so smoothly polished and so in tune with each other.

This pair was a particularly successful specimen. They seemed so well matched in their casual elegance, their confidence and joie de vivre, that they even appeared to look alike, although Kate's photographic eye told her that their features were not all that similar. The man, for instance, was a lot larger than his female companion, although he managed to give off the same air of compact energy. His hair was several shades lighter, but it was slicked back and slightly wet, as if he had recently emerged from the shower, so that it appeared to be the same color as hers. His eyes were dark blue and sparkly, and they crinkled up into enchanting slivers of good humor as he stood surveying his lover. He also had huge dimples in his pale olive cheeks, and his chin was just barely saved from being hopelessly Mitchumesque by the babylike softness of his full lips. Even from a distance she could see that his eyelashes were impossibly long.

Now he raised his head and lifted one finger to pinch the woman's cheek. "I could always find some trouble to get myself into, couldn't I? Even up here in the boonies." Kate could sense the mischievous twinkle in his eyes as he spoke.

The woman slapped his finger away. "Don't you dare! You just take care of business and wish me the best. It's the least you can do." She stood up on tiptoe and kissed him warmly on both cheeks. "Bye, darling!" she said, disengaging herself before he could hold her back. "Behave yourself, and I'll do the same."

The man leaned against the door frame again, crossing his arms over his chest and watching his companion as she dashed down the steps at the side of the porch. They were still not aware of Kate's presence. "Be good," he called out after her. "And don't forget to come home to the farm—with or without your excess baggage!"

The woman's tinkly laugh was cut short by the tinny slap of a car door, and a moment later an engine roared to life. Kate could not see the car at first, then a small green M.G. shot into view and out again as it sped off into the night. She stood still on the path until the sound had faded away entirely, listening to the silence settling around her and watching the man, who was posed in the doorway, staring off down the street, deep in somber thought.

Chapter Two

It was Kate who roused herself to move first, mustering her courage and luggage to proceed up the pathway to the porch. The man seemed truly surprised to see her materialize out of the night, and he visibly collected himself, standing up straight and putting a warm smile on his face.

"Well, hi there!" he called out cheerily. "Where did you come from?"

"New York," Kate said dryly. She was in no mood to explain that she'd been standing in front of him for five minutes.

He chuckled. "Seems like everyone's either coming from or going to New York."

"Hmm." Kate was trying to gauge how she would be able to get past him with all her luggage. He seemed to show no inclination to move out of the doorway to let her pass, so she was forced to stand in front of him and wait.

"Oh, hey, I'll take those for you," he said, suddenly realizing her predicament. He reached out to grab her duffel, but Kate pulled back.

"Oh, no, don't bother," she told him, staggering a step from the force of the duffel falling back against her leg. "I can manage for now, and then the porter can bring them up to my room when I check in."

The man threw back his head and laughed, revealing fine white teeth. When he lifted his head again, a lock of thick straight hair, still slightly damp, fell across his eyebrow, and he flicked it aside. "I'm the porter," he told her with a gleeful twinkle. "I'm also the checker-inner, cook, housemaid and general factotum—at least for the time being."

Kate was surprised. She had assumed he was another guest. He didn't strike her as the country-innkeeper type. He was too slick, too well dressed, with his casual corduroy pants and stylishly oversize white shirt. She reminded herself that many transplanted New Yorkers ran inns in Vermont, but she imagined that people like that usually had a predisposition to a quiet rural life-style. This man wasn't at all countrified and laid-back; on the contrary, he seemed to exude an urban energy she had always identified with confirmed city-dwellers, the kind who wouldn't be caught dead in overalls and plaid shirts.

Still, she liked his smile, and his laugh had been positively contagious. "You're the innkeeper?" In spite of her fatigue, Kate's gray-blue eyes sparkled with sudden humor. "Funny, you don't look—"

"Like an innkeeper." He nodded resignedly. "I know, I know. But I'm not a permanent innkeeper. It's just . . . just a phase I'm in, know what I mean? Besides, you don't look like you're from New York, either."

At first she thought he was making fun of her, since she obviously bore no resemblance to the sleek Manhattanite he had just kissed goodbye. But then he grinned and wriggled his eyebrows, which arched ironically over his deep-blue eyes. "Last time I was there the girls were wearing black lipstick."

She couldn't help returning that impish grin. "You must have been hanging out in a bad neighborhood."

"Heyyy." He drawled out the word with a heavy Brooklyn accent and an eloquent lift of his shoulders. "Is dere any odder kinda neighborhood in da Big Apple? Last time I was there that was all they were offering."

Kate smiled again, a bit shyly this time. "You haven't been there in a while, then," she replied, wondering where she was getting the courage to exchange light banter with this absolute stranger.

He pursed his lips and nodded. "It's been a while," he agreed, and once again reached for her bags. "Now, if you'll just relinquish your hold on these things, I'll see what we can do about getting you settled." His arm slid sensuously up her shoulder to remove the duffel-bag strap, and Kate was startled to feel goose bumps rising in its wake. She was sure the gesture had been unconscious—men like that thought nothing of random intimacies. He wasn't even looking at her. Nevertheless, the heat of his touch was palpable, even through the thick down of her coat.

But he took the duffel bag from her without lingering or behaving as if he had in any way noticed Kate's reaction to his touch. He turned and moved briskly into the entry hall, with Kate behind him. The house was warm and cheerful inside, with polished wide-plank floors that reflected the light from a huge flagstone fireplace just off the central hallway. The chintz curtains were a sunny persimmon-and-blue print and the walls were painted a pale cinnamon with bright white woodwork. The furniture was old and well used, but in good shape—two large camel-back couches that flanked the fireplace looked particularly appealing. Suddenly Kate realized how tired she was. There was no one in the room, but she could hear the faint babble of voices floating down the darkened hallway.

The man walked over to a small desk tucked into a niche beneath the stairs. "I'm not too sure we have anything available, but maybe..."

"Oh, but I have a reservation."

He looked up quizzically. "A reservation? Nina didn't say anything about any reservations coming in tonight."

Kate felt a familiar lump in her throat. "I have my confirmation right here...somewhere..." She began riffling through her pocketbook and, when that produced nothing, lifted her other bag off her shoulder and began rummaging in its depths. "I know I have it...they gave it to me at the office, and I'm sure..." She began to lift out pencils, erasers, rulers and assorted implements, piling them absentmindedly on the desk in front of her.

"What is this, the contents of Van Gogh's studio at Arles?"

Kate looked up, her expression bleak, unable to appreciate his wry grin as he surveyed the mess she had made. His esoteric allusion was totally lost on her at the moment. "I can't find it!" she said, an edge of hysteria in her voice. Not having a reservation had always been one of her worst fears about traveling.

"Hey, hey, not to worry!" His expression immediately became one of concern. "Believe me, if there's been a mix-up, it's sure to be Nina's fault. Unless, that is, it's my fault, which is also quite likely, except that I haven't been running this place for more than—" he checked his heavy Rolex "—oh, six minutes or so. So it couldn't have been me. Of course, around here you never know."

Kate listened to his monologue with increasing consternation, especially when she noticed that expressively arched brow lifting along with the corners of his generous mouth. She also noticed, irrelevantly, that his lips were impossibly red and full for a man and that his eyes were not exactly dark blue but more a blue gray...soft and inviting.

But he clearly had no more idea what was going on with her reservation than she did. The only difference between them was that he had a place to sleep for the night, while she might well find herself out in the cold. Again.

"I want to talk to Nina," she said. In a situation like this, she reminded herself firmly, go right to the top.

He clicked his tongue sympathetically. "Can't. Nina's probably halfway to New York by now. Bet she's even got her black lipstick out already." He grinned and began whistling a few bars from "New York, New York," shaking his head and scrunching up his eyes as if listening to an entire symphonic accompaniment.

But Kate was in no mood for his shenanigans. Nina was obviously the lover he had just sent off into the night, and she had left him in charge without any instructions, any information, or even the smallest inkling of how to run an inn. It occurred to her that the redoubtable Nina was not much of an innkeeper herself.

She took a deep breath. "Look. I definitely have a reservation for two nights at the Stonecroft Inn in Putnam Falls, Vermont. This *is* the Stonecroft Inn in Putnam Falls, isn't it?"

Her attempt at imperiousness did not faze him in the least. He raised his chin proudly. "None other. The fabulous Stonecroft Inn, in scenic, quaint, screamingly appropriate Putnam Falls, Vermont. *The* place for leaf peeping, maple sugaring, great bargains in wool blankets and adequate skiing—if you're something of a klutz with no love for great heights. The big-time skiers go farther north, as well they should." He paused and looked down at her. "I hate skiing," he confided in a completely different tone of voice. "It's so...undignified, don't you think?" Behind the desk, he assumed a hilariously awkward, knock-kneed pose. "All crunched up like that with your knees kissing. And those outfits! They make you feel like a stuffed kielbasa—not exactly my idea of *le style chic*—know what I mean? Besides, it gets *cold* out there!" He shivered dramatically, but Kate maintained her level gaze, determined not to give in to his attempts to placate her or make her laugh.

"All I want," she said, speaking in a low, clear voice to control her agitation, "is a room. My room. The room that was supposed to be waiting for me."

He stared at her as if only just realizing her predicament. Kate continued to meet his gaze unblinkingly, although she had the uncomfortable feeling he was cataloging her jet-black hair in its unwieldly pageboy, her pale complexion with the too-large mouth and her deep-set gray blue eyes, as if he were planning to commit them to his own photographic memory bank. Suddenly he started out of his reverie, and Kate began to breathe again.

"A room, a room! My kingdom for a room! Yes, I'm sure Nina got things messed up—she's not exactly the world's most organized person these days. But you just stand by and old Nick'll take care of everything for you." He reached under the desk and pulled out a black notebook, which he opened and began leafing through rapidly, his expression one of intense scholarly concentration. In spite of herself, Kate could not help watching him, fascinated by his chameleonlike ability to switch moods and personalities in the blink of an eye.

"All right, we've got Anderson in A, and the Coopers in suite B. The guy in C—I don't know his name, but I'm sure you don't want to share a bed with him." He looked up briefly, and his lips twitched when he saw the horrified expression that crossed Kate's face. "No, no, no. What you want," he went on, as if trying to convince her of the fact, "is a room to yourself. So. We've got suite D and rooms E and F occupied—that rock-and-roll group from Burlington on a road tour— and that leaves—" he planted his hands firmly on both sides of the opened notebook "—that leaves not a whole lot, my late little lady. Not a whole lot at all, I'm afraid."

Kate could feel tears welling up beneath her eyelids, but she refused to let them spill out. Still, it was too risky to open her mouth, so she concentrated on picking up the supplies she had spread out on the desk and placing them back in her bag. I'll tell him he has to find me another place to stay, she thought bitterly. I'll tell him he has to drive me to another place. He has to drive me back to New York if there's no room in this godforsaken place. I'll tell him what I think of him and his scatterbrained girlfriend—as soon as I can trust myself to speak.

But she didn't have to say a word. He suddenly slammed the book shut with such vehemence that Kate jumped and spilled a handful of lead pencils and erasers back onto the floor.

"I have it!" he yelled triumphantly. "I've got the solution." He came around the front of the desk and bent to help her pick up her things. Kate, who had been relieved to crouch down out of range of his manic intensity, wished he wouldn't be so helpful. She tried to tell him that she could manage herself, but the fact that she seemed to keep on dropping things as fast as she picked them up wasn't convincing. And every time his busy hands brushed against hers, she felt a jolt of electricity that made her fumble even more. Fortunately, he wasn't paying the least attention to her.

"You see," he rattled on blithely, "most of our rooms are closed up, this being the off-season of an off year, and heat costing what it does, know what I mean? But there is one room, one little room, that's nice and toasty warm, and just right for a tired little artist from the Big Apple named—what did you say your name was?"

Having finally gotten her recalcitrant materials back into the bag, Kate looked up. "I didn't," she reminded him wearily. His energy was slightly dizzying, much like the sunlight when it dipped and peeked through lacy trees. "But it's Kate. Kate Palmer."

He smiled. "Ah. Kate Palmer," he said softly, as if tasting the words on his tongue. "Yes." He seemed satisfied with the flavor of her name and held his hand out across the opened supply bag. "I'm Nick. Nick Capstein. And I'm pleased to make your acquaintance, Ms.

Kate Palmer. Very pleased indeed." He took her hand and shook it solemnly.

"Pleased to meet you, too," Kate replied automatically, but her voice trailed off slightly as she became aware that he was not letting go of her hand. He held it clasped beneath his, his grip soft but unyielding and his gaze direct and unwavering, as if he were seeing her for the first time. Kate was more flustered than ever by the electromagnetism of his touch, but she did not want to admit it. She forced herself to look right into his eyes, despite her trembling hand and the traitorous heat she could feel rising in her pale cheeks.

After a heartbeat of eternity, Nick cocked his head with winning appeal. "Wanna see it?"

For a moment she could not tear her gaze away from the captivating expression in his eyes. Not dark blue, more slate. A sort of Prussian blue with a lot of black, maybe a dash of charcoal . . . "See what?"

"The room, of course. Don't you want to see the room?" He seemed as eager to please as a little boy, but his wistful grin was undeniably sensual.

Kate stared at him again, at a loss for words. There was something theatrical about him, something intense and extreme, which attracted and fascinated her but also made her a little nervous. It was possible, after all, that he was putting her on, and she did not like to feel that she was being played with. She considered telling him that she wouldn't stay at his poorly run hostel for all the tea in China, then promptly dismissed the retort as an unproductive bit of overacting. Besides, she *did* have a reservation at his inn—Nina's inn—and she would be the only one to suffer if she refused his offer. "I'd love to see it," she said with a sigh.

The wistfulness vanished as Nick gave her a lazy grin. "I knew you would," he said, and stood up. "Now, you grab your magic bag of tricks here—" he handed her her supply bag and purse "—and I'll take the rest." He shouldered the duffel and Kate's coat, apparently not noticing its resemblance to the garment scorned by his lover. "Now, *madame*, if you'll just follow me." He turned on his heel with a flourish and sailed up the stairs ahead of her.

At the top of the first landing the cinnamon-colored paint gave way to wallpaper covered with tiny blue flowers and wainscoting painted a shiny colonial blue. The carpeting was a thick and inviting powder blue. Overall, the effect was warm and cozy, and through some of the slightly open doors that led off the hall, Kate caught glimpses of rooms similarly flowered and inviting. Each one was slightly different, but they all looked as if someone with good taste had taken a lot of time with them. Kate's spirits began to rise. But then Nick turned another corner and took her up yet another flight of stairs. This one was uncarpeted and considerably darker than the first flight. Kate made a face. Clearly the quaint luxury of the first two floors was not to be hers tonight. Well, she supposed she was lucky to have a bed at all.

Directly at the top of the stairs was a white-painted door. Nick pulled a large key ring from his pants pocket and began fumbling with the lock. He tried several keys without success, and she could hear him muttering under his breath. Kate began to feel sorry for herself again and to long for the familiar if limited comforts of her little one-room walk-up on East Ninetieth Street.

At last the door swung inward, and Nick mounted the rest of the stairs and entered the room. Looking up, all

Kate could see was blackness. "The light, the light," she could hear him muttering to himself, and then a muffled curse as he banged into a piece of furniture. Finally a switch was pulled and a bare bulb suspended from the ceiling illuminated the space. Cautiously, Kate walked up and into the room.

It was clearly an attic, with steeply pitched ceilings converging on three sides all the way down to the floor. On the fourth side a small gable jutted out, with three small multipaned windows staring out into the night. But the walls had been finished and were painted a pale pink, and curtains printed with a delicate floral spray of pink and green hung across the windows. Wallpaper in a similar and equally faded pattern covered the slanting ceilings.

The floor was bare but it had been painted white, and a rag rug in faded tones of green and white formed a circle in the middle of the room, which was quite large if one discounted the tentlike configuration of the ceilings. Tucked into the gable was a narrow wrought-iron bed with an impossibly thick-looking mattress covered by a patchwork quilt. Aside from the bed, a dresser and a small table, the room was bare and clearly had not been used for some time.

"I know it's not much," Nick said, moving around and making an attempt to clear away some of the dust with his shirtsleeve. "But it's warm, because it gets heat from the lower floors, and it's clean, or at least fairly clean, because I cleaned it myself last time I was up here." He laughed, and for the first time Kate detected a note of self-consciousness creeping into his voice. "Don't ask me why, because I had no idea it was ever going to be used." He walked over to the windows and bent down to peer out. "I just liked the way it looked, I guess," he said, almost to himself. He stayed at the window for a long moment, lost in thought, while Kate stood in the middle of the room and watched him.

Then he straightened, so suddenly that he bumped his head on the ceiling. "Ouch! Anyway," he went on with an apologetic grin, "it's all we've got—for tonight, at least. Do you think you can make do up here for one night? I know it's not what you expected, but..." His voice trailed off, and he smiled wistfully again.

But Kate adored the room. Somehow, despite all the difficulties she had encountered that evening, she was able to appreciate the fact that it was special. Even with the bare overhead bulb, she could sense its quiet charm, the soft innocence and tranquillity. Although the space lacked the well-designed luxury of the second-floor guest rooms, it was the kind of room in which she had often envisioned herself as a young girl—and even as an adult, in the dreary monotony of her Manhattan studio apartment. Already in her mind's eye the contours of the space were so familiar that she could imagine herself rearranging things to suit her needs—room for a work-table positioned just beneath those three little windows for maximum northern exposure, a few prints on the walls, some potted geraniums... It was a room so well suited to her particular tastes that, had she been so inclined, she would have suspected some sort of predestination in the course of the events that had brought her here.

Kate walked over to the bedside table and switched on the tiny light, which, with its small, fluted shade, gave off a soft pink glow. Then she went back to the middle of the room and switched off the overhead light. There, that was right. She could not help smiling as she faced

Nick, who had been watching her quietly all along. "It's perfect," she said.

Nick nodded. "I can see that," he said gently, his voice full of surprise. He shook his head and laughed. "You're right, Kate Palmer. This is your room, and it was ready for you after all."

They stood smiling at each other, their faces softened by the warm pink light. Kate was fascinated by the depth of his dimples, which ran up either side of his cheeks and seemed to cup the dim glow in their recesses. His eyes were a sleepy, smoky blue, but they, too, seemed to catch and hold the light. Then Nick's mobile expression underwent yet another abrupt transformation. "Oh, hey, I just realized something!" He slapped a hand to his forehead.

"What?" Kate was sure he had just remembered the room was to go to someone else.

"I forgot you probably haven't eaten. I'm supposed to offer you light refreshment. 'Incoming guests have probably been on the road for some time,'" he recited, casting his eyes upward to remember the words. "'It is always a good policy to offer them some light refreshment after they've gotten settled in their room. It needn't be an elaborate repast, but it will certainly add to their opinion of your inn, and probably to the amount of the final bill as well.'" He stopped reciting and shrugged at her. "That's what it says in the *Innkeeper's Manual*. Nina made me read it to her last night." He bowed and swept his hand out before him with a flourish. "So, Miss Incoming Guest, if you'd care for some light refreshment, which may not be elaborate and will certainly *not* add to your final bill—" he winked "—I'd be obliged if you would follow me once more." He straightened. "Unless, of course, you'd rather just settle in here."

Kate looked around her one more time. She did look forward to the prospect of settling in, of pulling back the bedcovers and plumping up the pillows so that she could look out the windows while she lay there. But Nick was right, she was hungry—suddenly so hungry that she felt a light refreshment might not be enough. "I think I would like a little something," she said demurely, and walked ahead of him onto the stairs, hoping she didn't look too clumsy clumping down the narrow uncarpeted treads in her boots.

Back on the first floor, Nick led the way through the living room and dining room, which was a cheerful yellow and blue with lots of windows and several small tables set with place mats and silverware. "Do you serve meals here?" Kate inquired.

"We serve breakfast every morning," he said over his shoulder. "And we're supposed to offer dinner as well, but ever since Nina took over no one's been brave enough to tax her culinary skills that far."

Kate was surprised at his cheerful dismissal of Nina's talents. She wondered what had brought the couple to Putnam Falls, if neither of them had the calling to be innkeepers. Clearly Nick was a rank novice at the job, and Nina, if her sudden absence and lack of planning were typical, was not exactly down-home material, either. They were a puzzling pair, but Kate was too tired to come up with any explanations.

Off to the left of the dining room was a small dark bar, complete with a pool table and blinking neon beer sign hanging over the counter. Inside, Kate could hear the babble of voices and the sound of music issuing from what was obviously an expensive stereo system. As she listened to it, Nick began to sing along with the music, hunching over and slipping into a jive strut, pelvis thrust

forward, fingers snapping. He sang the words to an old
Smokey Robinson ballad as fervently as if he had in-
vented them himself. Kate was embarrassed for him, and
then, when he spun around neatly on one foot and began singing directly to her, she was embarrassed for
herself. Fortunately they reached the kitchen before he
could go on much farther.

After the old-fashioned homeyness of the other
rooms, the kitchen was something of a shock. Large and
bright, with white tiles and gleaming stainless-steel ap-
pliances, it seemed adequate for full-size restaurant use,
although it was obviously not getting much use lately.

"Now," said Nick briskly, moving to the huge dou-
ble-door refrigerator and pulling both sides open.
"What strikes your fancy, Kate?"

Kate tried to peer past him to see what there was inside. "I don't know," she said, feeling awkward.
"Whatever you've got, I guess."

He turned around and gave her a wicked grin. "I was
hoping you'd say that." He chuckled mischievously.
"That gives me carte blanche to work up one of my
magnificent culinary events." He turned back to the
fridge after wriggling his brows dangerously. "Now let's
see, we've got salami and pastrami, and I know there are
some eggs, and there's cream cheese, and—oh, that terrific herbed cheese spread Nina got over in Brattleboro
the other day." He bent down. "Now, where did she
hide the onion? Ah, yes, here it is... And then I'll need
lettuce and tomato and some mustard—which mustard,
I wonder?" He turned and surveyed Kate, who had
perched on a stool next to a spotless stainless-steel
counter and was watching the growing pile of food beside him with mounting alarm. Nick spun around to face
her. "What kind of mustard are you, anyway?" He

narrowed his eyes and let them travel up and down her body, making Kate feel terribly self-conscious about her wrinkled ecru silk blouse, which was not well-tucked into her plaid skirt. Her boots hid most of her legs, which she believed were her best feature, but she felt unnaturally exposed under his expert scrutiny and cleared her throat uneasily.

Nick seemed to have his own agenda, though, for after a moment he pronounced, "Grey Poupon!" with absolute authority and turned back to his rummaging. Kate, who happened to love Grey Poupon, decided to settle back and let nature, or Nick, take its course.

Soon the pristine countertops by the stove and near the refrigerator were scattered with the debris of Nick's culinary efforts. He seemed to be everywhere at once—cutting, rolling, sautéing, stacking, transferring food as if playing an elaborate juggling game with the mountain of edibles he had chosen. Kate, who had been worried that she might not get enough to eat, now saw that she would not be able to make even a dent in the meal. "I'm not *that* hungry," she said at one point, trying to sound casual as she watched a platter of fried eggplant grow beside the stove at an alarming rate.

"Nonsense," he replied without even turning away from the stove. "Everyone's hungry at 10:00 p.m. It's in our genes."

There was no arguing with either his words or his tone, so she fell silent again. It was like watching a three-ring circus, complete with color, spectacle, some daredevil risks—Nick flourished the knives with breathtaking carelessness—and even music. He kept on breaking into snatches of song, and each was accompanied by an uncanny imitation of the singer who had made it popular. He even managed to pull off a fairly good rendition of

Martha and the Vandellas singing "Heat Wave," and the flames from the broiler, where a concoction of eggs, salami and cheese was sizzling under a roaring blaze, added an appropriate glow to his face. Kate was mesmerized.

In what seemed like no time at all, there was food in front of her. Aside from the eggplant and the omelet, which looked as if it contained at least a dozen eggs, there were bagels and three kinds of cheese spreads, a bowl of some cold marinated vegetables that resembled ratatouille and an entire garden's worth of sliced lettuce, tomatoes and onions piled onto a wooden platter. Kate blanched at the sight of it all.

"Don't panic," Nick said, seating himself on a stool on the other side of the counter. "What you can't eat, I'll eat. And what we don't eat, the Ravening Beasts in the bar certainly will. So just dig in."

"Ravening beasts?" Kate paused, a slice of fried eggplant halfway to her mouth, as a particularly shrill hoot of laughter floated in from the bar. It did sound vaguely primordial.

Nick nodded vigorously, his mouth full. "That's the name of the band that's staying here. The Ravening Beasts. Cute, huh?" He winked and kept on chewing. "Try some of that," he said, indicating the egg concoction.

Kate obediently dug her fork into it. It smelled delicious and had a wonderful pizzalike gooeyness beneath the fluffy egg crust. "This is terrific!" she said after savoring a mouthful. "You're very good."

Nick's grin threatened to split his face in two. "I know," he said, and acknowledged the feast in front of them with a sweep of his hand. "I call all this Nick's

Famous Nocturnal Nosh." He cocked his head. "You do know what a nosh is, don't you, Katepalmer?"

Kate liked the way he said her name all together, as if it were one word. "Of course I do," she replied primly. "A nosh is a snack or a meal. It's Yiddish. I may not be Jewish, but I did grow up in New York, you know."

He was looking at her and grinning as if he had some special secret joke. The dimples seemed bottomless, but they made Kate smile back automatically. "You never know," he murmured. "You just never know. So, what brings a dyed-in-the-wool New Yorker up to the wilds of central Vermont? With enough art supplies to paint Killington Mountain to boot."

"I work for Simmond's, the auction house on Madison Avenue and Twenty-third." Kate just assumed he knew the city well enough to be able to place this information in the proper context. He appeared suitably informed, so she went on. "I'm in their catalog department, actually. I do renderings for them. You know—drawings, sketches of the pieces they acquire for resale." Another sage nod encouraged her to continue. "Anyway, Simmond's has just purchased an estate lot of furniture from somewhere up here, and the pieces are going to be on display at a public auction over the next few days. So I'm here to draw them for the catalog." She took another bite of her omelet.

"Which auction house?" Nick asked.

"I think it's called Tate's. It's supposed to be right here in town. At least I *hope* it's right in town." The thought of another struggle on the morrow made her chew more slowly.

"Sure! That's Bob Tate. He's right over across from the post office. You won't have any problem finding it." He smiled encouragingly. "But why are these things on display at Tate's if Simmond's has already bought them?" he inquired, his attention seemingly on the steeple of lettuce, tomato and onion he was constructing atop a cheese-laden bagel.

"Well, technically because the public is supposed to be able to bid competitively for any of the pieces, even though Simmond's has already purchased them from the estate. But it's really a moot issue because the entire lot has to be sold as a unit and nobody could afford to buy them all except another auction house. Usually the big houses conduct their business before the pieces ever get to the auction floor, even though, by law, the public does have to get a chance to see them. Anyway, it's good for Simmond's because the interested buyers who come to these auctions learn that subsequently they can go to Simmond's with a bid and do business there."

"Sounds like a pretty elaborate system to me," Nick observed.

"It is. That is, I don't know much about that end of the business; my job is to see to it that the pieces wind up in the catalog looking like they're supposed to look. That's why they sent me here."

"Sort of like 'Have pencil, will travel,' eh?"

She smiled at the image of herself as a peripatetic artist, wandering from place to place to execute her works. It didn't fit what she knew about herself, but she liked it just the same. "What about you?" she asked. "What brings you to Putnam Falls?"

Nick jumped up, went to the fridge and emerged with two bottles of Canadian ale. He opened them both and handed one to Kate without even asking if she wanted it. Kate, who was not a beer drinker, lifted it to her lips and drank thirstily. It tasted divine—cold and bitter and refreshing.

"Ah, yes! That's the sixty-four-million-dollar question. What is Nicholas Capstein doing in Putnam Falls, Vermont?" He waved his beer bottle in front of her. "You know, you're not the only person who's asked that question. Why, at this very moment, there are probably dozens of curious and confused Manhattanites saying to themselves—or each other—'What in the world is Nick Capstein doing in Putnam Falls? I mean, he's as out of place there as a fish out of water, as a bagel without cream cheese, as—'" He broke off and shrugged. "Trouble is, none of them are very interested in the answer to that question. And even if they were, I'm not sure Nick Capstein could answer it for them." He shook his head. "He can't even answer it for himself."

Kate was surprised by this outburst and the unexpected undercurrent of bitterness with which it was delivered. Nick Capstein did not seem the type to let himself be trapped into a situation that did not suit him. "I'm interested," she said simply.

He stopped chewing and stared over his bagel at her. His eyes narrowed and moved across her features with the peculiar searching gesture she had noticed before. "You know," he said softly, more to himself than to her, "I do believe you are." He shook his head and snorted gently, as if amazed by this revelation.

Kate, emboldened by this, decided to press on. She was more curious about him than she cared to admit. "I suppose," she said carefully, "it's because of your girlfriend."

"My girlfriend?" He seemed genuinely puzzled.

Immediately Kate realized that she had made a gaffe. People like Nick did not call their mates girlfriends. That was too passé, too jejune. "Lady," perhaps, or "lover," or some other sophisticated shorthand, but not "girl-friend." "I mean your... Nina?"

"Ah, yes. Nina. Well, you could definitely say that I'm here because of Nina. After all, if she wasn't stuck up here, I certainly would never have—" He broke off and jabbed half a bagel in the air. "Wait a minute. Do you think Nina is my... that we're lovers?"

Kate blushed furiously. Not only had she said it wrong, but she was apparently way off base and had overstepped the bounds of acceptable behavior as well. "Well, I..."

Nick hooted with sudden laughter, throwing back his head and offering another glimpse of those bright, even teeth. Kate was surprised. *Now* what had she done?

"Nina my lover?" he said, still gasping. "Oh, my dear Katepalmer, that is most definitely not the case. My God, Nina is...she and I would probably kill each other within thirty seconds if we...after all, we've been at each other's throats for thirty-five years, give or take a few. But Nina and I as a couple?" He chuckled again and then, seeing Kate's expression, sobered instantly. "We're not lovers," he said. "Nina is my sister. My big sister—well, by about eighteen months, although she'd prefer it to be the other way around."

"Oh. Oh!" Suddenly it all fell into place for Kate—their fond banter at the door, the apparent mutual concern and, above all, that similarity in manner and appearance. She should have known there was a family resemblance, although it wasn't so much in their features as in their carriage and style. She felt foolish. Camera eye, huh? she asked herself dryly. Aloud, she said with a little giggle, "I'm sorry. I just thought...I was mistaken."

"Hey, no big deal. I guess it's a natural mistake to make. After all, Nina and I are pretty close and affectionate—when we're not hating each other's guts. I can see where you'd think we were attached in some way. The truth of the matter is that this is Nina's inn. Or rather, it was her husband's inn—her ex-husband's, I should say—and Nina got it in the divorce settlement. Her husband is Bob Tate—the auctioneer you'll meet tomorrow. He's a Vermont boy, born and bred. I told Nina right from the start that it wouldn't last, but would she listen to baby brother? Oh, no, not Nimble Nina, the chameleon of Sheepshead Bay. She insisted that she wanted to get away from the rat race and live on a farm. But no suitable gentlemen farmers showed up. Just Bob Tate and his inn and auction house. At the time, I guess it seemed to be an acceptable alternative. When Nina decides she wants something, she usually gets it, or some variation thereof.

"Anyway, when the divorce came through she got the inn, but not much else and, being perennially strapped for cash, she realized that her only alternative was to stay up here and run it for a while. Of course that defeated her whole purpose, which was to take the money and run like a rabbit back to Nueva York, but...well, Nina never did think ahead too well." He chuckled ruefully.

"But..." He still hadn't told her what brought *him* up to Vermont, but Kate wasn't sure there was a delicate way to press him further. She had the feeling Nick would have offered her the story by now if he'd wanted it known. He had certainly told her everything else of remote relevance.

"No buts, young lady," he said, slipping again into one of his theatrical personas. This one was lively and bustling, not unlike a harried parent. "You haven't eaten nearly enough. Now I want to see some real action on that omelet, understand? Young things fresh from the city have no idea how debilitating this clear mountain air can be. All those years of soot and pollution, then you get up here and your body just can't take it. You need fuel, girl, and plenty of it, to help you over these first few grueling hours of adjustment. It can be brutal, believe me." As he spoke he was gathering things and putting them on Kate's plate until it was once again piled high. Kate, who had just eaten more in one sitting than she remembered having done in a very long time, actually groaned. Nick heard her and grinned.

"Ah," he said, patting his chest in satisfaction. "That's what I like to hear. A satisfied customer. That's music to an innkeeper's ear."

Having apparently finished eating himself, he now sat back and folded his arms across his chest to watch Kate's progress. His hair, which had obviously had plenty of time to dry, was still slicked back, although the recalcitrant lock occasionally fell forward over his high forehead, causing him to flick it back absentmindedly. As she chewed slowly, Kate found herself wondering whether he had put something on his hair to make it stay back. It looked soft and silky, especially the piece that fell forward now and then. Small details like that about a person often held her attention, and Nick Capstein had more than his share.

But there was no way she could eat another morsel, even if it did allow her the opportunity to scrutinize his features for later review. Taking a deep breath, she pushed the plate away from her, prepared to confront the issue if he tried to get her to eat even more. "That's it," she said with what she hoped was convincing finality. "I simply cannot eat another bite. It was delicious,

Nick, really, but—'' she put her fingertips over her small belly ''—I just can't fit another thing, honest.''

He cocked his head in mock severity. "Are you sure?" he inquired sternly.

"I'm sure."

"All right, then, the remains go to the Ravening Beasts—and whichever other guests happen to be howling in the lounge at the moment." He cleaned off their plates and dumped them in the sink, then gathered the uneaten food onto a huge wooden platter to bring into the bar. He lifted the overloaded platter and headed swiftly out the kitchen door. Suddenly he seemed to remember something, because he stopped and turned around in the hallway. "Oh, hey, listen, you want to come into the lounge and join us? The guys are just playing some old Motown music." He rolled his eyes and hips in a sinuous, synchronized motion. "My favorite." He took two more steps toward the bar and stopped again. "I mean, I assumed you'd be bushed after the ride and everything else. I guess you probably want to go up to your cozy little nest and settle in, don't you? Course, if you'd like to join us . . ." He waited politely for her reply.

Kate stood uncertainly in the middle of the kitchen. From the lounge came the faint throb of music and the sound of subdued laughter. She found the invitation appealing and was still sufficiently under the spell of Nick's energy to want to follow him inside. But he did not seem overeager for her company, was no longer focusing all his attention on her; now he appeared anxious to join the other patrons in the bar. She could tell that he was aching to move to the insistent four-beat of the Motown hit issuing from the stereo.

Anyway, she reminded herself, she was tired, and she did want to escape to her attic room. "No, thanks," she said at last, trying to sound light and offhand and not betray her indecision. "I am tired. I think I'll just go on up."

He grinned dazzlingly. "Suit yourself," he replied. "I'll see you in the morning, Katepalmer. Sweet dreams." Then, with a wink, he was gone.

Chapter Three

Kate woke up the following morning with sunlight streaming into her eyes. It took her a moment to remember where she was, but then a slow smile spread across her face and she stretched luxuriously under the warm quilt. She was in *her* attic room, and it was even more perfect in the morning light than it had been at night.

Last night she had been too exhausted to draw the curtains, and this morning she was glad she hadn't. Sunshine fell across her bed and onto the wide, white-washed floorboards, the little windowpanes creating an intricate grid pattern of light. The pale circle of the rug was covered with tiny motes of dancing dust, and reflections shimmered off the floral print paper on the slanted ceiling walls. The walls themselves were transmuted by the light into the warmest shade of peach so that the entire space seemed to vibrate with coziness.

Kate found herself wondering which color paints she would have to mix together to reproduce the effect in watercolor—not that it could ever be reproduced, even if she were to attempt it.

She sighed and snuggled down deeper. The bed was not the firmest she had ever slept on, but she could tell, from the way her body conformed to the slightly saggy mattress, that she had slept deeply and without moving through the night. Now she felt completely rested, but far too relaxed to jump out of bed and begin her day. Normally, on a business trip in a strange place she would be nervous and eager to get to work, especially on the first day. But this morning she could barely command the energy necessary to get up, let alone work herself into a nervous anticipation about the work ahead.

She turned back to the windows and stared out, trying to gauge the time. The sun was slanted low in the sky, casting bright nets of light across the field below her window. Every bare bush and tree was thrown into sharp relief, and everything seemed to shimmer in the quiet morning air. She judged that it was very cold and probably still quite early. There was no sign of any life outside although, considering that her view gave onto little more than a dried-out field and a thick stand of bare poplar trees, she could hardly expect to find the place bustling with activity.

Still, she thought it was a beautiful scene and once again found herself trying to translate it into a watercolor palette. She examined the view intently for a few more seconds, then shut her eyes resolutely. Yes, there was a lot of ocher in the field, and some burnt umber, with a touch of Prussian blue and gray because it was still early spring and the morning frost was apparent. Because the scene sloped away from her treetop perspective, she would add highlights of eggshell white to the top of the page, and then, where the trees rose up from the flat bowl of the earth...

Of course she had no watercolors, and it was ridiculous to consider wasting her time in artistic daydreaming. Regardless of the early hour, Kate thought, she really *should* get up and get her bearings on the day. But somehow she couldn't bring herself to move or even to open her eyes and refocus them on more practical matters. She switched her mind's eye to the room itself and went over the scene once more. She loved the way the spindly legs of the dresser cast elegant shadows onto the floor and imagined herself capturing the nuances of jade and dusty green in the thick braiding of the rug.

Well, she couldn't paint the scene right now, but why not sketch it? After all, she had her photographic memory to rely on, but that wasn't as much fun as putting pencil to paper, and at that moment the only thing worth getting out of bed for was the prospect of grabbing her sketch pad and colored pencils from her bag and scurrying back beneath the covers with them to have a little fun. After all, it was still early, and she didn't have *that* much to do to get ready for the day since Nick Capstein could direct her right to the Tate auction house. Besides, she deserved to indulge herself every once in a while.

Nick Capstein. Just thinking about his name made her smile. It seemed to suit him, just as he had made her name sound as if it suited her so well. His name reminded her of someone quick and bright and droll...just like him, although she couldn't recall even meeting any other Nicks who fit that description. She closed her eyes and remembered him in the kitchen, shifting expertly from sink to stove to counter, whistling some ridiculous song through his teeth while his hands moved in a blur of activity to put out that outrageous midnight snack.

Taking a deep breath, Kate flung back the covers and touched her bare toes to the floor. She gasped at the cold, then charged across the room to the dresser, where her supply bag lay half-open. Away from the warmth generated by the sunlight, the room was really cold, and she could feel the goose bumps rising beneath her long flannel nightgown. Giggling and shivering, she grabbed her things and raced back across the room, jumping into bed with both feet so that the iron bedstead groaned in protest.

She warmed up quickly enough, though, and propping her back up with the old feather pillow, she spread her sketch pad open on her knees and contemplated the blank page before her with delight. She felt as if she were a schoolgirl playing hooky, although she reminded herself dryly that spending an extra half hour in bed sketching would hardly be considered a major crime.

Soon, however, she was totally engrossed in her work. It had been a long time since she'd allowed herself the luxury of drawing what she wanted to draw and not what Simmond's paid her to draw. Even the memory of Carl's condescending attitude faded from her mind as she attacked the page. Rather than relying on her photographic skill, she kept her eyes open wide and shifted her focus swiftly back and forth between paper and subject, sketching in the basic shapes, which she would later use her camera eye to complete.

Before she knew it, she had four sheets of paper filled with detailed renditions—two of the scene from her window and two of her room itself. One interior in particular delighted her, for it seemed to capture the unique warmth of the room and the soft filter of sunlight reflecting off all the crazily angled surfaces. And she had to admit she liked what she had done with the tilted perspective down onto the field below; somehow, she thought, she had managed to give the effect of depth with a minimum of stroke work and no messy cross-hatching. Of course, it wasn't what she would call a work of art, but she had to admit she liked it.

Satisfied at last, Kate put her pad away and got dressed, wearing a wool challis dress with a dropped waist and a pair of low brown heels. She liked the soft mauve-and-blue floral print of the dress and defended the use of shoes rather than boots by reminding herself that there was no snow on the ground and that she would, in any case, be spending the entire day inside. She did not allow herself to reflect on what possible reaction Nick Capstein might have to her shapely and unusually long legs.

The air in the second-floor hallway was a bit warmer than that in her room, but it was still very quiet, and Kate trod lightly on the thick carpet so as not to disturb the other guests, whom she assumed would still be sleeping. Down on the first floor it was also quiet, but she could hear the unmistakable sounds of music issuing forth from the kitchen. He was singing an old song, "He's a Rebel," and Kate unconsciously sang the familiar words along with him. She giggled at Nick's high falsetto, then stopped as she heard a crash and a curse. She waited in the empty dining room to hear what would follow, suddenly shy about coming face-to-face with him again.

But it was Nick who came in and found her standing somewhat uncertainly in the middle of the dining room, trailing her long fingers absently across the top of one of the tables. The sunlight, falling obliquely across the room over the tops of the crisp café curtains, had gotten all tangled up in Kate's straight dark hair, glinting highlights of warm russet and chestnut and casting soft, secretive shadows across her high, pale cheekbones. Her light-colored eyes widened beneath their dark lashes as she looked at him, and then, just as he was trying to figure out whether they were blue or gray or some indecipherable cloud hue, they seemed to glaze over so that she appeared to be looking directly at him without seeing him at all. He noticed that she moistened her lips absently and that despite the unerring stillness of her posture, her fingers kept sweeping idly back and forth across the polished oak surface of the table. He couldn't imagine what she was seeing, or not seeing, behind that small, compelling face, but he didn't mind taking advantage of the moment to admire her legs, which were long and elegant and extremely alluring, in spite of the rather clunky brown pumps she wore.

Almost without realizing it, Kate had begun an automatic "photo session" as soon as Nick stepped into the room. He was wearing a bright red V-neck sweater that brought out the high color in his complexion, and the fanciful deep blue of his eyes sparkled as clearly as a morning lake. His dark-brown corduroy pants were well cut and obviously expensive, but the sneakers he wore beneath them were old and battered and had a spot of something that looked a lot like butter or egg on the left toe. He also held a towel wrapped around his right thumb.

"Good morning, Sunshine," Nick said in an uncharacteristically soft voice. "Sleep well?"

Kate blinked twice, wondering if he had noticed her staring. "I slept deliciously, thank you." She looked around the empty dining room. "I suppose I'm too early for breakfast?"

He cocked his head quizzically, fondling his injured thumb in his left hand. "Early? Sunshine, everybody's been up and at 'em for hours already."

"What?"

"Well, everyone but the Ravening Beasts. I think they turn to stone if they get up before the sun goes down, or something like that."

"What time is it?" she inquired, trying to overcome her confusion. She should have looked at her watch, but it was buried somewhere so deep in her bag that she hadn't bothered.

"Oh, about 10:00 a.m., give or take an hour."

"Ten! But that's impossible!" It was difficult to reorient herself to this information, since she'd been so certain that it was before eight at the latest. "Omigosh, I'll be late! I'll be late for the auction!" She turned blindly and began to leave the room in a panic.

"Whoa, not so fast." Nick crossed the room and blocked her path. "The auction doesn't start until eleven-thirty—I checked for you. Besides, you can't leave without a good breakfast, can you?" He grinned disarmingly. "Remember what I told you about city girls who try to jump into country living too fast? Bad for the circulation—very bad."

In spite of her anxiety, Kate had to smile. "As if I didn't eat enough last night to last me for a week in the country." Her smile disappeared. "But really, I have to get myself together here. I've got to—"

"You've got to sit down and have a cup of coffee, at least," Nick finished firmly, taking her by the shoulders and steering her back toward the kitchen. "It's illegal in

Vermont for an innkeeper to let a guest leave without a cup of coffee, did you know that?''

"I had no idea.'' She allowed herself to be propelled into the kitchen but stopped at the sight of a huge frying pan in the middle of the floor, its contents splattered all over the room. "What on earth happened?''

"Oh, just a little accident.'' Nick picked up the pan and set it on the counter, then poured her a cup of coffee from the automatic pot. "Forgot to turn off the heat before I picked the thing up off the stove.'' He held up his still shrouded thumb.

"Ooh, is it bad?'' Kate shivered; she had little tolerance for physical discomfort of any kind. "Maybe you should do something to it.''

"Like operate?'' He set down the coffee, along with cream and sugar and a plate of delicious-looking muffins, in front of the stool she had occupied last night. "Nah, I'll live.'' He poured himself another cup and sat opposite her. "So tell me, Sleeping Beauty, what did you think of your little nest?''

In spite of her determination to drink and run, Kate smiled dreamily and launched into a description of how lovely it had been to wake up in her room. "I really do appreciate your giving it to me,'' she said, unconsciously nibbling on a muffin.

"Hey, we owed you, remember?'' Still, he seemed pleased. "But I'm glad it suited you so well. Really I am.'' He folded his arms across his chest and smiled broadly at her, watching her eat. "Now, why don't you finish up and go get your things together while I clean this mess. Then we'll hustle over to Bob Tate's and see what's what.''

"You don't have to take me there,'' Kate protested weakly, wondering how she'd managed to eat an entire blueberry-pineapple muffin without knowing she'd done it. "Just tell me where to go and I'll be on my way. You must have lots to do around here."

He put his hands on his hips and glared at her. "Plenty to do? I've been busting my... working like a dog since 6:00 a.m.—practically the middle of the night! Who do you think baked those muffins you're eating— the Keebler elves?"

"I'm sorry, I— You really baked these?" Kate couldn't contain her surprise. "They're delicious!" She had to restrain herself from taking another.

The glare disappeared at once. "Yeah, they're good, aren't they? I just started with a basic recipe, then added a few little items of my own, like the pineapple and the tequila."

Kate almost choked. "Tequila?"

"Well, I thought the batter seemed a little tame.... Anyway, after doing that and making scrambled eggs for six hungry hikers, I'm not about to spend the rest of my day making beds and dusting. By tonight they'll all be too tired to care what they're sleeping on. Besides, it's always easier to fall into an unmade bed, don't you think?"

Kate smiled at the sincerity with which this observation was offered. "Always." She herself would never think of leaving her apartment with the bed unmade, but when Nick explained it, it made sense. Everything he did seemed to make sense in an offhand, spontaneous way. He seemed to do everything so nonchalantly, by the seat of his pants, yet he was surprisingly competent at his tasks. She didn't know many men who could whip up scrambled eggs and muffins for a crowd. She didn't know many women who could, either, for that matter—herself included.

"Besides," Nick went on, taking one more muffin off the plate and putting it in front of Kate before clearing the table, "I have business of my own to conduct at Tate's."

"Well, if you're sure..." Kate herself wasn't sure about the prospect of having Nick as an escort. It was fine to fall in with his craziness here at the inn, but at Tate's she would have to buckle down and get serious, and he would definitely be a distraction. Besides, she wasn't so sure he wasn't just inventing business in order to be polite and helpful, and she hated to think of him going out of his way on her behalf.

"Sure, I'm sure." Nick busied himself noisily at the sink. "Believe me, I wouldn't spend any more time with old Bob Tate than I absolutely have to. There's no love lost between me and my ex-bro-in-law." He waved a soapy hand in her direction. "Now go on, get going, get going! You're the one who doesn't want to be late, aren't you?"

Obediently, Kate hurried out of the room, unaware that Nick was watching her long legs recede down the hall, soap dripping from his hands and a bemused smile on his face.

When she came downstairs ten minutes later, she found Nick in the hallway, struggling to fit a beautiful rolltop desk through the open front door.

"What's that for?" she inquired. He had put on a smoke-colored leather jacket over his red sweater, and her artist's eye was caught by the way the sunlight flowed over its buttery surface and danced through his slicked-back hair.

"For Bob Tate," he replied, grunting slightly as he maneuvered the desk. "That is, if I don't ruin it trying to squeeze it through the keyhole here. Can't sell damaged goods to old Bob, that's for damn sure.''

The desk was elegant—an antique rolltop in warm cherry with delicate scrollwork etched into the legs. The top was open, revealing a rabbit's warren of small drawers and compartments, each one a promise of secret delights, almost begging to be explored. Kate was enchanted with the graceful proportions of the piece.

''Why on earth are you selling it?'' she asked, coming forward and trying to help him ease the back end through the door without nicking it.

''Need the scratch,'' he said, and then, seeing her look of incomprehension, ''the money, the dough.''

''Oh.'' Kate felt it had been indelicate of her to ask and she looked away, embarrassed. But Nick appeared to have no such compunctions.

''Yeah, my sister has really made mincemeat of the bookkeeping around this place,'' he told her amiably. ''She spent a fortune redecorating it when she first got here, never stopping to think that little things like taxes and mortgages had to be paid before she could go crazy at Laura Ashley. So now it's April, and the boys from the IRS are breathing down her neck, and she hasn't got the proverbial pot to—'' he looked up and winked ''—so I'm just doing a little creative accounting here, getting rid of an extra dust collector in exchange for what I hope will be a pretty piece of change.''

''But it's so lovely,'' Kate remarked, watching as he lifted the desk off the porch and onto the front walk. The sunlight turned the wood a deep, rich honey red, and she ran her fingers gently over the polished surface. ''All those lovely secret compartments, so perfectly done! It seems a shame to sell something so beautiful.''

"That's exactly what I'm hoping they'll say over at Tate's," Nick told her, rubbing his hands together briskly before bending down to hoist the piece once again. "Besides, the thing was obviously built for a midget." He bent down and pretended to be sitting so that she could see the way his muscular thighs knocked against the underside of the desk. Then he stood and lifted it in his arms. "A midget who liked to hide things," he conceded, making a face, "but a short person nonetheless."

"Isn't Nina going to miss it?" Kate felt obligated to speak up for the desk, although whether it was on Nina's behalf or because she hated to see it go she could not say.

Nick was walking down the path, but he turned and cocked his head at her. "What is this, save the seals or something? It's just a desk, not my firstborn."

He gave her a quizzical grin, but Kate was embarrassed. "I'm sorry," she murmured. "I shouldn't have stuck my nose in."

He grinned. "You've got a cute nose for sticking, Katie, and a nice big heart to go with it. But don't worry about the desk. Nina will breathe a sigh of relief when she realizes she doesn't have to abandon her Bloomingdale's charge card to pay the taxes, and ex-hubby Bob will probably be so glad to see a family heirloom out of the clutches of us Philistine Capsteins that he'll buy it himself for a very nice price."

Kate still felt awkward, but his smile was so enchanting that it removed much of the sting from his gentle reproach. "Anyway," he added softly, "it doesn't do to get too attached to things, does it?"

Kate thought fleetingly of the attic room. "No," she said, smiling shyly. "It doesn't."

He met her gaze for a moment, still smiling, before shaking his head and taking a few more steps forward. "Now, if you'll be so kind as to open the back of the pickup before I drop my taxes..."

Kate, who had been standing motionlessly, was galvanized into action. "Oh. Oh!" She moved forward to pass him, but her big bag brushed against the desk, making him stagger back a bit. "Oh, God, I'm sorry! Are you all right?" She turned back and reached out with her free arm to steady him.

"No, no, that's okay!" He took another step out of her reach. "Just...get...the back open, please?"

Kate rushed forward again and opened the rear panel of the battered pickup, her face burning at her own clumsiness. Nick maneuvered the desk onto an old quilt that lay in the bottom, then slammed the door with a look of satisfaction.

"Well, all right!" he said, slapping his hands together cheerfully. He looked at Kate and winked. "Now, what do you say we go sell our souls?"

Tate's auction house was in a huge old building behind the post office in the center of town. Kate, used to the rarefied air of New York auction houses, was surprised when Nick pulled up in front of the ramshackle, barnlike structure.

"This is it?"

Nick nodded. "This is the place. Hard to believe Bob Tate rakes in a fortune here selling fake antiques to gullible city slickers, isn't it? Present company excepted, of course." He got out of the truck and opened the rear gate to pull the desk out. "Now, let's just hope Sticky-Fingers Tate doesn't make a fuss about auctioning off something that once belonged to him."

"Why would he do that?" Kate inquired, following him out and automatically taking one end of the desk to help.

Nick shrugged. "Maybe because of me. He thinks I'm responsible for Nina's relapse into big, bad, city ways." He looked toward the entrance to the auction house with rueful anticipation. "Hates my guts, as a matter of fact."

Kate quailed. She didn't like the idea of being witness to any sort of public conflict, especially when it involved someone she knew. And she had an inkling that Nick might be the sort who enjoyed fanning the flames of such a spectacle.

"Why don't you let me help you get this thing inside?" she suggested, hoping she could take his mind off any such confrontation.

Nick agreed, even though the desk was more difficult to manipulate with her help than it would have been alone. With much huffing and puffing, and with Nick calling out instructions as if they were carrying the Mona Lisa, they managed to get the desk up the ramp and inside the building.

They were maneuvering it down the aisle to the auction stage when Kate heard her name being called out. She turned and saw the chief field buyer from Simmond's regarding her with mild astonishment. "Oh, hello, Mr. Pietro," she said, instantly aware of her flushed cheeks and disheveled hair. She was not aware of the unusual sparkle in her eyes, although that was what struck Mr. Pietro most of all.

"What are you doing with that clever little desk?" Mr. Pietro asked. The sight of the normally subdued Kate Palmer staggering happily under the weight of a piece of furniture that was attached at the other end to a total stranger quite astonished him.

"I'm... just helping... Nick... Mr. Capstein, this is Albert Pietro, my boss. Mr. Pietro, this is Nick Capstein, my, uh..." Kate had no idea why she was at a loss for words, nor why it should seem so difficult to explain Nick Capstein to someone such as Albert Pietro.

But Nick didn't notice her predicament. "Pleased to meet you, Al," he said amiably. Somehow he managed to free his right hand, twist it over the top of the desk and offer it to Mr. Pietro, who automatically extended his in return. Nick gave it an affable shake. "Katie and I are just lugging this baby onto the block for sale."

"Katie?" Mr. Pietro blinked. It was clear that he could not envision her being called anything but Miss Palmer.

"Mr. Capstein runs the inn where I'm staying," Kate mumbled, aware that her cheeks were burning. "He offered... I was just..."

Nick looked from Kate to Mr. Pietro and winked broadly. "You just can't get good help these days, know what I mean, Al? So I figured anyone with a set of legs like Katie's could be put to good use."

Mr. Pietro gaped. Kate opened her mouth to protest but found herself grinning instead, and Nick plunged blithely on.

"Now if you'd decided to stay at the inn instead of that dry little Tinkertoy over in Sutton Valley, maybe you'd have gotten a little workout, too." He looked at Mr. Pietro sympathetically.

"I...uh...the company arranged our lodgings," Mr. Pietro replied apologetically, and now it was Kate's turn to stare. She had no idea how Nick had known that the rest of the Simmond's party was staying at the Holiday

Inn in Sutton Valley. There had been a shortage of
rooms there, which was why Kate, the only female in the
group—and low person on the totem pole, so to speak—
had been relegated to the Stonecroft Inn.

She also had no idea how he had gotten Mr. Pietro to
apologize for something that was not his fault. It was not
like Albert Pietro to apologize to anyone for anything,
much less to an errant stranger for something over which
he had no control. He looked almost as flustered as Kate
and was clearly surprised by his own apology.

But Nick was apparently unfazed by the effect he was
having on both of them. He turned back to Kate and, in
a flawless imitation of a Bronx construction worker,
said, "Listen, honey. We gotta put this thing down before I bust something important, okay? Besides, how'm
I gonna pay the taxes with it if it's firewood?" He gave
Mr. Pietro a smart salute and reshouldered the burden.
"See ya, Al." And he moved forward, leaving Kate no
choice but to move with him. She could feel the astonished gaze of Mr. Pietro boring into her back.

They finally got the desk up to the auction area and set
it down. Kate realized she was out of breath. The desk
had not felt that heavy, but she felt warm and flustered.
She looked out over the dimly lit crowd and picked out
Mr. Pietro standing next to two other Simmond's employees. In their neat suits and clipped haircuts, they
looked out of place at Tate's, and Kate realized that she
had momentarily forgotten the purpose of her visit to the
auction house. She'd been so engrossed in Nick and his
business that she had not even thought about her own.
She was surprised by this unusual lapse and certain that
Mr. Pietro had recognized it. She was sure he and his
colleagues were staring at her and whispering about her

uncharacteristic behavior and her surprising companion.

Kate's reputation at work was as starched as Albert Pietro's suit—a situation she'd never tried to alter. Her colleagues tended to take her somewhat for granted, since her behavior was always so acceptably predictable. An occasional clumsiness was about her only claim to distinction at Simmond's, where everyone was expected to do their best without standing out in a crowd. Now she realized how little it took to stand out, and she felt a brief pang of resentment before her usual embarrassment overtook her.

"Hey, forget it." Nick's voice was so close to her ear that she started. "You didn't jump naked out of a cake or anything, did you?"

She looked at him, astonished that he had so accurately assessed her thoughts. He was perched lightly on the edge of the desk, smiling into her eyes.

"Oh, I didn't . . . I mean, I don't . . ." She broke off, as much confused by her own emotions as by the warm light in his eyes.

"What's the big deal?"

He was right. There was no big deal. Kate took a deep breath and returned his smile tremulously. "I had just . . . sort of forgotten he would be here, that's all," she admitted.

Nick leaned a little closer, and the twinkle in his eyes was dazzling. "I gotta confess, I'm glad to hear it," he whispered. "I mean, he seems a pretty forgettable type, don't you think?"

Kate, mesmerized by the light in his eyes, could only nod mutely. She really did have very little to do with Albert Pietro and his associates, and what they thought of her should not matter at all.

"Besides," Nick went on in that smooth, cajoling voice, "you have to admit you were having fun playing manual laborer, getting those lovely artist's hands all callused up and everything."

He picked up her left hand and cradled it in his. Of course it bore no sign of calluses, but he stroked it gently all the same. "You are having fun, aren't you, Katie?" he whispered, his voice suddenly serious.

Kate took a deep breath to steady herself. Nick's deep-blue eyes were covering her like a soft blanket, rocking her senses into a gentle state of pleasure. She wanted to close her eyes and stretch like a cat under the warmth of his gaze, but she didn't dare take them off his face. "I'm having a marvelous time," she admitted, although she wasn't quite sure what she had done that was so much fun.

"Great!" Nick clapped his hands together suddenly, making her jump again. "That means I'm doing my job," he added, and she realized that he must mean his job as host and innkeeper.

"Oh, yes. Your job," she echoed, slightly disappointed. "And I suppose I had better get to mine." She backed away awkwardly, still unwilling to relinquish that tempting stare. "They're probably... I mean, I'd better..." She gestured weakly toward Mr. Pietro at the back of the room.

Nick blinked once and cocked his head slightly. "Oh, yeah. Right. You go ahead to work. I'll stick my face in Bob's office and start the ball rolling."

He jumped off the table and headed for a small office off to the right. Kate watched him go, aware of the powerful grace of his walk. Then, with an effort, she pulled herself together and went off to confer with Mr. Pietro about the morning's duties.

There was a lot to do, and Kate didn't see Nick again for over an hour. An entire Hepplewhite dining-room set had to be sketched, along with several beds and an assortment of side tables. Seated at the side of the stage with her portable drawing board on her lap, Kate concentrated on the pieces in front of her; her charcoal pencil flew over the thick white vellum she used, recording every line in perfect detail. As usual, she lost track of her surroundings while she drew, focusing instead on the picture window of her mind's eye, which made it possible for her to draw an object from several angles without looking at it more than once.

The auction was well under way, but Kate was only vaguely aware of the noise of the proceedings. Bob Tate, a handsome, rather florid man in an expensive-looking cable-knit sweater, stood at the podium and offered piece after piece in the rapid-fire patois of the professional auctioneer. Mr. Pietro and his assistants labored over their computer printouts, checking each presold item closely before agreeing to top the highest individual bid. They also looked over several pieces that were not part of the presale agreement and occasionally came over to Kate to have her sketch an extra object in which they were interested.

She was so engrossed in her work that she didn't notice Nick standing and watching her over her shoulder. A low whistle of approval startled her, making her pencil skid across the page.

"Hey, you're good!" he said, observing as she used her rubber gum to eradicate the mark. "Those lines are perfect, just exactly right." He looked at Kate in astonishment. "You are really terrific!"

Kate was pleased at the sincerity of his praise. "Thanks. It's not much, really. I just draw what I see."

"Not many people can see with such precision. How do you get it so exact?"

Kate shrugged and looked critically at the Sheraton-style four-poster on the page. To her, it looked just like a four-poster bed—there was no nuance, no meaning to the lines beyond what they represented. "I just draw what I see," she repeated, and then, aware that this was an inadequate response, added, "I've had a lot of practice at it."

Nick crouched down at her knee, level with her drawing pad. He could not take his eyes off her hand, which was still moving with quick assurance across the page even while she spoke. "I was watching you, and you don't even look at what you're drawing. It's as if you have a little picture of that piece taped to your brain."

"I have a photographic memory, I guess," she admitted.

Nick looked up, delighted. "You do? Really? Hey, that's terrific! I mean, that's really unbelievable—a photographic memory, huh? Fabulous!"

Kate shrugged again, embarrassed at the lavish flow of his praise. Several people nearby had looked up with interest as he spoke. "It's not that special, really. A lot of people have it."

"I don't know anyone who has it," Nick said, looking at her with an ingenuous smile. "I thought it was just something the brainy kids in school made up to make it all look easy." Kate wondered if he was making fun of her, but his expression was too sincere. "How does it work? I mean, what happens in your brain to make it record that way? Are you aware of the process?"

Nobody had ever bothered to ask her such an involved question about her skill before, and she paused to think about it. "It's as if my mind is a camera, you know? It just automatically takes a picture of anything

I look at, if I look at it with a certain degree of concentration. It doesn't work if I just glance at something; I have to really look at it, even if it's just for a second. And there it is, printed on my brain. The drawing part is simple, really. I've been drawing all my life, and I guess I've developed a certain skill at drafting."

"I guess," echoed Nick, watching her face with disarming fascination.

"All I have to do is train my hand to copy what my brain sees. And this is what comes out." She looked at the bed on the page before her. "It's just a bed, though. It doesn't mean anything."

"What do you mean, it doesn't mean anything? It means a bed, doesn't it?"

"I mean—" Kate stopped. She couldn't explain what she meant. It was a bed all right. But it wasn't art. It was just a bed. A sudden, unwanted image of Carl's face flashed before her eyes, and she blinked to make it disappear.

Nick was still shaking his head slowly in disbelief. "Can you do it when you're not drawing? I mean, make pictures in your mind just for fun?"

Kate blushed. "I used to a lot, when I was a kid. I still do, sometimes."

"How? Tell me about it."

His interest was so intense that Kate found herself slipping into her camera-eye state to show him. "I just close my eyes, like this, and I can see whatever it is I want to see."

He laughed quietly. "God, that must be a blast. To be able to close your eyes and paint perfect pictures in your mind. What a gas!" Kate opened her eyes. "No! Don't open them yet!" He put his fingers lightly over her eyelids, and she could feel the heat of his hand. "Can you see me, Katie?" he asked gently.

Kate nodded. She could see nothing else. The electric tension in his body seemed to be radiating from his fingertips through her eyeballs and right down to the pit of her stomach, making her vision of him vibrate in front of her.

"Tell me. What do you see?"

"I ... I see you," she said, feeling a little foolish. "You're wearing a red sweater and ..." She stopped, embarrassed and inexplicably out of breath.

"No. I mean, what do you really see?" he asked in an intent whisper. His voice was very close, very low and husky. "A bed is a bed is a bed. But what am I? Can you see that?"

Kate swallowed. His image was so clear in her mind that she was embarrassed by the intimacy of her vision. The texture of his skin, smooth and even-toned, the inviting fullness of his lower lip, were remarkably, almost palpably, clear. "Your eyes," she stammered, not sure of what she was going to say to this remarkable man. "They're an incredible shade of blue ... not really blue, but sort of blue gray like ... like twilight, only brighter." She took a deep breath. "I think you see a lot with those eyes. You ... see things clearly, too, but in a different way than I do. I see things, but I think you see behind them." She stopped, ashamed of herself for talking like that. "They would be very hard to capture, those eyes. I don't know if I could ever paint them."

The pressure of his fingers on her eyes had turned into a caress. Kate drew in her breath as he trailed them along the side of her cheek and down to her chin. The fingers rested lightly on her neck for a moment, feeling the charged pulse just above her collarbone, then lifted gently away. "You never know until you try," Nick said to her. "You just never know about anything until you give it a try."

Chapter Four

Miss Palmer?"

Kate and Nick both started at the sound of her name. It was Edward Sampson, one of Mr. Pietro's assistants. He was looking at them with a sort of mystified disapproval, and he glanced back over his shoulder toward Mr. Pietro as if unsure how to handle his assignment.

"Mr. Pietro wants you to give us a sketch of that," he said at last, gesturing toward the item on the auction block. "If you're not too busy." His eyes darted warily toward Nick, who looked amused but remained silent.

Kate turned her eyes to the podium and was startled to see Nick's cherry desk sitting in lonesome splendor beneath the single spotlight. "But that's..."

"That's a nice piece," Nick finished for her. "Looks like a real beauty." He cocked his head meditatively, his eyes bright. "You folks interested in acquiring it?"

"We might be," Sampson admitted cautiously.

"Good idea. And don't worry," Nick assured him dismissively. "Kate'll give you something spectacular for your catalog, won't you, Katie?"

Kate agreed, and Sampson returned to his seat. "But Nick, that's your desk!" she protested when he was out of hearing.

"Not for long, I hope," Nick told her, crouching down beside her again. "I hope it'll be Simmond's in a few minutes." He spoke without looking at her, his full attention now on the podium.

Although she knew it was irrational, Kate did not want the desk to be sold to her employers. Somehow she could not imagine anything related to Nick Capstein's reality being neatly encapsulated in a Simmond's catalog. He was so different from anyone she had ever encountered that she couldn't make the connection between his outlandish approach to the world and the orderly universe of her life at Simmond's. Besides, she had already developed a rather proprietary interest in the little desk. "I don't think..." she began hesitantly, then stopped because she wasn't sure what she was going to say.

But Nick clearly had other ideas. "No buts," he told her, his eyes scanning the small crowd shrewdly. "Even if old Albert doesn't buy it for Simmond's, his interest will drive the price way up." He turned and gave her a brief, dazzling grin. "Besides, if Simmond's buys it, you can always help me steal it back, right?"

Kate's jaw dropped and Nick chuckled. "Just kidding, Princess. Larceny isn't my cup of tea, either. Now quit catching flies and start drawing."

He removed the sheet of paper with the four-poster on it and pointed to the clean surface beneath. Automatically Kate began to draw every detail of the little cherry

desk. She didn't even have to look at it to remember its
sweet proportions, the inviting busyness of its many
compartments, the soft warmth of the wood grain. Her
practised eye didn't miss a thing, even though she drew
with her eyes trained on Nick, who stood up, thrust his
hands in his pockets and waited with evident anticipation for the bidding to begin.

Up on the podium, Bob Tate had picked up the mi-
crophone. "This item isn't on the sales list—it's a...last-
minute acquisition."

He frowned, but Kate wasn't sure whether it was from
a reluctance to sell his ex-possession or because he disliked the present owner. He refused to look in Nick's
direction as he continued in a rapid, nasal, auctioneer's
twang. "We've got here a solid cherry writing desk circa
1840 with twelve compartments, three of them secret.
Tongue-and-groove   construction,   wooden   nails
throughout. Turned spindle legs, hand-carved rolltop,
inlaid writing panel—a fine item, folks. Let's have a nice
opening bid."

His sarcasm was evident to Kate, but the assembled
buyers seemed very interested in the piece in spite of
Tate's sullenness. The first bid was a respectable five
hundred dollars, and several hands went up to raise the
ante.

"Five hundred?" Nick muttered. "Christ, that won't
even pay the beverage tax."

Kate could sense his anxiety in the way he bounced
lightly up and down on his heels, and he seemed to be
whistling distractedly to himself while his lively eyes
darted around the room. As her hand moved across the
page with sure strokes, she found herself straining to
catch the tune and watching distractedly as his lips
pursed around the sound.

He had been right about Simmond's interest. As soon
as Albert's bid was registered, the price quickly rose to
a thousand dollars and then, in two-hundred-dollar in-
crements, to sixteen hundred. Nick was working to con-
ceal a smile, and his shoulders had joined the rhythmic
tattoo of his feet. Now Kate heard a smattering of syn-
copated melody and a few muttered lines of a Rolling
Stones song: "You Can't Always Get What You Want."

But if you tried, sometimes you could. Kate smiled to
herself and turned her attention to her drawing. It was
important to her that this sketch be especially good, not
just in the mechanical rendering, but in the style as well.
She wanted to capture the naive elegance of the little
desk, the inviting warmth of its little cubbies and pi-
geonholes. She wanted it to be more than a photo image; she wanted Nick to like what he saw.

But Nick didn't seem to be paying any attention to her
or what she was doing. Kate was amazed at his ability to
focus so fully on one thing after another, apparently
without switching gears. He seemed to have forgotten
her existence as he stood watching and listening, his entire body alert to every nuance of action in the room. She
was intrigued with the way his eyes narrowed and widened slightly while his head swiveled back and forth to
catch the latest bid. A constant pulse of rhythm animated his every muscle so that each little motion was
inflected with an easy grace. It was impossible not to
stare at someone so finely balanced, so of a piece. Kate,
who was quick to notice clumsiness in others as well as
herself, marveled that Nick didn't attract more attention than he did. Almost without being aware of it, she
began a sketch of him next to the one of the desk. As was
her habit, she opened her eyes very wide for a moment
and then shut them, her fingers working with rapid as-

surance as she outlined the faintly backswept shape of his hair and his unexpectedly high cheekbones with the long crease of dimple on each side.

She was halfway done with his torso when she heard him hoot softly. "Hoo, boy!"

"What happened?" she inquired, aware that she'd not been paying attention to the bidding.

"Nothing at all." Nick glanced down at her upturned face and grinned. "I think we got ourselves a little bidding war going on here, that's all." He rubbed his hands together in anticipation. "Yep, this is going to be fun—not to mention profitable."

Kate stopped drawing in order to turn her attention to the podium. The bids were coming in furiously now, and she could see a faint sheen of perspiration across Bob Tate's high forehead. She looked over at Albert Pietro and saw his thin eyebrows drawn together in a tight knot—a sure sign that he was anxious as well.

"It seems like the bidding is going up faster than it should," she observed, noticing that Tate was rattling off figures faster than they seemed to be coming in.

Nick chuckled. "That's because old Bob's bidding on it himself."

"Is that allowed?" she asked in surprise.

"When you own the auction house, it is," he replied. "Besides, Bob can't bear the idea of losing. I offered to sell him the desk outright for two grand when I talked to him before the auction. But he was so eager to convince me there would be no action on it that he turned me down." He clucked sympathetically. "Now he's gonna have to pay twice what I asked."

Kate felt a momentary pang of regret on Bob Tate's behalf. If he was willing to bid market price on the desk, he must want it badly. She hoped that his would be the final bid. Then Nick would get the money Nina needed and the desk would have an appreciative owner. She felt it deserved that much, at least.

Suddenly a tall, burly man in a thick plaid shirt and blue jeans stood up and called out a bid. He had longish, receding gray hair and an unruly ruddy beard, and he eagerly jabbed his stubby thumb in the air to emphasize his intention. Kate saw Bob Tate pause and scowl at him before he took the new bid. ·

"Uh-oh," Nick muttered. "Now the real fireworks start."

"Who's that man?" she asked.

"His name is Daniel Avon, and he's Bob's nemesis. If Bob wants something, you can bet Dan Avon will try to buy it first."

"Why?"

Nick shrugged. "Beats me. Avon's a rich New York stockbroker who decided to chuck it all and become a backwoods boy. Moved up here a few years ago and bought a huge tract of land up on Calhoun Ridge—calls it Avon Farm, like it's always belonged to Avons. He's trying to out-Vermont all the Vermonters in the Green Mountain state, and Bob's always been his special target. My guess is he figures if a third-generation Vermonter like Tate wants something, it's probably worth having. And he's got the money to buy his authenticity." He snorted derisively. "He's also the only man in town richer than Bob Tate, and he's determined to keep it that way, backwoods or no backwoods."

Suddenly Nick cupped his hand over his mouth and, in a fairly convincing falsetto, called out a bid that was three hundred dollars higher than Avon's last bid. Bob Tate looked over at him sharply, but it was clear he couldn't tell if the bid had come from Nick or from someone else.

"Did I hear twenty-eight hundred?" he inquired testily. "Is that a bid? Who made that bid?"

"Nick," Kate hissed, "you can't bid on your own merchandise! You need to sell it, not buy it!"

Nick stared at her, his eyes wide with innocence. "That wasn't me," he exclaimed softly, pressing a hand to his breastbone. "I don't know *where* that came from."

But Daniel Avon had heard the bid, and without waiting for it to be confirmed, he raised his bid another two hundred dollars. A contented grin spread across Nick's face, and Kate saw Bob Tate throw him a daggered look before going on with the bidding.

"Nothing like a little juice to keep the ball rolling," he confided to her with glee.

"The auctioneer looks like he's ready to kill you," she murmured, appalled at his audaciousness.

"He should thank me," Nick responded. "Avon used to come over to the inn and try to talk Bob into selling the place to him, lock, stock and rolltop desk. Bob got a real kick out of making the guy salivate and then turning down his offers." He made a rueful face. "I think he had a pretty low opinion of city folk even back then."

"So why should he thank you?" asked Kate. She felt uneasy with Nick's blithe disregard for his ex-brother-in-law's feelings, although she suspected it stemmed from a protective sentiment concerning Nina.

"I just helped him raise the ante a little, that's all. If I know Bob, the cold hard cash'll win out over any sentimental attachments he might have to the desk."

He was right again. At Avon's three-thousand-dollar bid, Albert—with a frown of disapproval and a resigned shrug of his shoulders—dropped Simmond's out of the bidding. Bob Tate looked furious, but he, too, no longer added his own bid to the litany of numbers he called out. Daniel Avon was now the only one still bidding on the desk. He looked around the room, a little confused at the sudden lack of interest, and seemed surprised when Tate announced acerbically that the desk was his for three thousand dollars.

"I suppose you're satisfied," Kate remarked tartly. She hadn't liked the way the business had been conducted. But Nick looked down at her and grinned without a glimmer of remorse in his eyes.

"You bet. I get Nina's tax money, Bob gets his cut of the action, and old Dan Avon gets another slice of Vermont life."

"It doesn't bother you that the price was driven up out of all proportion to its worth?"

"Why should it? Avon can afford a dozen desks if he wants 'em. Serve him right to— Hey!" He caught sight of Kate's sketch of him at last. "That's me, isn't it?"

Kate, who had forgotten all about the sketch, was embarrassed and automatically put her hand over the sketch. "It's nothing," she said dismissively. But her mind's eye recalled the picture, and she felt that it was, after all, very good.

"Don't be a goose. Of course it's not nothing." He crouched down, removed her hand and examined the portrait more closely. "It's something—something really special. You've really captured something there, Katie." He looked up at her and winked. "Course, I'm not that handsome, but thanks all the same." His face was very close to hers, and his cajoling whisper was alarmingly seductive. "You're a very talented lady, you know that?" From the way his dark, sapphire eyes held hers, Kate was sure he was referring to something other than her art.

She squirmed inwardly. "Not really, it's just . . ."

"It's just you need to have a little more faith in yourself," he finished for her. He was still holding her hand, and Kate could feel her fingers growing damp and sweaty in his tender grasp. "Tell you what, Princess," he whispered seductively. "Whaddya say we take Nina's tax money and run away together to Formentera? You could paint, and I could—" He paused, and his eyes narrowed briefly as if over some private pain. "I could watch you," he finished.

Kate had been planning to tell him that she didn't approve of his underhanded method of driving up the bid—she had been to enough auctions to know that such practices were illegal. But under the melting scrutiny of his gaze her retort vanished, and she found herself smiling foolishly into his eyes.

"I don't even know where Formentera is," she said, aware that she was speaking in the same intimate whisper. They might have been alone in a dark nightclub instead of in the middle of a drafty barn.

"Does it matter?" he inquired with a gruff little catch in his voice. His eyes softened, and she was intensely aware of his full lower lip.

Kate felt the now familiar shortness of breath and heat rising in her cheeks. She was so surprised to find herself in the middle of a tête-à-tête with the likes of Nick Capstein that she could barely find her voice, let alone think of the right thing to say. Her brain told her that now was the appropriate moment for a clever remark, that Nick's meaningfully seductive gaze was something he turned on automatically without thinking much about its effect. But her heart could not help responding with an accelerated frisson of pleasure, and her mouth steadfastly refused to form the correct words. Instead, her lips parted slightly of their own accord, and she could almost feel the anticipatory pressure of a kiss.

The kiss never happened, however. After a moment Nick shook his head slightly and, raising one finger, tapped it lightly against his pursed lips. "Mustn't, mustn't," he sang warningly, and straightened up so suddenly that Kate reared back, causing the sketch of Nick and the desk to fall to the floor.

She bent down to retrieve it with shaky hands, but Nick was there first. "I'll take that," he told her, scooping the heavy vellum out of her grasp. "Simmond's won't be needing it now, and even if they did, I don't think they'd want to include me in their fall catalog."

"But, I..." She reached for the page, but Nick held it up out of her reach. She had to grab several times before he relinquished his hold on it.

"What's wrong? You want me to pay for it, is that it?" Nick's tone was suddenly flippant and mocking.

"Of course not!" Kate retorted, stung by the suggestion, and even more by his sudden change of mood.

"Then what?" His gaze held an unexpected challenge.

Kate looked at the sketch and then away. "It's not what I wanted," she murmured in embarrassment. "It's not right."

It was true. Although she knew the likeness was accurate, Kate realized that she had not quite been able to capture Nick's elegant, slouching style any more than she'd caught the sweet beauty of the little desk. She felt like crumpling the paper and tossing it away in frustration.

Nick reached out and ruffled his hand through her hair, pulling up a thick strand and then letting it slip slowly through his fingers. "Ah, Katie," he said with a sigh. "Why are you so hard on yourself?"

Kate was astonished. How could he be so...so perceptive about someone he barely knew? she thought wonderingly. And what more did those piercing sapphire eyes see when they looked at her?

He was gazing down at her with a sidelong, knowing smile, his fingers still toying with the ends of her hair. "You are, you know. It's a perfectly good sketch, and I'd be happy to pay you real money for it, seeing as I've just come into a good chunk of three grand." He chuckled dryly. "But I'll tell you what I'll do. I'll make you a trade. That sketch in exchange for dinner tonight." He looked around surreptitiously, then bent close to her as if they were making some clandestine arrangement. "Whaddya say? Do we have a deal, or what?"

Kate didn't know whether to laugh or cry. In the space of a few minutes she felt as if she'd been put through a month's worth of emotional postures. Nick Capstein left her feeling dazed and exhausted and even less sure of herself than usual. She had absolutely no idea what to make of him.

But she did know that she didn't want it to stop. And he must have seen that, because he gave a satisfied pat to his stomach and straightened. "Ding!" he said in perfect imitation of a game-show host's hucksterish glee. "That's the buzzer! Your time's up, Miss Palmer. I'm afraid we'll have to assume that's a yes answer."

Kate managed a wan smile. "It's a yes," she said, wishing he would slow down and give her a chance to catch up with his outrageous patter. But his grin was so infectious that her own broadened. "It's definitely a yes," she repeated in a stronger voice.

"Good." Nick looked up. "Uh-oh, here comes Mountain Man Avon. Get set for a heavy dose of good ole boy." He spun around and instantly assumed a hearty, welcoming pose as Daniel Avon approached. "Daniel, my man, good to see you!" He clapped the big man on the back, and Avon responded with a grimace that was half smile, half snarl.

"Paid a pretty penny for that desk of your sister's," he said accusingly.

"Ah, well, it's worth every cent, you know. Benjamin Franklin's grandson sat at that desk, did you know that?"

Kate's eyes widened. Why hadn't Nick mentioned that to her before? Simmond's would probably have bid considerably more for a desk with such historic value.

But Daniel Avon was not so easily persuaded. "Like hell he did," Avon scoffed. "Only grandson to sit at that thing was Bob Tate himself—he told me it was his grandfather's the first time I saw the piece up at his inn."

He placed a strong emphasis on the last two words, but Nick remained unfazed. "Surely you don't believe everything old Bobby tells you, do you, Dan? My God, he has the worst habit of talking things down—doesn't want anybody to know what a fortune he had tied up in that old inn. Course, now that he gets a commission off the sale of the desk..." He cocked his head. "You sure he didn't mention Ben Franklin's grandson?"

"Listen, Capstein. I know you and your tricks. It's people like you come up here and ruin the natural beauty of this state."

"You mean ex-New Yorkers like me, Dan?" he inquired innocently. "That's funny. I thought you were an ex-New Yorker yourself." He looked down at Kate and explained with exaggerated patience, "Being an ex-New Yorker is like being an ex-con around these parts, Kate. Definitely a no-no."

Avon was not amused. "I hear that loud music coming from your place till all hours of the night. You and your sister have no respect for the beauty of this area. You think it's just an outpost of Manhattan—another place to raise hell."

Nick cocked his head. "What's the matter, Avon? Your cows complaining?"

Kate had to duck her head to hide a smile. Daniel Avon was a little too pompous for her taste, and she was enjoying Nick's audacious baiting, even though she hoped it wouldn't escalate into a scene.

Avon shook his head in disgust. "People like you don't deserve to have a place like the Stonecroft Inn. You don't care a hoot for historic integrity. You don't care for anything but your own good time." His scowl swept over Kate as if she were equally responsible for this depraved state of affairs. "You got no respect for people, either, Capstein. You don't belong around here."

"Unlike you natives, right, Dan?"

The scowl got uglier. "I'll have you know my grandfather was born in these parts. Avons have had land in Vermont for two generations."

Nick snorted. "They owned a pig farm near White River Junction, Dan. And neither generation could wait to get out."

Avon actually took a threatening step toward Nick, who immediately put up his hands in a placating gesture. "All right, all right. Truce. You've got the desk, and the world is a little safer for Vermonters now that us ugly city slickers have lost control of a little bit of history. So what do you want with me?"

Avon was still disgruntled, but Nick's sudden change of tack caught him off balance. "I need to know about the secret compartments," he grumbled. "Can't seem to make 'em work, and Tate won't give me the time of day on 'em."

Nick grinned. "I do declare," he drawled, "you Vermont boys got a funny way of asking for help, you know that? But never mind—fortunately we depraved New Yorkers are only too glad to help, aren't we, Kate?"

Without waiting for a reply, he picked up Kate's sketch of the desk and showed it to Avon. "It just so happens Katie made us a very neat little sketch of your desk, Dan. You can clearly see where all three secret compartments are located. These two are pretty easy to figure out—they just align with the grooves in the wood, and you open them by pressing the little cherry knob." He pointed to the desk while Avon squinted at the paper. "But you see here? Where the two planes of wood come together at an angle? This compartment is the real surprise."

"I don't see any secret compartment," Avon grumbled.

"That's because it's so secret," Nick replied matter-of-factly. "But if you'll look real close, you'll notice that our lovely artist-in-residence here has exactly duplicated the tiny inlaid knob. You just press on that piece right there and that opens the super-de-duper secret drawer. See?" It was clear that Avon didn't, and Kate herself wasn't sure she knew what Nick was talking about. She craned her neck to see what she had drawn, but he was waving his fingers in a general sweep across the page and it was impossible to tell exactly what he was referring to. She wondered if he did himself, but Nick didn't seem to notice the confusion his explanation was causing.

"So, Dan, you're all set," he said with finality. "Now you've got Ben Franklin's desk all for your very own. The secret of the last drawer has been handed down by word of mouth from generation to generation. It's a pleasure to be able to pass it on to you." He bowed neatly, and Kate saw the sparkle of amusement in his eyes as he lowered his head. Catching her eye, he winked broadly, and she had to suppress the urge to giggle. "Now you've got someplace to hide your illegal drugs and stuff, right?" he inquired lightly.

It was meant to be a joke, of course, but Dan Avon clearly had no sense of humor about it. He grew very still and very red in the face, and it seemed as if his small eyes would bulge out of his head. He looked as if he might explode at any moment and was barely containing his rage. Even Nick was taken aback by this inordinate display. But after a few frozen seconds, Avon somehow managed to pull himself together.

"Don't be a fool, Capstein," he muttered stiffly, his voice filled with disgust. "*You* may have used the desk for such purposes, but I can assure you I won't." His eyes traveled back to the picture and then rested shrewdly on Kate for a moment, as if he were trying to assess her position in this madness. Kate knew he had been outraged by Nick's flippant suggestion, but she thought he might also be confused by the rush and whir of his chatter. In an odd way, she could sympathize with him. It was hard to tell when Nick was serious.

"You draw this?" he inquired gruffly, fixing her with his most intimidating glare.

"Yes, I did," she replied in a meek voice.

"Not a bad likeness of me, either, is it?" Nick said proudly. "Whaddya think, Avon, is it me?" He jutted his chin out and offered Avon his handsome profile.

Avon seemed to be debating whether or not he could get away with landing his right fist on the proffered chin. Kate found herself holding her breath. "A picture is no good," he growled at last. "You'll have to show me on the desk itself."

"Sorry, Dan," Nick said. "No can do."

"What do you mean, no can do?" Avon glowered.

"I mean, a lesson isn't included in the purchase price. Besides, figuring it out for yourself is part of the fun, don't you think?" His glittering eyes held an unmistakable challenge.

"Why, you little..." Avon took a threatening step forward and clenched his fists. Kate sucked in her breath and shrank into herself. She had suspected Nick liked to get himself into outrageous situations, but this was a bit much! She shut her eyes and waited for the blow to land.

But it didn't. At the last moment, Avon apparently decided not to make even more of a scene. "You'll be sorry for this, Capstein," he muttered as he backed away. "One of these days you'll be sorry." With that, he turned on his heel and lumbered off to claim his prize from the auction block.

Kate, whose heart would not stop racing, stared after him. Then she stared at Nick, who was watching Avon go with a strange expression on his face. "Why wouldn't you show him?" she inquired incredulously.

Nick kept on staring at Avon's back. His brows were drawn tight across his eyes, and he seemed to be struggling with some private dilemma. Suddenly he raised his hand and swiped it dismissively through the air. "Ah, forget it," he said. "It's not worth the trouble." And he spun around and walked rapidly toward the door, leaving Kate to wonder if he had been answering her question or his own.

is so right, there was no sign of his true self in it. He was
the one bit of reason to even attempt the business. She
found it almost impossible to concentrate on drawing
furniture against Nick's sharp moods and sunny smiles.
"Welcome," he called suddenly, with a sunny smile,
when he arrived and went up bundled packages from Lisa's
in a rush to the studio. She laid aside the drawing and
flounced happily.

Chapter Five

In Nick's absence, Albert Pietro recovered his poise and
commandeered Kate to fill in the details on a whole set
of dining-room furniture in the back room. She was kept
busy on this project for the rest of the morning and most
of the afternoon. By the time she had finished, there was
still no sign of Nick at Tate's. She had no idea where he
had disappeared to, or why.

She went back to the Stonecroft Inn by herself, wishing he wasn't so abrupt in his comings and goings and
wondering why he had left without telling her. He had
seemed defeated all of a sudden—angry—although she
did not know what he was angry about. At Dan Avon?
At himself? Maybe she had done something? No, it
couldn't be that; all she had done was watch.

He was so perplexing, she mused, so mercurial, that
she had no idea how to place him in her mind. She had
drawn his picture with her usual accuracy, but the real

Nick Capstein, she was sure, defied description, just as he defied convention. Kate sighed and turned back to her work. She doubted whether he really meant to keep their dinner date. It would be like him, she thought, to make plans so offhandedly that he forgot all about them. Look at what had happened to her room reservation.

Ah, well, she told herself, I won't be surprised if nothing comes of it. Or disappointed. But she knew that wasn't true. She would be disappointed. Already she felt slightly deflated, as if, in Nick's absence, the world had once again assumed its normal humdrum proportions. She tucked his sketch firmly into the back of her notebook without daring to look at it again. *If* she and Nick actually had dinner later on, she would have to give it to him, but she knew its flat accuracy would always be a reproach to her, because she had so clearly failed to capture Nick's incandescent charm. He had probably just said he liked it to be polite, just as he had probably made the dinner invitation to be polite. After all, what could they possibly have in common? She should be glad if there was no dinner after all—what on earth would she find to talk about with Nick Capstein? Kate decided she would not be disappointed; she would be relieved.

When she finally returned to the inn, Nick was not in evidence, and Kate was sure she had been right about the invitation. Then she found a note tacked to the door of her attic room: Gone to buy provisions for the Ravening Beasts. Be back in time to pick you up for dinner at eight. Save yourself for me. Nick.

Kate looked at the note and laughed softly. As relieved as she had been a moment ago, she was now equally relieved—and more than a little elated—that she was going to spend the evening with him after all. Nick seemed to imbue even this scrawled message with his own private brand of energy. She lay across her bed and looked at the headlong tilt of his cursive, imagining him tossing off the note as he ran out the door. He had a remarkable ability to do two things at once and make it look easy.

Kate did not have that skill. She tended to concentrate on one thing at a time, and she concentrated on getting dressed for dinner with exceptional care. A shower in the erratic little bath on the second floor took quite a while and required much patience; afterward, she sat and brushed her hair meditatively for almost an hour until it dried into loose, shining waves. She never tired of the view from her little windows, and as she watched and brushed, dusk melted into night with exquisite precision.

After some deliberation, Kate decided to wear her rose mohair sweater with the cowl neck and a charcoal skirt. She didn't have much to choose from, but she liked the way the sweater made her pale skin bloom and the neckline revealed the slender line of her throat to some advantage. She was awkward with the little makeup she used, but she managed to apply mascara, shadow and blush to her satisfaction.

To Nick's, apparently, as well. "Whew!" he whistled softly when she appeared shyly in the lobby. He shook his head slowly and smiled, and Kate could tell he was genuinely pleased. His surveillance made her feel even rosier, as if a sunlamp were bathing her in its warmth.

"You look lovely," he said after a moment of silent appreciation. "I mean, really, really pretty."

"You seem surprised," Kate remarked with a nervous shadow of a smile.

Nick frowned. "That's not right," he chided gently. "That's not what you're supposed to say when a man tells you how pretty you are."

Kate fluttered her hands. "What should I have said?"

"How about 'Thank you'?" he prompted with a dry little smile.

"Thank you," she repeated obediently, but his expression made her smile in earnest. "Thank you very much," she added with a quick curtsy.

Nick seemed satisfied. He adjusted the collar of his shirt and cleared his throat. "You might also mention how nice your date is looking this evening," he suggested, looking airily up at the ceiling.

Kate chuckled. "You're looking rather nice yourself, Nick," she told him.

And he was. He wore a well-cut dark sports jacket over a crisp white shirt and thick tweed trousers. A maroon silk necktie was knotted rakishly at his throat, and Kate realized that his flair for clothes extended beyond his usual casual outfits. Only his footwear belied the suave formality of his attire—black Reebok hightops peeked from beneath his cuffs.

"*I* thought so," he murmured, and then stepped forward and tucked her arm into the crook of his elbow. "So, sweet Kate, now that we're both looking so fine, shall we go forth to sample the myriad delights of this exotic and stimulating Vermont kingdom?"

"A lovely idea," she agreed, already feeling heady with the success of the evening. "Where shall we start?"

Nick looked at her sideways and winked. "Well, since there's only one place open within a twenty-mile radius that serves edible food—besides this one, of course..."

"Of course."

"I suggest we start there." He opened the door with a flourish. "What do you think?"

Kate smiled, thinking how much she was enjoying this silly conversation. "I think that's a marvelous idea," she said, and swept past him into the cold night, unaware of the dazzling effect of her smile.

The Bear and Claw looked inauspicious from the outside—more like a roadhouse bar than a gourmet restaurant. But inside it offered a pleasant surprise, with a welcoming fire and deep banquette seating that looked cozy and inviting. Nick was apparently known and expected, for he was greeted by name and conducted to a private table with a full view of the hearth.

"A bottle of Perrier-Jouet, Clive," he instructed the maître d' with an airy wave of his hand.

"What'd you do, win the lottery?" Clive inquired tartly.

Nick looked shocked. "I'll have you know this is by way of being a very special celebration," he said. "The lady and I have just completed important business and artistic negotiations, and we're in dire need of refreshment. Besides, it's none of your damn business how I'm gonna pay for it."

Clive shrugged with dry humor. "I just have to make sure you *do* pay, Nick."

Nick rose in his seat and made a vaguely menacing gesture. "My good man, are you suggesting...?"

"Relax." Clive patted him down good-naturedly. "I know you got the money. You sold Avon that little desk, and now you think you own the town." He arched his brow speculatively at Kate. "Perrier-Jouet it is, then." And he walked away.

Nick clicked his teeth together in mock exasperation. "That's what happens in a small town," he confided. "You can't burp without everyone hearing about it."

Kate giggled. "I think you're probably a major topic of conversation around here no matter what you do," she said.

He slouched back, rested his arms along the back of the banquette and looked at her. "You think so? And why is that?"

He was watching her with such penetrating energy that Kate felt a slight nervousness returning. "I guess it's because you...you're so..." She smiled as she searched for the right word.

"Such a depraved New Yorker?" he prompted with a wry grimace.

"Not exactly. Although Daniel Avon must get some satisfaction from thinking you are."

"Just warped, then, huh? A little..."

Just then the champagne arrived, nestled in an elegant silver urn filled with ice. After it had been set down beside their table, Nick waved the waiter away, preferring to uncork it himself as he spoke. He seemed to be getting some private satisfaction out of describing himself derogatorily. "A little off the beaten path, as they say up here?"

"Of course not!" Kate retorted immediately. Something about his tone of voice made her bristle. "You're just—" she spread her palms helplessly "—you're just a very unique person, that's all."

"Unique weird or unique nice?"

She managed to keep her eyes on his. "Unique nice," she said firmly.

Nick smiled and handed her a glass. "You know something, Katepalmer?" He looked at her with such intensity that she shivered suddenly. "So are you."

"Oh, I'm not—" she began, but he silenced her by clinking his fluted champagne glass against hers.

"To being a very unique-nice person," he toasted with an odd gruffness in his voice. He was suddenly serious, and Kate had to lean forward to hear him. "To two very unique-nice people. To us."

"To us," echoed Kate wistfully, and they both drank.

Nick drained his glass at once. He refilled it and topped off Kate's without asking. Then he leaned back again and rested his free hand along the banquette near her ear. She had the feeling, from the way he smiled at her, that he was well aware of the astounding effect those nearby fingers were having on her.

"So, Kate, do you know any depraved New Yorkers? Any unique-weird folks, off-the-beaten-path types, back home in the Big Apple?" The question was vaguely challenging.

"Uh, no. Not really. That is, I—" She shook her head. "I keep pretty busy at work," she added, as if this explained it all.

Nick pursed his lips. "Seems like old Albert is pretty left of center, if you know what I mean."

Kate had to laugh. "Albert Pietro is about as middle of the road as you can get," she said, surprising herself by the conviction in her voice. "As a matter of fact, everybody at Simmond's is pretty...is pretty..."

"Boring?"

"No!" Kate felt obliged to come to the defense of her colleagues. "I mean...they may not be...it may not be the most exciting place in the world to work, but it's not boring."

"So you like your job."

"Of course I do." Kate automatically allowed Nick to refill her glass once more, although she had only taken a few sips. Then she saw, by his slight smile, that she had not sounded convincing. "Well, it's not perfect, but it's fairly interesting."

"How interesting?"

Kate shifted uncomfortably and realized that this motion had brought her to within a hair's breadth of Nick's fingertips. She froze. "Well, I get to do a lot of drawing, and that's good. I travel a bit, and see lots of lovely antiques." It sounded lame, even to her.

"Do you get much time to do your own work?"

"My own work?" Her eyes widened, turning to pale-blue crystal in the reflected firelight.

"Your own work. Your own art. The stuff you make up out of your head."

Kate blinked. Was it possible that he even knew her secret insecurities about her art? That she would not allow herself to explore the limits of her own creativity because she was afraid there might be nothing there? Carl Masters may have contributed to her insecurities, but the seeds themselves had been sown long ago. Still, Nick could not have known this. He was merely making small talk—dinner conversation.

"I don't really have much time for that," she mumbled.

His brows lifted quizzically. "Really? What do you do with your free time, then?"

Kate sensed he was probing, but she wasn't sure for what. And she didn't want to tell him that her free time was largely frittered away by the exigencies of daily life in a big city. What little free time she had was spent doing nothing very exciting with her small circle of friends or else alone in the precious privacy of her tiny apartment. Carl's departure had been somewhat of a relief to her after enduring years of his subtle contempt. But she was lonely without him—without the familiarity of his presence—which was why she had allowed the relationship to go on for so long.

Still, her life had never seemed so circumscribed to her as it did now, when subjected to the reflected scrutiny of someone like Nick Capstein. Nick, she was sure, never rested for a moment when in New York. His life would be a whirlwind of events both professional and social, all of them exciting and breathless and . . . off the beaten path. In spite of her discomfort, Kate smiled.

"Why the secret smile, Kate?" he asked immediately, and she sensed rather than saw his fingertips edge closer to the nape of her neck.

"I was just thinking," she said, making an effort to concentrate on her words, "how different your life must be from mine. In New York, I mean."

"Oh, I'm not so sure it's different," he said musingly. "I might do different things than you do, but I think, a lot of the time, I might feel the way you do."

Kate blinked. "What way is that?"

He pursed his lips. "You know. A little restless, a little unfocused, like maybe there's something better out there if I only had the energy to try for it."

Kate was sure she had never felt that way before in her life, but suddenly it seemed as if that were exactly the way she sometimes felt after all. She was so surprised by this revelation that she forgot to ask Nick the logical questions—such as what he did for a living. Instead, she took a moment to think about this new perspective. And while she did, she became aware of a slight stirring in her heavy hair.

With a soft intake of breath, she waited for Nick's fingertips to make contact with the skin behind her ear. When it came, it was so tentative that she could barely discern the touch from her anticipation of it. Then she felt the backs of his fingers trailing gently along the rounded column of her neck, and she heard him sigh in wonder. Her whole body seemed to vibrate with the sound.

"You are so soft," he murmured, shaking his head. "So incredibly soft." His eyes were half-closed and he seemed very far away. But his touch was warm and intimate as his fingers explored the front of her throat and up under her chin.

He didn't open his eyes until he felt her nervous swallow, and then, when he did, he was smiling dreamily. "Katepalmer," he said, savoring the syllables of her name, "I'm afraid I've totally forgotten what we were talking about."

"So have I," she whispered, staring at him with parted lips. She felt strangely separated from herself, or from the usual person who was Kate Palmer. That Kate Palmer was watching in disbelief as this one sat next to Nick Capstein, their silhouettes bathed in golden firelight, looking exactly like the couples she had often seen sitting in the windows of elegant bistros in New York. She was fascinated as this couple, their eyes locked in some intricate silent dialogue, moved their heads closer and closer together. She looked on in astonishment as their lips simultaneously moistened and made contact, their faces tipped elegantly to receive the kiss without any awkward adjustment of nose or chin.

It wasn't until she felt his lips on hers that Kate jumped back into her own body in time to receive the distinct impression of heat and light as it emanated from

Nick's lips and flowed down her throat like nectar. The hand that had played around her throat brought her closer so that she could feel the starched rustle of Nick's shirt against her cheek and smell his exotic after-shave. His mouth felt full and pillowy, the lips as tender as they had looked to her artist's eye. But she had not imagined that he would taste so good or make her feel so...so liquid, so weak.

It was not a long kiss and, she reflected later, had probably seemed quite circumspect from the dining room's point of view. But for Kate it had been earth-shaking in the most romantic way. Her narrow romantic history had not prepared her for anything like Nick Capstein's first kiss. Nor did it prepare her for what came after. Pulling away with obvious reluctance and looking at her with an almost palpable sensuality, Nick took a slow, deep breath and smiled shakily.

"I'm starving," he murmured. "Let's eat."

And to Kate's great astonishment, she found she was, too. She was sure the powerful effects of his embrace would render her senseless and unable to eat, but once she'd recovered her composure, which took several minutes—minutes filled with Nick's gay, irreverent chatter—she discovered that she was absolutely raven-ous. She could not understand why Nick had chosen to undercut such a provocative moment, but it suddenly didn't matter that he had. Hey, she thought to herself proudly, I'm handling this pretty well. I'm doing just fine!

And she was. She began to laugh at Nick's lunatic comments on their dining companions, then offer some of her own—shyly at first, but then, aware of Nick's delight in her dry humor, with more assurance. In the remote corners of her mind Kate felt that she had suddenly and inexplicably become somebody else—somebody self-assured and pretty and fun. "This isn't you," whispered a little voice. "You're not like this." But she was having far too much fun to care.

Nick had ordered an incredible amount of food. "Do you always eat so much?" she inquired as the waiter placed dish after dish before them.

"Why not?" Nick rubbed his hands together and surveyed the table's bounty with relish.

"I'd get big as a house if I ate like this all the time," she replied.

"Bull. You're a naturally thin person—you just don't trust your body enough to test it out." He thrust a warm roll slathered with butter in her direction. "Here. Try this on for size."

"How do you know if I'm naturally thin?" asked Kate, taking a bite. "Mmm, this is delicious."

"My recipe," he said offhandedly. "I traded it for one of the chef's specialties—that omelet we had last night." He took a huge bite of roll and went on talking without missing a beat. "How do I know? I look, that's how I know. You may have a photographic memory, Miss Kate, but I . . . I happen to have a particular genius for women's bodies." He rolled his eyes and winked. "I'm sort of like an idiot savant, you know? I don't know much, but what I know, I know rea-l-l-lly well." He glanced under the banquette at her long legs. "You're a beautiful woman," he added in a more serious tone of voice. "You don't know it, but that doesn't make you any less beautiful. Maybe it even makes you more beautiful. So have some cream of asparagus soup, and enjoy."

Kate was nonplussed. Did he really think her beautiful? With her broad shoulders and heavy eyebrows and too-full lower lip? She could not believe it. But Nick had a way of making a person believe whatever he said, and tonight was a night to suspend disbelief. "Thank you," she said simply, and opened her mouth to taste the soup.

More wine was served with the veal course, and Nick ordered a heady almond liqueur with the coffee—more alcohol than Kate had imbibed in a long, long time. As the meal drew to a close she found herself getting more and more giddy. Everything seemed dangerously off balance, but deliciously so. She had a sudden flash of Nina standing at the door of the inn and giggling about something dangerously delicious. So *this* was how such people lived—on the edge, without any kind of commonplace routine to keep them tethered to the earth. Everything—the restaurant, the food, the wine—seemed to have a special tint of brilliance about it. Even Nick, who tended to glow in the most mundane circumstances, was particularly incandescent. Kate knew it was the wine, but it was something more, besides. Nick had woven a magic spell, and even though she knew it was magic—not real—she was loving every minute of it.

Exactly how far from her own reality she had ventured was made clear to her as they were leaving the Bear and Claw. Threading her way ahead of Nick through the now crowded restaurant, she suddenly found herself face-to-face with her colleagues from Simmond's, who had obviously come in after them.

"Albert!" She stopped so suddenly that Nick bumped into her from behind. "I mean, Mr. Pietro!" Her face grew hot as she looked around the table at the startled faces above the neat business suits. "What are you all doing here?"

"We worked quite late on the inventory," said Mr. Pietro, his face expressing disapproval, as though Kate should have been there with them. "We were told this was the only decent place to eat after 8:00 p.m."

"It's very good," said Kate, and discovered that she was having difficulty remembering how to conduct an ordinary conversation. I must be tipsier than I thought, she thought, and made an effort to pull herself together. "I can recommend the cream of asparagus soup, and the veal, and..." She stopped as she realized that none of the men around the table were listening. Instead they were staring—staring at her, and at Nick, who for once seemed strangely quiet.

"Yes, we noticed that you seemed to be... enjoying yourself," said Mr. Pietro after a pause that seemed to go on forever.

"Oh," Kate said lamely. She felt her knees falter and wondered how she could explain her outrageously unprofessional behavior to the satisfaction of these dour young men. Then, aware of Nick behind her, she realized that she didn't owe them any explanation at all. She was off duty and could do whatever she liked.

The fact that she had never done anything like this before should be of no concern—not, at least, to Albert Pietro and company. She straightened and added in a stronger voice, "As a matter of fact, I haven't enjoyed myself so much in years." She bent down to her employer and said in a loud whisper, "I really recommend the Perrier-Jouet, Albert. Although I don't imagine Simmond's would enjoy seeing it on your expense account."

Mr. Pietro sucked in his breath sharply, and Kate heard Nick bite back a snicker. "They certainly would not," Albert sniffed.

Nick leaned across Kate's shoulder. "Hey, Al," he said conspiratorially. "Maybe, just this once, you

could . . . you know . . . cheat a little? The accounting office'd never know the diff, would they?" He looked
around the table, and Kate could almost feel the ingenuous glitter of his eyes. "Hell," he added more loudly
still, "Katie and I'll never tell 'em you're padding the
bill. Will we, Katie?"

The look of shock on her colleagues' faces was enough
to make Kate quail, but she felt Nick's warm hand at the
small of her back. "No," she echoed. "We'll never tell."

Nick started to propel her away from the silent group.
"Go ahead, guys, live it up a little. After all, you gotta
do something to make up for being incarcerated at the
Holiday Inn, don't you?"

And before Kate could hear any of them reply, he
marshaled her out into the night.

The frosty air hit her like a cold shower, but instead of
sobering her up, it only made her feel more giddy. She
looked at Nick and grinned widely. "I . . . you . . . I can't
believe . . ." she began, and collapsed into giggles.

Nick tucked her shoulder under his arm and drew her
close as they hurried across the parking lot. The cold was
taking her breath away, and the laughter wasn't helping. By the time they got into the car, she was gasping.
"What?" he asked, looking at her fondly. "What can't
you believe?"

Kate used her knuckle to wipe the tears out of her
eyes. "I can't believe you told Albert Pietro to cheat on
his bill. Albert Pietro has never cheated on anything in
his life, I'm sure of it! Oh, the look on his face . . ." She
began to giggle again.

"Well, maybe it's time he did a little cheating. Loosen
him up a little, know what I mean?" He reached out and
brushed her hair away from her coat, letting his fingers
rest briefly on the back of her neck. "I think everyone

could use a little loosening up now and then, don't you agree?''

He was smiling, but his voice was so gentle and serious that Kate stopped laughing. She stared at him for a moment, suddenly shy again before that penetrating gaze. She knew that Nick wanted something from her, but she wasn't sure what. "Y-yes," she stammered awkwardly. "Yes, you're right."

He watched her for so long that she finally turned to face the front of the car so he wouldn't see her burning cheeks. Her newfound confidence had suddenly left her, and she was herself again, shy and unsure.

Nick started the car, and they drove back to the inn in silence. Kate felt herself sobering up, but she was still totally unable to read her companion's mood or intent. Once again, she felt that she was out of her depth with Nick, out of her league. She didn't know what he wanted—what he meant.

Nick pulled the car into the lot at the Stonecroft Inn, and Kate got out at once. Suddenly she longed for the comfort of her little attic room, and she started up the flagstone path to the front door. But Nick took her hand from behind and made her stop.

"No," he said with a gentle shake of his head. "Not yet."

Kate's heart was hammering so loudly she was sure he would hear it. "Not yet?" she repeated dumbly.

"I want you to see something first. Out back."

"But it's cold out!"

He pulled on her hand. "We'll survive. Come on."

Kate allowed him to pull her around the gravel path to the back of the main house. The ground was dark and very hard, and she slipped a little on the hoarfrost that covered the grass. But Nick tucked her arm more firmly into his and supported her as they walked away from the house into the moonlight.

They were standing in the field that Kate could see from her attic window, in the middle of the landscape she had painted that morning. The air was so cold it felt like ice water pouring down her throat, and she gasped a little as she inhaled. The moonlight had converted the field and the trees beyond into a negative image of the scene she had sketched: the bowl of earth was black and the trees tipped in silver. The sky rose above them like an arch of black velvet, and the moon made a path before their feet that stretched invitingly into the dark distance beyond.

"Stairway to the stars," Nick sang, then added softly, "Nice, isn't it?"

"It's beautiful," Kate whispered, not wanting to shatter the pristine beauty with her voice. "It's breathtaking."

"I knew you'd think so," he said, sounding pleased. "Cold?"

She shook her head. "I don't mind."

For a while they just stood there and looked out across the field, unaware of anything but the beauty of the scene before them. Kate felt as if she had walked into a painting, and suddenly she knew what was missing from her landscape sketches: she had drawn what she saw—and not what she had experienced.

"You could do it justice," Nick murmured against her ear. "With your eye, I know you could."

This time she was not surprised that he had read her thoughts. "I'd like to try," she said. "I'd really love to try. But it's not my eye that's important. It's... something else."

She was not aware that Nick was watching her profile instead of the landscape or that he seemed about to say something more. She didn't notice the bittersweet mingling of melancholy and desire in his eyes as he watched her watching, watched her drinking in the sights with a look of rapt wonder on her face.

After a while he shook her gently out of her reverie. "Come on, let's go in. You're shivering."

Kate looked down and realized that she was. She let him lead her through the back door to the inn and up the stairs, unwilling to say anything that might disturb the mood. Magic had befallen her again.

When they reached the top of her narrow stairs, Nick opened the door to her room. He stepped in and let her come up behind him. The room was flooded in the same silver moonlight, and neither of them moved to turn on the light. Kate was filled with a breathless anticipation that had nothing to do with the cold. She turned to face Nick, waiting, wondering what would happen next.

Nick, too, seemed to be wondering. His expression was unreadable, and he seemed oddly indecisive. What did he want? What was he waiting for? she wondered. Kate knew she could never bring herself to make the first move, could not even make herself take the two steps necessary to move into the circle of his arms. Too much was holding her back—insecurity, shyness, confusion. She didn't know what was expected of her, or even what to expect, with a man like Nick Capstein. She felt as if she were floating in a sea of molten-silver light, and she didn't know if she would sink into it or swim for shore. All she knew was that if he made one move—one gesture to look, to show that he wanted her—she would gladly have fallen into his arms. So she stood there, awkward and lovely as a colt, waiting to see what would happen.

At last Nick smiled. And his smile was like a release: in a moment, she was in his embrace. His hands spread against the soft material of her sweater, kneading the slight ridge of her spine beneath with a sort of hungry fascination. He held her so close against him that she could barely breathe. But she didn't think about breathing. She thought only that she had waited too long to touch those lips, to feel those hands, to relish the weight of his hard chest pressing against her breasts. She wanted to place her hands on his body, to begin exploring that exhilarating terrain; but she simply did not know where to begin.

Instead, with her arms raised but not yet touching him, she opened her mouth beneath the pressure of his, and she heard him moan low in his throat—the dark sound of desire. Her heart beat so passionately that she could feel it throbbing in her temples. It seemed as if Nick might lift her off the floor and devour her where he stood. She would not have minded if he had. She stood there with her arms open and her heart singing. She was his to the very core of her being.

But suddenly something changed. Nick did not stop kissing her, but it was no longer the passionate embrace she so eagerly sought. Instead, he relinquished his hold on her mouth until his lips were barely, chastely, brushing against hers. His hands still grasped her possessively, but they slipped upward and across her neck until they were merely resting on her shoulders. Confused, Kate let her hands drop back to her sides without having caressed him, as she so longed to do.

His lips were still tender, and they lingered on hers as if reluctant to part, but after a moment more he pulled away. Kate felt groggy and dazzled at the same time. What was happening here? Why had he kissed her? Why pull away?

He was still smiling, but there was a painful expression in his eyes. "This is the last thing on earth I need," he murmured ruefully. "I'm not the type to wish upon a lucky star." He ran one finger longingly down her face from her temple to her chin, gazing at the rapt, open face before him. Then he placed it over her lips before she could ask him what he meant. He just shook his head minutely, as if in answer to her unspoken questions, but he did not explain himself. Instead, he let out his breath in a deep sigh.

"Say good-night, Kate," he whispered, and moved his fingertip away.

"Good night, Kate," she echoed obediently, and didn't even see him smile as he left. She did hear him humming softly under his breath as he left, but she didn't recognize the song until later.

He'd been humming a Neil Sedaka tune that had been a hit when she was just a child. But she knew the title: "Go Away, Little Girl, Before I Beg You to Stay."

Chapter Six

Kate lay awake for hours after he left, trying to decipher his cryptic message. What had he meant, about wishing on a lucky star? What was the last thing in the world he needed? A simple kiss? Another woman? A commitment?

A roll in the hay?

For although the term was crude, she could not deny that that was exactly what she'd wanted to happen—not *expected* to happen necessarily, because she was too unsure of herself and of him to feel that strongly about it. But she had definitely wanted contact of a carnal nature. Now, lying awake in her austere little wrought-iron bed, she berated herself for not having made herself clear sooner. She should have touched him, she chastised herself. She should have let him know how she felt.

Not that it would have mattered that she wanted him—not to Nick Capstein. Someone like Kate Palmer was the last thing in the world he needed. He was used to excitement, flamboyance, unpredictability. What did he want with the awkward attentions of a shy, insecure art illustrator whose idea of a good time was crying over an old Greta Garbo film?

Kate knew she was being hard on herself, but her frustration could only vent itself in castigation. Still, even in her moments of deepest doubt, she suspected that she was wrong about Nick. There *had* been something he wanted of her, or with her. She was almost sure of it. She had sensed a melancholy, almost painful longing, a deep poignancy, in his kisses, even though they'd ended in such disturbing chastity. Of course she could have been wrong, but it seemed as if Nick really *had* liked her, really had enjoyed their evening together. But why? What had he found so fascinating in her that she couldn't find in herself?

Kate did not dislike who she was, but she had been aware of her limitations ever since childhood, when it had seemed to her that nothing she did was good enough for her revered, remote father. Her affair with Carl Masters, the only long-term sexual relationship she'd ever had, had only reinforced her insecurities.

In a way, her shortcomings were something of a comfort to her. They allowed her to circumnavigate many of the thornier issues of her existence, such as what to do about her career and her aspirations, and even how to deal with love—or the lack of it—in her life. Despite her insecurities, she had never really regretted being Kate Palmer. And then Nick had come along, and although she still did not regret who she was, she suddenly felt as if she were being seen through some magical prism that only Nick held. If he was an enigma, then so was she— as seen by Nick. Who was the Katepalmer he seemed to enjoy so much? What was it that so delighted him about her, and how had he made it seem as if, for one magical evening, she delighted in that stranger who was herself?

Questions, so many questions. Kate didn't know when she had felt so muddled, so immersed in a confused state of pleasure-pain. She felt as blind as a teenager again, shipwrecked on the shoals of her own conflicting emotions. And the biggest question of all kept on repeating itself like a broken record despite her efforts to ignore it. If Nick *had* liked her so much—and she felt that he truly had—why hadn't he stayed to finish what had been started? Her sexual experience was limited, but she was neither an innocent nor a prude. She knew her slow response might have been partly to blame, but there had been something else—some darkness that had haunted his eyes as he'd murmured those strange remarks and gone humming down the stairs. What had it been? What had made him change his mind at the last minute? What private demons rose before him at such inopportune moments? Surely a man such as Nick Capstein wasn't cursed with the insecurities of a Kate Palmer.

Kate tossed and turned for hours, trying to thrash out some rational answers that would offer relief. All she succeeded in doing was giving herself a headache. Looking out her window didn't help, either; the landscape was all too familiar, embossed on her mind's eye forever, along with the sensation of icy-cold starlight and a warm, comforting arm around her shoulders. But closing her eyes was equally dangerous. Like a curse come back to haunt her, the image reproduced itself with razor-sharp clarity on her photographic eye. That bowl of cold earth, the silvery moonlight and Nick's lips coming closer to cover hers with his warm, spicy kisses....

* * *

She didn't know how it got to be morning, but she was glad to see the sun. Somehow, it made everything seem brighter and less confusing. It had snowed a little in the predawn hours, and a thin blanket of snow covered the world in a sparkling shower of light. Kate got right out of bed, shivered through her morning ablutions and managed to convince herself that there was nothing all that much to get worked up about. She'd had an enjoyable evening with an unusual man, and it hadn't quite led to a roll in the hay. That was it. Period. Back to reality.

She marched resolutely down to the dining room, all ready to see Nick through clear eyes, and was somewhat disappointed to find that he wasn't there. One of the Ravening Beasts, looking as if he hadn't slept at all, presided over the coffeepot and muffins.

"Nick's split," he growled before Kate could even open her mouth to ask. "Went off to see some guy about some syrup—I don't know. Told me to serve coffee to the guests." He cocked his bleary eyes at Kate. "You a guest?"

"Yes," she said firmly, and held out her coffee cup. I'm glad he isn't here, she told herself as she sat down at a table in the vacant dining room. Now I can just get out of here and get to work, and everything will be back to normal. This thought seemed rather soothing, and she sipped her coffee serenely, gazing out at the front porch of the inn. The parking lot was empty; no surprise entrances likely, she decided with relief. She was even glad there were no tequila muffins to tempt her into insober thoughts. Just plain old English muffins and toast. She could resist English muffins. No surprises there, either.

Kate was just about finished with her coffee when she felt his lips on the back of her neck. "Good morning, you delicious person."

Her cup clattered to the saucer and then tipped over, sending a trickle of coffee across the checkered tablecloth. "What are you doing here?" she cried, jumping to her feet.

Nick shrugged, arms crossed complacently over his chest. "I run the joint, remember?"

Kate looked down at the coffee dripping onto the floor, feeling betrayed. "I thought . . . he said you were out," she finished lamely, indicating the sleepy Beast with a wan gesture.

"I came in the back way and went straight upstairs," he said, producing a napkin from out of the air and wiping up the spill in one efficient sweep. He looked over his shoulder as he bent to mop the wide planks. "I was hoping to sneak up on you in bed," he whispered devilishly.

Kate gaped. She was more at sea than ever, and embarrassed to boot. His eyes, she thought irreverently, were an impossible color.

"But no matter," said Nick, straightening and ushering Kate out of the dining room. "Everything's all set for the day, anyway. I've taken care of every detail."

"What details?" she asked, and he grinned at the tone of bewildered dismay in her voice.

"The details of our country outing, of course," he said, steering her out into the hall. "I've got the lunch packed, the car all gassed up, and I spoke to Spike Johnson up over in Atwell's Peak—he's doing a sugaring run today, and he says we're welcome to come and watch as long as we don't expect him to talk to us."

"A sugaring run?"

Nick reached out and pinched her cheek as if she were a sweet but silly child. "Ah, you poor city kid, you," he said, clucking sympathetically. "Don't even know what a sugaring run is." He put his hands on his hips and slipped effortlessly into a perfect Southern drawl. "An' jes' where do y'all think Aunt Jemima gits her maple syrup from, honey chile? Maple bees?"

In spite of her confusion, Kate had to smile. "Maple bees?" she spluttered, and burst into a high cascade of laughter.

Nick looked as if she had given him a gift. "To tell you the truth, I didn't know about sugaring, either, until last spring. Like everyone else, I figured the syrup came from plastic bottles with log cabins on them. But it seems there are these trees, and they put little taps into them, and this stuff comes out..."

"Sap. And they boil it down over wood fires and make it into maple syrup," Kate finished for him. "Honestly, Nick, I'm not that insulated from Mother Nature."

"You're not? Boy, you sure are full of surprises." They grinned at each other, and Nick took a step closer to Kate. "Did you sleep well last night?" he asked, his voice soft.

"Not very," she admitted shyly.

"That's good," he murmured in a gravelly voice. "I'm glad you didn't. I didn't, either." His eyes held a smoky promise that caught in Kate's throat like wood fire. "Not a wink."

She swallowed. There it was again—that arrested sensual tension that crackled in the air between them. She had the feeling she should do something about it— did women in Nick's circle make the first move? She could barely bring herself to contemplate the audacity of doing so. Nick was watching her with wry anticipation, as if he knew she were having trouble but wasn't going to help her out. She felt that she had failed in some way.

But Nick didn't seem to think so. "Well," he went on cheerfully, bustling away, "let's get this show on the road. We've got a big day ahead of us." He picked up a big wicker basket and headed toward the door.

"Wait!" Kate stopped cold in her tracks.

He spun around impatiently. "What?"

"I can't go with you. I've got to work today," she wailed. For a few moments, he had made her completely forget about her responsibilities. "I've got to go to Tate's and finish doing the illustrations for Mr. Pietro."

Nick looked exasperated. "What? More scribbling?"

She nodded miserably. "There are three more rooms full of furniture. I've got to get them done. We're supposed to finish today and return to New York tonight."

Nick stood disconsolately in the doorway. "Wait a minute, wait a minute. You mean you've got to wait around there all day while the stuff gets auctioned off just so you can draw it up?" She nodded. "Well, why don't you just go tomorrow and do it? Tomorrow is Sunday. Surely Simmond's wouldn't mind if you worked on your own time, would they?"

"No . . ."

"After all, the furniture isn't going anywhere, is it?"

"No, but . . ."

"And it really doesn't matter if you do your bit while Albert's there or not, as long as you know which pieces to draw, right?" Nick seemed to be warming to his own idea. "As a matter of fact, it'd probably be a hell of a lot easier without that old sourpuss breathing down your neck." He cocked his head and pursed his lips. "Am I right or am I right?"

"Well . . ." Kate was dubious.

"Well, what?" he demanded.

"Well . . . that's not the way we usually do it."

Nick put down the basket, walked back to Kate and placed his hands firmly on her shoulders. "Now, Kate," he said patiently, gazing deep into her eyes, "you know as well as I do that's a lousy reason not to do it differently." He smiled beguilingly. "We're not usual people, are we?"

I am, Kate thought, but the enticing light in Nick's eyes made it impossible for her to admit it. "What will I do about Albert?" she asked him.

Without taking his eyes off her face, Nick reached out and took the receiver off the phone that stood on a nearby table. "You'll call him, that's what you'll do," he replied reasonably. "You'll call him and tell him you just can't make it today." He winked gently. "Make up some excuse."

"But what?" The idea of improvising—of lying, really—filled her with dread.

He shrugged lightly. "I don't know. But you'll think of something. I know you will." He turned and dialed *O.* "Operator, give me the Holiday Inn in Sutton Valley, please." He waited for a moment, smiling into Kate's eyes, then held out the phone. "Here you go, old girl. Give Albert the old heave-ho and let's blow this two-bit joint."

Kate gasped for a moment and then, hearing the receptionist's voice, found herself asking to be connected to Mr. Pietro's room. The phone was picked up on the second ring, and she took a deep breath. Here we go, she thought.

"Uh, hello, Mr. Pietro? Um ... this is Kate."

"Yes, Miss Palmer?" His voice, coolly acidic, somehow gave her the courage to go on.

"Mr. Pietro, I'm afraid I won't be able to make it to the auction house this morning."

"What?" He sounded as if she'd just confessed to a multiple murder.

"I'll be able to do the necessary sketches tomorrow," she rushed on, afraid of losing momentum. "Just leave me a list of what you want, and I'll be happy to take care of it."

Mr. Pietro was clearly unconvinced. "But Miss Palmer, this is...highly irregular. I really don't see how..." He droned on while Kate, staring into Nick's smiling face, found herself growing unexpectedly irritated by his imperious whine.

"I'm sorry, Albert," she interrupted boldly. "But it's just impossible for me to do it, and that's that."

Nick opened his mouth in a little "oh" of surprise and mimed applause. There was silence on the other end of the line.

"Kate, is something the matter with you?" Mr. Pietro asked at last. He sounded a little frightened. "You've been acting very oddly. Very, very oddly."

Kate listened and watched Nick. "Perhaps," she said softly. "But there's nothing the matter. Nothing the matter at all." She smiled at Nick. "Just leave a list of the pieces you want sketched in Mr. Tate's office. I'll have them for you back in the city on Monday morning. Goodbye, Mr. Pietro." And she gave the receiver back to Nick.

He cradled it and, leaning forward, chucked her gently under the chin. "That's my Kate," he murmured, fingering her jaw lightly. "I knew you could do it."

"It was easy," she said, and realized that was true.

Nick wriggled his eyebrows diabolically. "And it gets easier every time, little girl." He picked up the picnic basket and started to leave again. "Oh, wait!" He spun around. "I nearly forgot." He reached around behind the hall table and brought out Kate's sketchbook and pencils.

"Where'd you get those?" she asked, surprised.

"I told you. I snuck up to your room. But you weren't there, worse luck. So I grabbed these instead."

"What for?"

"So you can use them, what else?" He tucked the things under his free arm and picked up the picnic basket once more. "You're not going to let a beautiful day like this go by without drawing it, are you?" And he walked out the door ahead of her.

"No," murmured Kate as she moved to follow him. "I suppose I'm not."

Several hours later Kate and Nick were sitting on a rough wooden trestle table outside a tiny shack high up in the woods. They had finished the thick ham sandwiches, bread-and-butter pickles and whiskey-spiked coffee Nick had brought and topped it off with hot, sticky maple syrup poured over fresh snow, a specialty of Spike Johnson's sugar shack. Kate felt full and warm and perfectly content to be sitting there and breathing in the spun-sugar air. It was colder than down in the valley, but the sun sparkled through the maple-tree branches and dappled their faces with warmth, and the heat from the sugar shack created a hot, sweet mist that was thick enough to taste.

"Well," said Nick, pulling a last bit of candied syrup from between his teeth, "what do you think of Spike's setup here?"

Kate looked through the open door of the shack, where a small man in a heavy rubber apron and boots was slowly stirring the sugar pans with a huge wooden ladle. "I think it's amazing," she replied. "All that work in that boiling-hot little shack, all those hours standing over the pans, for just a few gallons of syrup." She licked her lips, still sticky from the maple treat. "Not that it isn't worth it," she added.

"That's why they call it Vermont gold," he told her. "Spike's been at the steam pans all night, and he'll probably stay all night tonight."

"Why such a marathon?"

"When the sap runs, it runs, and it's got to be tended then and there. Has to do with the weather and the trees' leafing cycle. If you're too early, it's too cold and there's no sap. Too late, and the trees go into bud—no sap." He peered into the dark interior, where Spike, looking like an apparition from another century, was wrapped in clouds of steam and smoke. "It's hard work, but I think Spike loves it." He smiled. "Matter of fact, I know he does. Nothing could get him off this mountain when the sap's running."

"How did you meet him?" Kate asked. Johnson had been friendly and seemed pleased at their arrival, but he had spoken very little to Nick and even less to Kate, who seemed to embarrass him. He had gone about his business while they stood nearby and watched, Nick doing all the talking.

The taciturn man with grubby fingernails seemed like the last person Nick would have for a friend, but the two men obviously liked each other. They shared a kind of quiet intimacy that Kate found surprising. It even made her a little jealous: for all his rustic roughness, Spike Johnson seemed to understand Nick Capstein better than she did.

"I met him at the bar in town," Nick said with a grin. "Aside from the local chief of police, who figures he can keep an eye on his citizens best by drinking with them, he's the only man in Putnam Falls who can knock back a quart of Johnny Walker and keep his mouth shut." He raised his voice. "Isn't that right, Spike?"

From inside the steamy shack came a taciturn grunt. "Ayep."

Nick chuckled. "When I first came up here, I was, shall we say, eager to lose myself in the local customs? Meaning the local custom of drinking yourself silly on a Saturday night. Spike here figured my soul needed saving one Saturday when I was being particularly obnoxious at the tavern, and he brought me up here with him. Said the sugar fumes'd kill the alcohol and set me straight." He inhaled the air deeply. "Personally, I think you get higher from snorting all this sugar smoke than you would with a case of Scotch, but I'm not about to tell that to Spike."

Kate sniffed. The air was damp with the smell of syrup, and she was beginning to feel rather light-headed from it all. "I don't know how he stays in there so long," she whispered. "You'd think his insides would get glued together the way my teeth are now."

Nick laughed. "Maybe that's the secret to Spike's levelheadedness. Anyway, he considers it his duty as a Vermonter to spend weeks alone in there every spring. It's a ritual for him, kind of like a religion." He shook his head, no longer smiling. "I wish I had something as sweet and dependable to believe in."

Kate looked at him, surprised by this sudden revelation. "Don't you?"

He shook his head. "Nope. I used to. But then—" He broke off and stared sightlessly before him. "Then the real world reminded me that I wasn't living in a sugar shack." Now his voice was bitter.

Kate watched him for a moment in silence. "Nick," she said softly at last, "tell me about your life."

He turned to her and smiled that slow, lazy smile. "No, no. It's not a good story for a beautiful early-spring day in the woods." He reached out as if to touch her, then let his hand drop. "It's not a good story for you."

"Try me," she said steadily.

He looked quizzical. "You really want to know?"

"You make it sound like a deep, dark secret," she observed.

He lifted his eyebrows. "It's not, really. Just shallow and a little bit muddy is all. Actually, there's not that much to tell—I mean, they're not gonna come running to me begging for the movie rights or anything."

Kate placed her hands over his lips in a gesture she had learned from him. "Tell me anyway," she said with a little smile. "I really do want to know."

He looked at her speculatively, half smiling still. Then he nodded slowly several times. "Okay, I believe you really do." He got off the trestle table and, putting his arms around her waist, lifted her down. "But not here. Let's go for a walk, and I'll sing you the ballad of ol' Nicky C. Don't forget to take your sketch pad with you. There's a great vantage point up the mountain just a little ways. I don't want you to miss it."

Kate wondered why he was insisting so adamantly that she draw. She could sense that he was nervous, an unusual state for Nick Capstein. But she understood that state all too well. She suspected that he wanted her to have something to do while he talked. So she took her pad and pencils, and they headed off up the snowy path. She noticed he didn't bother to say goodbye to Spike, and Spike didn't even seem to notice their departure. Apparently such niceties were not necessary between them.

They walked for ten minutes through the woods, their boots crunching on the thin layer of hard-packed snow. Kate had reluctantly worn her down coat over her wool pants and thick Icelandic sweater and had been relieved when Nick had put a heavy down parka over his tan chinos and crewneck. Away from the heat of the sugar shack, the forest canopy blocked out the sun, and she was glad of the warmth. She was also glad of Nick's silent but confident presence. She didn't have much experience in the deep woods, and every snapped twig made her look around nervously.

Then Nick suddenly veered off the path, at a spot where the trees seemed to close in to a wall of snow-covered branches and green pine needles. He lifted the boughs of a thick juniper bush aside and pointed to a sunny circle of light about ten feet away on the other side.

"You go ahead. I'll hold the branches." Then, seeing her hesitate, he grinned. "Don't worry. There are no bears waiting to gobble you up. Not even raccoons. I promise."

Kate held her breath and ducked under the tunnel of leaves, which seemed endless. She was glad to hear that Nick was right behind her, although she still wasn't certain she was going to like his choice of seating arrangements. But when she got out of the tunnel and straightened on the other side, she gasped at the view.

"Pretty incredible, isn't it?" Nick came up beside her and put his arm across her shoulder.

Kate could not speak but shook her head in slow amazement. They were standing on a shelf of rock, covered with soft pine and moss, which seemed to have appeared with no warning from out of the gradual slope of the mountainside. An overhanging ledge had protected the ground from snow, but not from the warming rays of the early-afternoon sun, which slanted in on them with all the drama of stage lighting. The promontory overlooked a vast panorama of hills and slopes and tilting fields, each one a different shade of gray, brown and white, like the soft flanks of a huge, gentle beast. In the middle of this scene was a perfectly round pond, shimmering with thick white ice. It was surrounded by a sentinal force of miniature fir trees in perfect formation. Several houses were nestled into nooks and crannies below them, looking like babes cradled in the motherly arms of the soft earth. Despite the lack of greenery and the blanket of snow, the scene appeared warm and lush.

Kate let out her breath slowly. "How did you ever find this place? It's perfect!"

Nick laughed. "To tell you the truth, the first time I found it I was looking for somewhere to be sick. When I saw it, though, I recovered my equilibrium at once. Now, it's sort of my secret hideout. You know, like a fort or a tree house for a kid." He shrugged, oddly shy. "I've never shown it to anyone before."

Kate wanted to reach up and stroke his cheek but didn't dare. Instead she sat down and opened her sketchbook. "I'll draw," she told him. "You talk." Suddenly she couldn't wait to get her fingers around a pencil, to try to bring the scene to life on paper. She was also eager to hear Nick's tale.

"Good." He sat down beside her and waited until she was settled with her sketchbook open and her pencils ready. "There really isn't much to tell you, though. I'm a New Yorker, born and bred. Dropped out of college to go on tour as the road manager of a rock-and-roll band that opened concerts for the Grateful Dead."

He picked up a pinecone and chucked it over the edge. Kate could hear it bump and crackle down the mountainside, but she didn't bother to look and see where it had landed. Although she was listening closely to Nick, her mind's eye was already working feverishly, trying to determine the best way to begin her first sketch. Should she include the pond and that tall narrow house over there? Or the slope of hillside to the right that held a little corral full of lazy horses pawing silently at the still earth? She decided on the pond and began to draw rapidly. There was no need for her to speak.

"God, that was a wild time. You name it, I did it. Luckily, I didn't do it all, or I wouldn't be here to tell you about it." He sighed. "Got out of that after a while, and started hanging around studios with my musician friends. I had this idea I should be in the music business, but I had no idea where to start. I wanted to be something, but I didn't know what. I certainly couldn't be a musician without any training, although I must admit I've always been a frustrated singer."

Kate looked at him from beneath her lashes and smiled. "I could have told you that."

He chuckled, "I'll bet you could. Anyway, to make a long story short, I got involved in promotion, and then with the production end of the business. Got into music videos when they first came out, and made myself a pretty good living off it, too." He took a deep breath. "I had this partner—have this partner, I should say. He handled the business end, I took care of the production. We made a great team, Jared and me. He was the money man, I did the inside business—took care of the musicians, set up studio sessions, arranged for production teams. Even Nina got in on the act, after her divorce. She and Jared hooked up, and she turned out to be a pretty good PR person." He laughed shortly. "She talks a good game, just like her brother. But we did well for ourselves. It's a tight little world, the New York music scene, but we did well."

Kate, drawing rapidly with small, sure strokes, listened carefully even though she kept her eyes on the scene before her. Nick's words evoked an image that was in complete contrast with the bucolic landscape, but she could imagine it as clearly as what she saw before her. She saw Nick lounging in a studio, his hair slicked back and a cigarette between his lips—even though he had never smoked in her presence. She saw him squinting and pulsing his shoulders rhythmically to the beat of the music. She saw him throw back his head and laugh at someone's clever joke, then bend over and whisper into the ear of a stylish woman who showed a row of perfect white teeth as she smiled up at him invitingly.

It was an alien world to her, but a fascinating one. Kate had to force herself to concentrate on the view in front of her and not on the one in her mind's eye. She had never been much good at creating imaginary visions, but this one was complete to the last detail. She was even jealous of the woman.

But Nick was there, with her, on the ledge overlooking a winter paradise, not bopping to some secret beat in the city. Kate shook her head to clear it of the invasive image. If she could just get herself to apply that creative energy to the scene she was drawing, maybe it would grow into something other than a dry architectural rendering of perfection.

"It all sounds lovely," she murmured, because he had stopped talking for a while.

"It sounded lovely to me, too," he resumed. "It was lovely. I had everything I wanted—or everything I thought I wanted." He shrugged and threw another pinecone. "And then it all just seemed to collapse."

Kate stopped drawing and looked at him. His face was drawn into a closed drum of memory. "What happened?" she asked softly.

He took a deep breath before continuing. "You know, I've thought about it and thought about it, and I'm still not sure. There never really was one moment that I could put my finger on and say, Yeah, this is why it happened. I mean, there I was, knee deep in the big time, having the time of my life—or so I thought. Boy, I said to myself, this is it, Nick. This is where you really belong." He laughed sharply. "I tell you, Katie, when you're involved in that much material success, you can get lulled into believing you really do live in fairyland."

Kate kept her eyes on her work. She had the feeling Nick hadn't talked this way to anyone in a long time, and that she might ruin it if she spoke. Anyway, she couldn't have told Nick that she was being lulled into a fairyland of his making, sitting there with him on that sylvan ridge.

"Of course it couldn't last. Somehow I knew it couldn't last, even though I wanted it to. I started getting this—you know, this feeling, this sense, that I wasn't happy, even though I kept telling myself I was crazy not to be. It was as if I were trying to upset my own apple-cart; as if I were fooling myself."

Kate swallowed. She knew that feeling all too well.

"At first," he went on, "I just put it down to over-kill—you know, to having too much of a good thing. I thought it would pass if I just laid off the scene a little bit, took some time to be alone, so I didn't have to be Nick Capstein, Supersmile, a hundred percent of the day." His beautiful lips turned up in a brief, bitter grimace. "Trouble is, it got so I could barely drag myself to the next studio session, or the next gig. I mean, I was burned-out."

He shook his head and sighed slowly. Kate watched his profile as he squinted into the light. "It sounds like you couldn't have been very happy doing it in the first place," she offered softly.

Nick nodded and let his breath out through his nose in a self-deprecating snort. "Yep. You could say that. You could definitely say that." He turned and regarded her with his head cocked to one side. "I should have known you would be this easy to talk to, Katepalmer," he murmured in a much gentler voice. "I should have known you would understand."

"I think I do," she replied, thinking about her own life and wondering if perhaps she understood Nick so well because she suffered from some of the same symptoms. But she put that thought firmly out of her mind and regarded her paper, waiting for him to go on.

"Anyway, that wasn't all there was to it. It got worse—much worse. I began to lose respect for what I was doing, and patience with everybody I worked with. Especially Jared Cooper." Another impatient snort. "Jared." His voice was an odd mixture of forbearance and exasperation. "If ever there was a proverbial straw that broke the camel's back, it was dear old Jared. While I was drifting further and further away from the business, old Jared was getting in deeper and deeper. He got himself involved in some get-rich-and-famous-quick scheme, and started revving his engines in hyperdrive.''

He paused to collect his thoughts. ''In a way, it was partly my fault. I know I didn't exactly lend an interested ear when he started babbling away about making a million dollars and getting big-name acts. I mean, Jared can be hard to listen to at the best of times, but when he got like this... Well, I wasn't ready to hear it and I gave him a pretty clear signal that whatever it was, I wasn't interested.'' He shook his head ruefully. ''That was a big mistake.''

''What happened?''

''I don't know. At first he got sort of cocky, like, 'You don't want to make a million bucks? Then I'll do it myself.' And he started running around like a crazy man with some pretty unsavory characters.'' A glint of dry humor appeared in his eyes. ''And when I say someone's unsavory, you'd better believe it. Anyway, Jared suddenly disappeared. I mean, he was around town, I knew, but he didn't show up at the studio or at any of the usual haunts. Even Nina got worried, and she tried to get me to keep tabs on him. Nina loves Jared but she knows that when he gets started, he can jump in way over his head. Of course, by the time I opened my eyes and looked around, it was too late. Jared started acting very nervous, very secretive and jumpy. He wouldn't talk much to Nina, and he certainly wouldn't talk to me. I had blown it, but somehow I couldn't make myself care enough to do anything about it.

''Nina got so fed up with both of us that she came back up here to get away. I stayed in the city and tried to pretend that nothing was wrong—with Jared or with me." He shook his head as if amazed. "I tried—I really tried to work up a modicum of interest in my job, in my business, in the life I'd been living so well for so long. But you know, I just couldn't seem to manage. It was all so...so wrong."

Kate had stopped drawing and was staring out over the plateau. "I know what you mean," she whispered, but Nick was too wrapped up in his own tale to notice her wistful tone.

"And then one day, about a week ago, Jared really did disappear. Came up here to visit Nina for one night and then just split."

"He just left? Without telling you?"

"That's about the size of it. Not a word, not a note, not even a postcard. He did manage to get his paws on a good chunk of the business account, of course. Jared's impulsive, but he always manages to think carefully when it comes to money."

"What do you think he needed the money for?"

"You mean besides plane fare?" Nick shrugged. "He was in some trouble, that much I figured out. There wasn't that much money to take, so he must have needed it badly."

Kate was both fascinated and repelled by the images Nick's story conjured. It was like something out of a cheap novel—fast living, secret deals, sudden disappearances. If anyone but Nick had told such a tale, she would have been openly skeptical. "What kind of trouble was he in?"

"Don't know," he replied shortly. "Still don't know. I followed Nina up here, and I've been socked in ever since." He turned to her so suddenly that she started. "But you know what's even worse? I didn't care. I mean, here was this guy I had cast my lot with, worked with, practically lived with, for God's sake, and I really couldn't bring myself to care what happened to him. Do you know what that means?''

Kate spoke hesitantly, taken aback by his sudden vehemence. ''That you weren't happy?''

He didn't appear to have heard her at first. ''It means that I'm no better than a—'' He broke off. ''What did you say?''

''I said it must mean that you were very unhappy living that life, to have lost interest in it that way.'' It seemed a very simple explanation to her—obvious and clear.

But Nick reacted strangely to her statement. For a long moment he stared at her so intently that she was afraid she'd insulted him. But something about his gaze made it impossible for her to drop her eyes. It was as if he were trying to read himself in their luminous depths, and she suddenly wanted very much for him to see what she saw.

''You're right,'' he whispered at last. ''You're absolutely right. I was very unhappy with that life—with myself.'' He sounded as if he had never really entertained the notion before. ''It doesn't make it right—my not caring about Jared—but that's exactly the way it was.''

''It doesn't sound like Jared cared too much about you,'' Kate pointed out stoutly. ''After all, he took the money and left, didn't he?''

''What?'' Nick was still staring. ''Oh, yeah, Jared. We'll find out his story when Nina gets back from New York with him.'' He didn't sound as if he was very interested in Jared.

"He's back?" In spite of the power of Nick's compelling blue gaze, Kate was dying to know the rest of the story.

Nick nodded. "Yep. Called and told Nina she had to come and get him, quick. She had to drive all the way down to the city to pick him up at a coffee shop on Twenty-third Street, for God's sake. Typical Jared melodrama." But Nick didn't seem as bitter as he had a few moments ago. And he was still staring at Kate with a mysterious little lift of amusement playing across his mouth. "Katepalmer, you really might be my lucky star, did you know that?"

Kate was flustered and decided to keep her mind on the story rather than risk venturing into more dangerous areas. "Well, then, everything is settled, isn't it?"

"What do you mean?"

"I mean, once you find out what happened to Jared, you can let him know how you feel about the business. Maybe you can work something out."

"And then?"

She was a little surprised. "Then? Why, then you can go on and do what you really want to do."

The tension between them snapped abruptly as Nick dropped his eyes.

"Ah, yes What I really want." He turned and stared off into the mountains across the valley. The sun had slipped farther into the western sky, and although their ledge was still warm, it was tinted now in the roseate glow of late afternoon. Nick's profile was tipped with gold, but his eyes were shadowed in the crease of his brow. When he spoke, his voice was once again hard and faintly derisive. "That, my dear Kate, is the big question. What does Nick Capstein really want?"

She could think of no adequate reply to this and no explanation for his volatile change in mood, so she turned silently back to her drawing. She had completed the scene, with the pond just off center on her page and the edge of the tall farmhouse beyond it jutting up into the top of the picture like a church spire. It was a gentle picture, like the roll of the land beneath her, but it evoked none of the peace she saw in the scene. Instead, it was filled with unruly lines and curves, and bright, hard edges that seemed to jump off the page. The tip of a tree stabbed into the cloudless sky, and the fir-tree circle was full of menace.

Kate realized with surprise that she had let her emotional response to Nick's story color her work. It was the first time in her memory that she had produced a drawing so alive, so untamed and unsettling. She stared at it as if it had been done by a hand other than her own.

Nick leaned forward and saw it, too. "My God," he breathed, "if I had your vision, your talent..."

"Oh," she said automatically, "it's not really very good."

He grabbed her arm so fast that she cried out, and he pulled her around to face him. "Don't say that, Kate," he said in a low, urgent voice. "Don't *ever* say that about yourself."

Kate was bewildered by his vehemence. "But—"

"But nothing. Just don't do it!" He must have realized he was scaring her, because he softened his hold on her arm. "Don't you see? The whole point is that when you know what you want, what you are, you have to grab life and live it, regardless of the consequences. You have a great gift, do you know that? Do you know how many people long for a gift, for something to show them the way through their life? You have it, and yet you're afraid to use it.''

His voice dropped further. ''You shouldn't be afraid, Kate. Believe me, I know what it does to you. Don't be afraid to go for what you really want. At least you have something to go for.''

Kate was subdued by this outburst, because it was so true. ''But I don't *know* what I really want,'' she told him. ''That's just it.''

''Aw, sure you do. You know.''

''No, I don't think I do,'' she insisted, shaking her head. She looked up at him beseechingly. ''I'm not like you, Nick. You may not have made the right career choice, but you always seem to know what you're about. Right or wrong, at least you know yourself, what you want, who you are. You knew when it was right, and you knew when it was wrong.'' She shook her head, fighting back the unexpected tears. ''I don't know that. I really don't.''

Nick scrunched forward on the carpet of moss and pulled her back toward him. ''Sure you do,'' he said soothingly, wrapping his arm around her so that she leaned against his chest with her head nestled into the crook of his shoulder. With characteristic abruptness, he seemed to have forgotten all about his own dilemma in concentrating on hers. He stroked her hair absently. ''You just don't think you can do what you really want to do, that's all.''

''What do I really want to do?'' she inquired tremulously.

''Be an artist! Your own artist. Paint landscapes, do portraits, whatever!'' He gestured at the paper spread beside them. ''Look at what you drew just now. That's wonderful—that's incredible! Don't you know how good you are?''

"Yes, but . . .''

"But what? Why don't you cut loose and pursue your art seriously, Kate? Why do you stick yourself into a dry little box at Simmond's and only draw what other people tell you to draw? Why do you do that to yourself? Do you know?''

Kate drew a shuddering breath. She was perilously close to tears, but Nick's closeness was deeply comforting. She felt raw and rinsed out, as if she'd just been through a major emotional trauma. "Because I'm . . .''

"Because you're afraid." His fingers toyed with a lock of hair that fell against her cheek, and the back of his hand stroked her skin gently. She could feel his jaw moving against her temple as he talked. "I know. I know what it's like to be afraid. But it's no good, don't you see? It's not doing me any good, and it's not doing you any good, either." He kissed the top of her head. "You need to know how good you are at this. You need to put some confidence in your life. Some color, some magic." His hand dropped suddenly into her lap. "I'm telling you this for me, too, you know. We both need to put some magic in our lives."

Kate looked at her drawing and then at the hand in her lap. She picked it up with both of hers and turned it over, tracing the lines across the palm as if to read the future there. Futures could be predicted, but never, in her wildest imagination, would she have expected to find herself in this situation, sitting on a mountainside in the arms of a man like Nick Capstein. She had never dreamed she would be confronting her deepest fears about herself and listening calmly while he confronted his. But suddenly, sitting on the sun-warmed ledge above soft foothills that were dipping into dusk, she knew what Nick meant. She knew exactly what she needed.

"I know, Nick," she whispered, shifting in his arms so that her face leaned up to his. "I know what I need. I need you."

He looked down at her for a moment, uncomprehending. Then he shook his head. "I didn't dare," he whispered, his voice full of wonder. "I didn't dare think you'd want me the way I want you. But you do. My God, you do, don't you?" And, holding her face cupped in his hands, he brought his lips firmly down on hers.

This time the kiss was different, full of passionate promise, and Kate abandoned herself to it with a hungry moan. She shifted in his lap and wrapped her arms around his neck, holding him tightly to her as if afraid he might suddenly retreat again. She had never felt like this before, but she was certain it was right—it was more "her" than anything she had done in a long time. And in any case, she had no intention of stopping now.

Nick's mouth was warm and hard, his tongue dueling with hers in an exquisitely provocative dance of passion. They covered each other with kisses—short, fiery little bites of desire that fell like hot rain wherever they landed. As he kissed her, Nick smiled, and Kate placed her lips on his left dimple. Ah, how she had longed to do that!

At last he swung her around so that she was across his arms and bent hungrily to her mouth and throat. Kate thrust her hands into his hair and raked her fingers through its luxuriant thickness. It was cold and smooth in the chill air, but she could feel the heat of his pulse as it quickened beneath her touch. Her hands came away powdered with an infusion of maple dust.

"God," he gasped breathlessly between kisses, "this is crazy! This can't be happening—not to me!"

"Why not?" Her ragged voice surprised her; it sounded as if it belonged to someone else.

"Not with you, not here.... Not if we want to stop." He held her face tight and still. "Will you want me to stop, sweet Kate?" His eyes burned into hers.

"No," she breathed. "No. Please, no."

His smile was so full of sultry passion that she had an urge to bite at his full lower lip. "We might freeze to death out here," he warned her. "Are you sure?"

She knew he was not asking her about the weather. He was giving her a chance to change her mind. He realized this did not come naturally to her. But Kate did not want to stop. Having come this far was unprecedented; she would not—could not—turn back now. "I'm sure," she said, and returned his gaze, her eyes naked with candor and longing. "I'm very sure. Besides," she whispered, pulling him back down to her lips, "you'll keep me warm, Nick."

He chuckled deep in his throat—she could feel the rumble of pleasure. "Oh, yes," he breathed, settling her down beneath him on the carpet of moss. "You can bet your sweet self I'll do that."

She lay very still while he slipped his hands under her sweater and unbuttoned her blouse, only moving her head so that he could remove them. He gazed at her small breasts, at her heaving ribs, and for one awful instant Kate thought he would find her wanting. But his dimples creased and his eyes turned an even smokier blue. "So lovely," he murmured. "So very, very lovely. And you smell like maple syrup. Good enough to eat."

Then, just when the goose bumps began to rise on her bare flesh, he bent and covered her breasts with his kisses. Kate kept her eyes open wide as waves of sensation rolled across her chest and down in the pit of her stomach. The heat was incredible, the pleasure complete. "Oh," she whispered as if in prayer. "Oh, Nick."

Somehow he removed the rest of her clothing, and his, without ever exposing her body to the cruelty of the cold mountain air. She was covered always with his touch...by his gentle mouth, by his warm limbs and incredibly agile fingers as they played over her body as they would a drum. He had spread his coat beneath them, and now he took hers and pulled it over them, creating a downy cocoon of warm skin in which they could explore each other to their hearts' content. With Nick as her silent guide, her seeing eye, Kate began to read his body and respond to it with her own.

She felt the beauty of his torso—the hard musculature, the firm spine, the downy hair that sprinkled across his chest and loins. Shyly at first, and then more bravely as his touch fueled her desire to fever pitch, she began to touch him as he touched her—with intimate care and wonder. In spite of the cold, in spite of the hard forest floor, her once awkward limbs felt elegant and graceful as they basked in the heat of his lovemaking. On their own accord, her arms and legs wrapped around him, pulling him closer to the core of her need. With Nick leading the way, she was quickly becoming an adept at the language of love.

Then, like an acrobat, Nick rose up and thrust into her, and Kate forgot her shyness and wonder and clung to him in a passionate frenzy of sensation. They might have tipped off the mountain ledge, for all she knew of the world around them. There was only one reality for her at that moment. Nick was her world, and she reveled in him.

Chapter Seven

Hours later, they sped down the mountain in the pickup truck, Nick crooning "Bewitched, Bothered and Bewildered" all the way. He couldn't look at her—the night was too black and the mountain road too perilous for him to take his eyes off the road, but Kate could tell by his profile that he was smiling as he sang. She was smiling, too.

Yes, it was true. She was bewitched by him. Bewitched and bewildered, but at the moment, not at all bothered. As a matter of fact, her physical and mental states were just about as perfect as they could be. Her bones were still a little chilled, and she felt a bit sore, but nothing could disturb the magnanimous warmth that spread through her loins and suffused her entire being.

Kate chuckled as Nick continued his heartfelt rendition of the old classic. His obvious delight in her was as precious as her enchantment with him. Of course it was she who was beguiled, and even in her current state of bliss she was enough of a realist to acknowledge that beguilement was Nick's strong suit. She did not doubt the sincerity of his passion for her; she simply assumed it was not unique. Nick was a man of many passions, as quicksilver as the ever-changing color of his eyes and the expressions on his face. Kate, swept up in the torrent of his sudden and seemingly inexplicable fascination for her, did not care to think about repercussions of any kind. She only knew that she had to be a part of Nick's life as long as he wanted her. He may have been many things to many people—women in particular—but she had never felt this way before... ever.

They had stayed in their magical world until darkness fell, so absorbed in their ardent pursuit of ecstasy that neither perceived the sudden drop in temperature. When they finally noticed, it was completely dark—a thick velvet blackness that made Kate open her eyes very wide to make sure they were not closed. Fortunately Nick's key ring had a penlight attached to it, so they'd been able to stumble through the tunnel back to the path, giggling in whispers because the darkness was so absolute.

Spike Johnson was still at work over his sugary pans, and if he noticed that Nick and his lady friend returned as lovers, bound by an intimacy that went beyond touch, he did not remark on it. As a matter of fact, he uttered absolutely nothing beyond a friendly grunt of farewell when they got into the truck, lugging gallon jugs of syrup with them for the inn.

For Kate, the entire day had been a trip to fairyland, a spun-sugar fantasy right down to the scent of maple that still clung to her hair. The whole thing might have been a dream, she thought, until she licked her swollen lips. The sweet taste in her mouth was partly maple syrup, partly the memory of Nick's mouth and skin.

Although the ride down the curvy dirt road was scary, Kate was reluctant to see the flat, paved road back to town and the homey lights of the Stonecroft Inn. Nick had said they both needed some magic, and the day had been magic indeed. The trouble was she didn't want it to end yet, and she was afraid she would wake up—or he would—once they returned to the real world.

She needn't have worried. As soon as they pulled into the parking lot, the front door opened and a woman rushed out.

"Nick! Nick!" she shouted, waving her arms and dashing down the flagstone path toward the truck.

For a moment Kate's vision on the ledge revisited her: it was Nick's sleek urban lover, come to Vermont to re-claim him. But then she recognized the handsome face, the shining cap of hair. It was Nina.

"Damn!" Nick muttered when he saw her. "I'd for-gotten they were coming back tonight! They're the last thing I need." He started to get out of the car, but Nina flew to it and put her leather-gloved hands on the door, preventing him from opening it all the way.

"Nicky, wait a minute," she said breathlessly. Then, seeing Kate, she peered into the darkened cab. "Oh. You have someone with you." She withdrew automatically and threw Kate a distracted but charming smile. Kate was struck by the similarity between brother and sister and wondered how it could have escaped her before.

Nick grinned with the same automatic charm. "Hey, Nina. Welcome home. You rescue Wonder Boy?" He gave his sister an absentminded peck on the cheek, but Kate could tell he wasn't prepared for her return, and she wondered if it was because of Jared or because she,

Kate, was with him. Was he ashamed of her in front of his sleek sister? No, she reminded herself sternly. That was an unworthy thought.

"Listen, Nicky, before you get out—" Nina spoke breathlessly "—I have to tell you something."

Nick sat back, exasperated. "Nina, we want to go in. We're cold."

Nina threw Kate a more discerning glance, as if realizing she had dismissed her too easily. "Look. Things are worse than we thought, Nicky."

Nick's eyes narrowed, and his body tensed. "What do you mean, worse than we thought?"

Nina grimaced nervously. "I mean Jared really is in trouble. Big trouble."

"What'd he do, steal someone's idea for a video?"

Kate could tell Nick was trying to be flippant. She knew he was nervous about facing Jared, not only because he would have to deal with Jared's problems but because it would mean dealing with his own doubts as well. "Jared never was very original," he added with a light laugh.

But Nina was in no mood for banter. "It's worse than that, Nicholas."

Nick stopped smiling as soon as she used his full name. "How much worse?" he inquired, looking closely at his sister. He seemed to have forgotten all about Kate.

Nina's eyes, so like Nick's, flicked briefly over her brother's shoulder toward Kate and then returned to him. "Much," she said, her voice low, urgent. She stepped back so he could open the cab door. "You'd better come in and let him tell you about it."

Nick sighed heavily and got out of the car. "Okay," he muttered. "Guess it's time to face the music." He started walking up the drive with Nina but stopped after a few steps. "Hell. Wait a sec, Nin. I'll be right in."

Kate slumped against the seat, feeling deflated. He *had* forgotten all about her. How could he have switched gears so quickly, so completely? The only explanation she could find was that their time together hadn't meant as much to him as it had to her. The realization brought her back to earth with a painful thump.

But when he came around to her side of the car Nick's expression was contrite. "I'm sorry, sweet Kate. I got shanghaied for a minute there."

"It's all right," she murmured disconsolately.

He thrust out his lower lip, and Kate was reminded again of his resemblance to his sister. "No, it's not all right. I had planned to spend a lovely evening with you. I hadn't counted on having to listen to Jared's tale of woe. Not now. Not tonight." His eyes held the smoky promise she'd come to recognize, and seeing it made her feel a little better.

"But as you said, the sooner I get this behind me, the sooner I'll be able to get on with my life." He laughed shortly. "Whatever *that* is." He opened the door for her. "Well, come on, then. It's not going to be pretty, but let's get it over with."

He held out his hand, but Kate resisted. "Oh, I don't think I should," she told him.

He stopped, surprised. "Should what?"

"Should be there when you... when Jared and you talk."

He took her hand. "Why not? It's not like you don't know what's going on—any more than I do, that is. Nina makes it sound like Jared committed murder, but if I know him—and my sister—things have probably been blown up way out of proportion." He stopped and narrowed his eyes briefly. "I'm sure they can't be as bad as all that," he added softly, more to himself than to her. Inexplicably, she was filled with a nameless dread.

But if Nick felt the same foreboding, he seemed determined not to let it affect him. "Whatever melodrama Jared's got to tell, he can tell it to you, too, sweet Kate." He stroked her wrist cajolingly. "Besides, I want you to be there with me. After Jared talks, I'm going to do some talking. I'm going to tell him I want out. And I need you to be there when I do."

Kate looked at him and realized he was quite serious. She was torn between her desire to avoid what would surely be an awkward confrontation and her desire to stay next to Nick at all costs. He must have seen or sensed her conflict, because he leaned into the car and kissed her gently on the lips, then drew back and looked searchingly into her eyes. "Please?"

She knew she could not deny him when he asked like that. With a wan smile, she allowed him to help her out of the truck and up the path to the inn. In the hallway he paused and took a deep breath, and Kate could tell that he was as nervous as she was. More than that, he was afraid—not of what Jared had to say, but of his own ambivalence. Shyly, Kate squeezed his arm encouragingly.

He smiled down at her. "Sweet Kate," he murmured. Then he sighed heavily. "Well, here goes nothing."

Kate's first impression of Jared Cooper was that he was the most incredibly handsome man she had ever seen. Instinctively she understood Nina's attraction to him; he exuded a rich, sophisticated sensuality. Even wearing an unsteady half smile, he looked as if he'd stepped out of the pages of a men's fashion magazine. He was attractively lean, and even though he was perched on the arm of a nearby wing chair, she could tell he was taller than Nick. He wore a leather coat over a light-blue shirt and navy wool pants, and not a single sleek black hair was out of place. His eyes were Mediterranean blue, his jaw perfectly etched and his skin impossibly tanned.

But he was clearly ill at ease. His eyes darted from Nick to Kate to Nina, and his beautiful mouth twitched. He got up from the wing chair and then, apparently thinking better of it, sat down again on the upholstered arm. "Nicky!" he boomed in a deep voice, making a poor effort to sound hearty. "Good to see you, man!"

"Good to see you, too, Jared," said Nick with an amused little smile. "It's been a while."

Jared ignored this gibe. "Who's your friend, Nicky?" he inquired with false eagerness. "Aren't you going to introduce us?"

"This is Kate Palmer," said Nick, putting a proprietary arm around her shoulder. "Kate, Jared Cooper. And," he added as an afterthought, "my sister, Nina."

Jared gave Kate his dazzling model's smile, but Nina's greeting was more wary. She looked sharply from Kate to her brother but said nothing. Kate could barely manage to mumble the amenities—Jared's unctuousness and Nina's guardedness brought out all her insecurities. She was sure neither Jared nor Nina wanted her there, and she wished she had declined Nick's invitation to stay. There was an awkward moment of silence; while Nick guided Kate to sit by him on the sofa, Jared fidgeted handsomely, Nina looked impatiently from her brother to her lover, and Kate remained frozen beneath the weight of Nick's arm.

Only Nick looked at ease, but Kate thought he would probably look that way in any situation. Finally he

spoke. "Okay, Jared, let's hear it." He raised one hand
warningly. "But I want the whole truth, with none of
your usual fast talk. You talk honest, I'll talk honest.
You understand?"

Jared nodded and swallowed. "Of course I do, Nicky.
I'll be straight with you. I have to be straight with you—
I realize that now." He looked at Nina for reassurance
before going on. "First of all, I want to let you know
how sorry I am about the way I left. I really thought I
had no choice."

"I said, no bull!" Nick reminded him.

Jared nodded, took a deep breath, started to speak,
and then spread his hands helplessly in the air. "God,
Nicky, I would never have done it if I'd known it was
gonna come to this. I mean, I really didn't think it was
anything! It was one of those things that just happened,
know what I mean?"

Nick sighed patiently. "No, as a matter of fact I
don't."

But Jared didn't seem to be listening. "It was just like
I was there, and it was there, and before I knew it... But
then he came back, and ... how was I to know it was so
important to him? I never thought he'd get so ... so ..."
He broke off miserably.

"Who are you talking about, Jared?" Nick asked in
a heavy monotone, as if he were questioning a dull child.

"The guy I borrowed the money from," he replied, as
if Nick should have known. "You know, for that MTV
video thing we wanted to do."

"You mean the one *you* wanted to do. The one I said
was crass and commercial and I wouldn't touch with a
ten-foot pole."

Jared's eyes flashed with an instant's anger, but he
spoke placatingly. "You would have liked the project

once it got under way, Nicky, believe me. I know you thought it sounded awful, selling bubble gum with heavy metal, but I'm telling you, it would have been a great idea."

"Doesn't sound like it worked out too well after all," Nick pointed out.

"That's because I never got a chance to make it. Things got hot too fast."

"What got hot?" Nick narrowed his eyes. "Why'd you have to borrow money for this thing, anyway, Jared? I thought we were doing all right?"

"You thought!" For the first time Jared's bitterness surfaced. "What did you know—or care? This kind of project needs big money—and we didn't have big money."

Nick absorbed the attack without flinching, and Kate knew he felt he deserved it. "What about going to a bank?" he asked quietly.

"We're...we've been a little overextended lately at the banks," Jared mumbled.

"Overextended!" Nick's eyes flashed, but he controlled himself. "Okay, so what you're trying to tell me is that you didn't use the money for the video. What did you do with it besides taking a brief vacation?"

Jared flushed. "The money's not the problem. I can get my hands on the money."

Nick snorted. "Oh. Great. I'm glad money's not a problem," he said facetiously.

"Nick—stop it!" This came from Nina. Her nostrils were white and flaring. "You've got to listen."

"I'm trying to listen," he replied. "It's just that I don't seem to be hearing much that makes sense." Kate knew he was impatient because he was nervous himself about telling Jared he wanted to leave the business. She wished everybody would stop talking at cross-purposes so they could get it over with. But she didn't dare open her mouth.

"Go on, Jared," Nina commanded.

Jared was getting more and more upset. He took a deep breath and let it out shakily. "It's not the money, Nicky. I can give it back to him if that was all he wanted. But he doesn't! He wants the book."

"What book?" Nick asked reasonably.

"The one I took, of course," Jared snapped as if this were perfectly clear already. "But I didn't have the book. I got scared and hid it, and then I really got worried and...that's why I left, understand?"

"No, I don't!" Nick said sharply, but Jared was off on his frightened monologue again and didn't listen.

"Of course, soon as I got to Bermuda I realized it was a big mistake. I should have just come up here and gotten the book and given it back, but... Anyway, so I came back to do that, but it was too late. They were already waiting for me! I couldn't even get to my apartment!"

Nick was losing his patience as well. "For God's sake, Jared, will you please slow down and—"

"I mean, he was *there*, Nick!" Jared's perfect skin had turned a sickly shade of yellow, and his eyes bulged with fear, as if he saw something horrible before them. "He was actually in my home! I was on my way through the lobby and the doorman stopped me and said my friend was waiting and I said, 'What friend?' and he said, 'You know, the bald guy who told you to go on up—you did tell him it was okay, didn't you, Mr. Cooper?' And I said...and that's when I realized who it was. I don't know any other bald men—it had to be him! And I didn't have the damn book—it was up here in the desk! So I rushed outside and called Nina from the coffee shop...and I had to wait there—for *four* hours until she came to get me. I *still* think we were followed."

This nearly senseless torrent of words had been delivered in a breathless rush, and when Jared finally stopped, the room echoed with his nervous energy. Kate hardly dared to look at Nick, who was sitting very still beside her. She could feel his carefully measured breathing as he fought to control his temper.

Finally he turned to Nina. "Nina, do you mind translating that idiotic babble so I can figure out what the hell happened?"

Nina opened her mouth to reply, but Jared rushed on again. "I'm not babbling! I'm telling you we're in big trouble, Nick!"

"Not us! You!" Nick retorted angrily.

Jared's jaw snapped shut. He was taken aback by Nick's anger, as if he had not really expected anyone to blame him at all. He blinked twice, looked at Nina for help, then turned back to Nick. "Look," he said placatingly. "It doesn't really matter now, does it? I mean, I'm here, and all I have to do is get the book out of Nina's rolltop, and when he shows up I'll just—"

"When *who* shows up, for God's sake?" Nick nearly shouted.

"Martin DeVoe, of course!"

"Martin De—" Nick stood up suddenly, but Nina interrupted him.

"He's not coming here," she snapped. "He didn't follow us, Jared, I swear to you."

"I think you're wrong, Nin," Jared said, talking over Nick's shoulder. "He wants that book, and he wants it bad."

"What book!" Nick shouted so loudly that everyone jumped.

"His account book!" Jared shouted back, his voice shrill with fear.

"What the hell are you doing with Martin DeVoe's account book?" Nick demanded. Something in his voice made Kate really afraid for the first time.

Jared took a step backward, away from Nick. "I—I took it from his office when I went to borrow the money."

"You—" Nick broke off in shock and then suddenly lost control and lunged for Jared. "You *idiot!*"

Jared hollered, and Nina jumped forward to separate her brother and her lover. Everyone seemed to be shouting at once, so it was surprising that they heard Kate, who spoke in a low voice.

"The desk. It's gone."

All three of them heard her and stopped talking at once. They were frozen in a tableau that would have been ridiculous if things weren't so serious. Three pairs of eyes turned to stare at her.

"What did you say?" Nina made it sound as if Kate had spoken Swahili.

"Your rolltop desk," Kate whispered, and looked at Nick. She could not go on.

He stared back at her for a moment before it dawned on him. "Omigod!" He slapped his forehead with the ball of his hand. "The desk!"

Nina put her hands on her hips. "Nicky," she snapped, "do you mind telling me..." Then she stopped. Her mouth closed into a red line and her eyes narrowed. Suddenly she swung around and walked out of the room.

"I don't . . . What's . . ." Jared broke off when Nina reappeared.

"You did it!" she accused, glaring at Nick and Kate as if they were both responsible. "You sold the desk, didn't you?"

Now it was Nick's turn to spread his hands. "Nina, we needed the money."

"You sold my desk." Nina was now looking straight at Kate, who shifted uncomfortably beneath her accusing gaze as if she were responsible.

"Hell, Nin, it wasn't exactly a Capstein family heirloom. The IRS was breathing down your neck. I had to do something."

"You sold the desk?" Jared's voice was a high squeak of panic.

Nick turned to him and smiled halfheartedly. "That's about the size of it, buddy. The pretty little cherry number is gone."

"But you can't have sold it! You don't understand! If I don't have that book, he'll . . . he'll kill me! *I've got to have that book!*"

Kate was so sure he was going to faint that she actually stood up, automatically ready to catch him. Nina watched in shock from the doorway as Jared swayed sickly in his crocodile boots. Only Nick seemed unperturbed.

Then Jared managed to recover enough to sink back onto the chair. He looked green and shaken, but he was conscious.

Nick came and sat down, too. He was clearly back in command of himself and the situation. "Look, Jared, nobody's going to kill you. Martin DeVoe may be a scummy drug dealer, but he's not dumb, and he's not a killer." He crossed his arms over his chest. "But now that things have reached such dramatic proportions, maybe you should back up and tell us the whole story without fudging the details. I know I'm eager to hear it. Katie's ready to hear it." He raised his eyebrows at Nina. "Nin, are you ready?" She sat down without a word. "Good. Now talk."

Jared held his head in his hands, and his voice was muffled in misery. "When I first got the idea for the big video, I started going everywhere for money. Seemed like nobody in town thought it was worth investing in, and we were already stretched out at the banks. I know you weren't interested, Nicky, but—"

"Forget about me," Nick snapped. "Just tell me what happened."

"I knew we could have hit it big with these commercials, I just knew it! I thought if I could somehow get the money together to make one—just one—on my own, then everybody would see what a good idea it was." He shook his head, and Kate stared, wondering how his hair managed to stay so sleekly welded to his skull. "I was sure . . . so sure. So I went to a friend who knew . . . who suggested someone he thought might be able to help me out."

"You went to Martin DeVoe," muttered Nick, as if this fact were just sinking in. "You actually went to him for money when you knew . . . you knew . . ." He broke off and shook his head.

Jared peered out miserably between his fingers and nodded. "God, Nicky, I didn't think it mattered! It was just this one time, just a little money—what did it matter where I got it? Besides, I knew he needed a place to run some of his cash through the laundry. I figured it would work out to be mutually beneficial—know what I mean?"

Nick shook his head disgustedly, his lips pressed together so tightly that his dimples were granite etches in his cheeks. "You went to a goddamn drug pusher for money. Unbelievable!" Jared's head drooped farther, and Nick seemed to take pity on him. "Okay, so you went to borrow money from DeVoe. Then what happened?"

Jared made a visible effort to pull himself together. "So, there I was in his apartment—he's got a huge place in the East Village—really fantastic looking!—and he says sure, he'll give me the money. He says he's been thinking about getting into videos—'investing in something nice and legal,' was how he put it." He spread his hands. "You see, Nick, I really thought it was going to be all right then!"

"The book, Jared. Tell me about the book."

Jared swallowed. "So everything was going along, and I was telling him about my plans for the video, when . . . when he gets this phone call. And all of a sudden he gets really serious and keeps on saying 'Yes sir, yes, sir,' like he's talking to some Mr. Big—know what I mean? And then he gets very pale and nervous, and suddenly he tells the caller to hang on a minute and tells me he's going into another room for a minute, and would I please wait. So he puts the guy on hold and goes into the other room, and leaves me alone."

"Then what did you do?"

"Nothing. I mean, not at first. I figured he'd be right back. I saw the light on the phone, so I knew he was still talking to this guy from another extension." Jared shrugged. "I just sat there and looked around at all his neat stuff." He stopped.

"And then?" Nick prodded.

Another deep, ragged breath. "Then I got up and started wandering around the room. He was taking forever, and I was getting...restless, you know? So I sort of just walked around and looked at things." He stopped, but no one said anything. Finally he went on.

"I was just looking, you know, through the stuff on his desk. I was curious about how a drug dealer did business."

"Jeez!" Nick muttered, but Jared ignored him.

"I never thought about what I was looking at, not really. Just idle curiosity. But there it was, sitting on his desk, sort of stuck under a heavy marble paperweight, like maybe he had forgotten about it for a while. I had no idea what it was, or even what made me pick it up. It was just a little leatherbound notebook like the kind you get at a stationery store. You know, like an address book. It had a sort of beveled cover, and there was a pen stuck in the pages, like to mark his place. So I..." His voice trailed off again.

"So you stole it," Nick said wearily.

"I didn't! At least, not intentionally," Jared protested. "I mean, I just sort of picked it up to look at it— you know, natural curiosity... It was just a bunch of numbers, like dates and figures and stuff. Nothing exciting or anything."

"I'll bet," Nick muttered.

"And then, while I was looking at it, DeVoe suddenly came back into the room." Jared's face reflected his memory of that panicked moment, and Kate felt a brief stab of pity for him. "I didn't know what to do! I'd been so absorbed in...in what I was doing that I forgot to watch for the phone light to go off. Luckily, I had my back to him, so I just sort of slipped the book into my pocket."

"Lucky you," said Nick dryly.

"Well, what else could I do?" Jared whined. "Just hand it to him and apologize for snooping?"

"Yes, that's exactly what you could have done!" Nick snapped.

"No, I couldn't!"

"Why not?"

"Because I knew—" Jared sighed miserably "—I knew he would be mad if he saw that I had it. And I wanted him to lend me that money."

"So you just pretended nothing had happened and hoped he wouldn't notice it was missing?" Nick's voice was filled with disbelief.

"That's right. I was scared to death, but I just hoped...and he didn't notice! He didn't notice anything!" Now it was Jared's turn to sound disbelieving. "He looked kind of pale himself when he came back into the room, like he was nervous after that phone call. He told me he didn't have much time and sat down and wrote out a check on a Swiss account and that was that."

"And you left. With the money and the book."

"Nick, I wanted to put it back, but I didn't know how! I was stuck with it!"

Nick shook his head. "Then what did you do, Jared?"

Jared looked guilty. "At first I wasn't sure what I should do—throw it away, or mail it back, or what. I needed time to think. So when I came up here the last time I gave the book to Nina and told her it belonged to a friend of mine who'd asked me to hide it someplace."

Nick looked incredulously at his sister, who had the grace to drop her eyes briefly. "You knew about this?"

Nina shook her head defiantly. "Jared didn't give me the story—he just told me to hide it and then he split.

How was I to know what it was? It just looked like a little account book with a lot of numbers. I had no idea." She flashed an angry look at Jared.

Nick turned back to Jared with a snort of disbelief. "Why, you little... You were thinking about blackmailing DeVoe with the book, weren't you? That's why you didn't mail it back to him right away!"

Jared nodded miserably. "I...thought about it for a little while, yeah. But I couldn't figure out what the numbers meant, so I knew it wouldn't work. Besides, as soon as I gave it to Nina, I realized how much trouble I'd be in when DeVoe finally figured out I had his book. I mean, he gets a lot of traffic through his place, and he was pretty out of it after that phone call, but sooner or later he'd remember that I'd been in there when his book disappeared." He looked disconsolately at Nina. "So I split. I went to Bermuda—but I wasn't going to stay, I swear! I just wanted...I wanted a chance to think clearly, without being distracted." When he realized that neither Nick nor Nina believed this, he shrugged. "Okay, so I was scared. Wouldn't you be? And it turns out I was right to be scared, wasn't I? DeVoe was waiting for me in my apartment when I got back." He looked out the window nervously. "He's probably waiting for me right now—out there!"

Everyone turned instinctively to the window and the black night beyond. Kate felt a deep chill invade her bones in spite of the cozy warmth of the parlor.

Nick leaned forward, an incredulous smile on his lips. "Let me get this straight. You went to borrow money from a bald drug dealer named Martin DeVoe, and you stole some book of his that he wants back very badly— badly enough to follow you to your apartment and maybe even here?"

"He didn't follow us," Nina piped up. "I'm sure of it." She met her brother's glare defiantly. "You know I can drive fast when I want to," she told him. "I took all the back roads, too. Believe me, if he *had* been following us, he got very lost. If he's not still waiting for Jared in New York, he's halfway to Quebec by now." She smiled in triumph.

Nick looked at her disdainfully. "Even if you're right, how long do you think it will be before he figures out where Jared is? How long do you think it'll be before he shows up looking for his damned book?" Nick's expression was so harsh that even Nina was cowed. He stared at her for a moment and then turned back to Jared. "Hell, Jared! How could you be so dumb?"

Jared bristled. "It wasn't dumb, Nicky. Don't tell me I was being dumb. I just...didn't think, that's all. As soon as I realized what had happened, I knew I had to give it back."

Nick exploded. "Jared, you took the damn book four days ago! Then you left it with Nina and took off for Bermuda!"

"I came back, didn't I?" Jared was really angry. He narrowed his eyes and jabbed his finger accusingly into the air. "Haven't you ever done something you regretted before, Nick? Haven't you ever made a mistake?"

Nick did not reply, but Kate knew what he was thinking. He had made a mistake, all right. And it had just come back and blown up in his face. All four of them were silent for a tense moment or two, Jared and Nick and Nina glaring white-faced at each other, Kate sitting still and as unobtrusively as possible. She felt as if she'd stepped into an alien country, whose language and culture were virtually incomprehensible. The afternoon had been a magical mystery tour, too, but at least then she'd

had Nick's body, and her own, and the very real plea-
sures they had shared between them. At that moment,
Nick, Nina and Jared seemed so remote from Kate that
she felt she might as well have been alone in the room—
alone with a hidden time bomb that could go off at any
moment. She waited breathlessly, trying not to think
about what might happen next.

Nick shifted, pursed his lips and then let out his breath
loudly. "Oh, yeah, Jared. I've made mistakes." He
sounded calm, resigned and even a little amused at the
irony of his situation. "You better believe I've made
mistakes."

Somehow, with this confession, the air cleared and
everyone relaxed, except Kate. Jared pressed his advantage. "Look. I made a mess of it. I know that, and you
know that. But knowing doesn't change anything. The
question is, what are we going to do about it?"

"We?" Nick asked pointedly. Then, when both Jared
and Nina opened their mouths to speak at once, he put
up his hands to ward them off. "Yeah, yeah, I know.
We're partners. A team. Brothers to the end." He
snorted in exasperation. "I guess I'm in as deep as you
are whether I like it or not."

"I guess so," said Jared evenly.

There was another silence. Kate wished they would all
just keep quiet, not start talking again about drug dealers and account books and secret desk drawers. Her life
had been so calm and contained before, and now it
seemed to have tilted out of control—just like theirs.

The worst part of it was that Nick, too, seemed like a
stranger to her. The reality of his life, although he had
warned her about it earlier, was like some grim Gothic
plot. He had told her that he'd been involved in a crazy
world, but she hadn't really believed it. Up there on the

mountain, it had seemed so...so impossible, like a fairy tale. She had not believed someone like Nick existed, let alone people like Jared and Nina—or Martin DeVoe. Only Nick had been real; only he had mattered.

And now he seemed very far away and like a stranger. She knew she could never reclaim the magic of their afternoon together. She longed to escape to the relative safety of her attic room, where she could nurse her misery in isolation.

But Nick did not notice her misery; he was too busy struggling to manage his own. He took a deep breath and blew it out in a gust of resignation, spreading his fingers across his thighs. "Okay. So where do we go from here?"

"I don't know," said Jared, despondent again.

"I know! How about the police?" Nick asked brightly, as if he were suggesting they all go out for a pizza.

"No! No police!" Jared shook his head firmly. "We can't go to the police."

"Why not, for God's sake? Some guy's following you, threatening you, you go to the police."

"He *didn't* follow us," Nina interjected.

"Oh, be quiet, Nina, will you!" This came from Jared and surprised Nina into compliance. "He could have followed us, and even if he hadn't, Nick's right: it's just a matter of time before he does show up." He paused and cursed. "We've just got to get our hands on that desk. Fast!"

For the first time in an hour, Nick turned directly to Kate. His expression was a mixture of amusement and bitterness. "Well, sweet Kate, you've been very quiet all evening. What do you make of all this?"

Kate felt Nina and Jared turn their attention to her as if they had forgotten she existed. She thought Nick might have, too, for a while. In the space of an hour her world had turned upside down. Now, she faced a man whose background and motivations were once again obscure, whose actions were unpredictable and whose world was more than a little frightening. But he was still Nick, and he still had the power to captivate her. She had no idea how to respond to his question but she felt compelled to say something, to show them all that she wasn't as upset as she really was. She felt he was demanding it of her in some silent way, willing her to speak out when she would have preferred to take refuge in silent anonymity. "I think," she said at last in a small, clear voice, "that it's all very sad."

She heard Nina flounce back in her chair, exasperated. Jared barely suppressed a sneer. But Nick nodded gravely. "Yes, you're right. It is sad, isn't it?" He searched her face. "And it's worse than you thought, isn't it? My life, I mean."

"No. Yes. I don't know." She wished he wouldn't pin her with that penetrating gaze. She did not know how to lie to him.

Nick put his hand on her neck so that his fingertips brushed her cheek. He only pulled her a few inches closer to him, but the pitch of his voice and his compelling expression made it clear that he was talking for her ears alone. "Kate," he murmured. "My sweet, my lucky star. What do you think I should do? I would like...would very much welcome your opinion."

Kate was so surprised that she forgot her embarrassment. "I can't tell you what to do," she whispered. "All this is...completely unreal to me. I've never...I wouldn't know what to tell you, Nick."

"I know that. That's why I need your help. I need your seeing eye."

"My what?"

"Your seeing eye. Your clarity. Your simplicity. Your vision."

He was serious, she realized, and it suddenly occurred to her that his image of her had been fabricated from his own needs, just as her concept of him had been fashioned largely from her desires. He thought she was special, that she possessed some magical powers of observation and insight, just as she had invested him with the power to enchant, to bewitch. They had confided in each other up on their little ledge, but how little they really knew of each other! Was it possible that he had blinded himself to the shy, awkward Kate—the person she knew herself to be? Could he truly believe she was someone so different?

But what knowledge did he expect her to possess, what answers did he expect her to have? She was sure she did not have them, but she couldn't bring herself to tell him he was wrong about her. That would render whatever they had shared together null and void, and she was not ready to do that. In spite of everything, she was not yet ready to let go of the magic. "What do you want me to say, Nick?" she asked helplessly at last.

He shook his head. "I don't know. Just don't run away." Then, without warning, he smiled into her eyes. "You could just say hello, Kate. That'd be all right."

Kate stared for a long time at the man in front of her, trying to decipher him. He was asking her to give him strength, color, inspiration . . . as he had done for her. Part of her still wanted to run away from the responsibility, the challenge. But she was aware of another, new sensation—a feeling that maybe, just maybe, she could be what he saw her to be: strong, clear, simple. Perhaps it wasn't real, but did that really matter right now? And then, suddenly, it occurred to Kate that if Nick had created an idealized image of her, she might have done the same with him. He was no magician, no wizard of seduction. He was just a man—a warm, funny man who was suddenly in pain and in need.

No, she wouldn't run away. It was Saturday night. She could spend the weekend being what Nick wanted her to be. She was not yet ready to break the spell, and if this was the game she had to play... well, why not?

At that moment she did feel brave and clear, although her stomach was churning and her mouth was dry. But she made herself look directly at him, and she smiled into his eyes.

"Hello, Nick," she said softly. "I think I'll stay."

Chapter Eight

"So here's what we're gonna do," Nick said, hunching forward on the sofa and speaking in a conspiratorial whisper. "I'll go up to Avon Farm and get the book from Dan. He won't be real pleased to see me, but I'll try to convince him to be human for a change. You two," he continued sternly, looking at his sister and Jared, "stay here and lie low." He turned to Kate, and his expression softened. "You, too. You wait for me here." His voice caressed her, promising untold delights. Involuntarily, she shivered.

"I'm coming with you, Nicky," Nina interrupted them determinedly.

"Oh, no, you're not," he told her. "You've done plenty for one day, Mario Andretti. Besides, someone has to stay here and protect Jared." He cast his partner a withering look that Jared returned with perfect aplomb. "I don't want him out of your sight, Nina. Yours either, Kate."

Nina glared at her brother. "Nicky, don't be an idiot. Jared can take care of himself. And I'm coming with you."

"You are *not* coming with me," he said severely. "You asked me to take care of this mess, and that's what I'm doing. Is that understood?" Nina narrowed her eyes but did not protest, and Kate understood the dynamic between brother and sister: Nina was a spitfire, but if there was one person in the world she listened to, it was Nick. For his part, Nick could not stay angry at his sister for very long. "Besides, honey," he went on in a softer tone, "what if Jared's goon comes after him? Somebody has to guard the gates, and I can't think of a better person to put this guy off the scent than you."

"How am I supposed to do that?" she inquired petulantly.

Nick grinned. "I trust you. You'll figure something out."

Kate remembered her feeble attempt at fabricating an excuse for Albert Pietro on the telephone that morning. Nick seemed to expect women to think on their feet as quickly as he did. She assumed that, in his experience, they probably did. Certainly Nina would have no trouble inventing a good story on the spot, because she grinned in spite of herself.

"I guess I can manage that," she allowed.

"What about me?" Jared asked sourly. "Don't you think I can manage on my own?"

"Nope. Besides, Jared, I don't think you're gonna want to see this guy if he comes to the front door, are you?"

"You're right," Jared muttered. "I'll keep out of sight and let Nina handle it."

Kate realized that Jared was used to having people—women, especially—take care of his problems for him. The difference between Jared and Nick, she reflected, was that Jared deliberately traded on his good looks and charm, while Nick expected his women to be equal partners in his escapades. For a moment she thought about asking if she could go with him to Dan Avon's, but she realized that if he wasn't allowing Nina to accompany him, he certainly wouldn't let her come along.

"God, this is just like a Humphrey Bogart flick," Nina murmured, and Kate could see the sparkle of excitement in her eyes.

"Not exactly," Nick retorted dryly. "more like Tom Mix in the Wild West. Or the Keystone Kops."

Kate smiled because she knew that despite his wry tone, Nick was as stimulated by the prospect of action and adventure as Nina. Kate, too, had the sense of participating in a melodrama, but she wasn't nearly as delighted about it as Nina and Nick seemed to be. Unlike Nick, she was not convinced that Jared's life—possibly all of their lives—were not in real and immediate danger. If Martin DeVoe was a drug dealer and loan shark, why wouldn't he be capable of murder as well? In Kate's mind, there was very little difference, and she failed to see why Nick, despite his greater knowledge of such things, should distinguish between them.

She was scared. Yet she had agreed to stay, to throw in her lot—if only temporarily—with this compelling man and his sister. The old Kate Palmer—the real one—would never have willingly associated herself with danger, real or imagined, but the old Kate had not known Nick Capstein. So here she was, sitting with him in the warm parlor, listening to him plan some escapade that she would ordinarily have dismissed as impossible. It was frightening, but undeniably exciting, too, and Kate found herself leaning forward, eager to hear what Nick had to say.

"The fewer people descending on Avon's place, the better," he told them. "He's not gonna even want to see me, much less a posse of perverts from evil old Manhattan. I'll go alone and try to convince him to give up the book."

"Why won't he just let you have it?" Kate inquired. "After all, it's of no use to him, regardless of what he thinks of you."

Nick smiled to himself at the sparkle he saw in Kate's eyes, but he answered her question seriously. "You saw what he was like at the auction house. Dan Avon wouldn't miss an opportunity to make my life more difficult. That desk is his now, and on general principle he's not going to make it easy for me to get near it. He'd love to think that I'm suffering for something he could give me." He sighed and turned to his sister. "Where's the book, Nina—you remember which drawer you put it in?"

Nina shook her head. "One of the secret compartments. I just shoved it in and slammed the wood partition back into place. I didn't look to see which one. As a matter of fact," she admitted balefully, "I'm never sure where those damn things are or how they work."

"Oh, terrific—" Nick sat back heavily "—now I don't even know which drawer the damn thing's hidden in. I'm sure Avon hasn't figured out those compartments yet, and he's not going to be pleased when I start fiddling around with his precious new possession—especially after I told him I knew how they worked. He already trusts me about as far as he can throw his barn. He'll probably think I'm trying to sabotage it right under his nose, or pick up a stash or something like that!''

Kate looked at him in surprise. ''But I thought you did know how the drawers operated. You explained them to him from my picture, didn't you?''

Nick grimaced. ''I fudged the explanation, couldn't you tell? I know how two of them operate, and I can operate the third one once the panel has been slid back, but I can never figure out where the damn thing is. And with our luck, the book is probably in the third drawer.''

''See, Nicky? Now you *will* need me to come along. I'm the only one who'll be able to find that third drawer.'' Nina looked triumphant.

Nick seemed to consider it reluctantly, and Kate spoke shyly into the silence that ensued. ''I know where the drawer is, Nick.''

All three heads snapped around to look at her. ''How do *you* know?'' Nina asked accusingly.

''I saw it when we moved the desk out of here,'' she explained. ''And then, when I drew the sketch of it for Simmond's—'' She broke off and shrugged apologetically. ''I'm sure I could figure it out.''

''That's impossible,'' Jared said flatly. ''You just saw it once....''

''Twice, really,'' Kate corrected him automatically.

''Whatever. I've seen the thing a dozen times, and I still can't figure it out. Neither can Nicky. Nina's the only one who could possibly get the drawer open.'' He eyed Kate skeptically, and she blushed.

''Ah,'' Nick said proudly, ''but you don't know my Kate.'' He put his arm around her shoulder and pulled her against him, which made her blush even harder.

"This lovely child has a magic seeing eye. A photographic memory. I told you, she has vision."

Nina looked disgusted. "So you're gonna take her along instead of me, is that the deal?"

Nick pulled away so that he could see Kate's face. "Well," he said softly, "I had planned on going solo, but now that you mention it, maybe it's not a bad idea after all. What do you say, sweet Katepalmer? Are you game for a little live action? A taste of how we live here on the dark side of the moon?"

"Don't you think you're putting her in unnecessary danger, Nicky?" Nina demanded caustically.

"Whaddya mean, danger? Avon might be teed off, but he's not berserk. He won't use a shotgun on us." He squeezed Kate's shoulder reassuringly. "Besides, with Kate there, he might actually be easier to deal with. I think he liked her."

This was so patently untrue that Kate giggled. "I doubt it."

"But it might really help if you were there." Nick pressed on. "After all, you could take one look at the desk and remember exactly where the drawers are, couldn't you?"

"Probably." Kate didn't want to sound boastful in front of Nina and Jared—especially Nina. Besides, she wasn't at all sure she could envision the whereabouts of the third secret drawer. Her photographic memory had never been put to the test under pressure before, and she did not especially want to try it out under these conditions.

"Sure, you could. I know you could."

He looked at her with such confidence that Kate experienced a moment's paranoia. Was this all Nick had meant when he said he needed her vision? That he wanted her photographic eye to help him find the secret drawer? Could he possibly have engineered the entire scenario just to get her to come along and help him out? She remembered that he had allowed Nina to go to New York after Jared instead of going himself. Maybe he was a lot like Jared after all—letting women do his dirty work.

But she could not believe that, not with Nick gazing so appealingly into her eyes. He had meant what he said about wanting her just to be there. Anyway, she reminded herself, it had been her decision—her wanting to be with him—that had made her agree to stay on. And now, having committed herself that far, she felt compelled to venture further still. "You're right," she found herself saying. "I know I could."

Nick's eyes glittered. "Does that mean yes?" he asked her. "I mean, I don't want to push you or anything. It won't be dangerous, but it might be uncomfortable. And I know you don't like confrontations."

Kate was surprised to hear this. How did he know what she felt about confrontations? He put his lips briefly against her ear. "You can say no, you know. You've already done more than you know for me just by being here."

Kate sighed inwardly. As she always did when faced with those incredible eyes, she was feeling recklessly not herself. "I'll come with you," she told him.

"Then it's settled." Nick threw his sister a firm, warning glance, and Nina glowered back. Jared looked uncomfortable. She's jealous! Kate thought, and was surprised to find that she derived some small satisfaction out of this. "You two stay here and mind the fort," Nick instructed them. "Kate and I will go—right now."

So they went out again into the cold night. It was only eight-thirty, but it felt like the witching hour. Kate could barely remember getting up that morning. She had traveled light-years, it seemed, since then. Still, the butterflies in her stomach were not entirely uncomfortable, and she felt a thrill of complicity sitting beside Nick as they sped off into the blackness.

"I still have a few questions," she announced when they had left the lights of Putnam Falls behind them.

She could see him grin in the reflected glare of the headlights. "I was hoping someone would have the good sense to ask some," he admitted cheerfully. "Those two are so caught up in their own drama that they didn't even bother to think about it. Shoot."

"You don't really think this Martin DeVoe will stop once he has his book back, do you? I mean, guys like that...I don't know, but it seems to me he won't just go away and leave Jared alone just because he has what he wants. It seems to me he'll still be pretty annoyed."

"You're absolutely right," Nick replied promptly.

"Well, uh, doesn't that mean, he might...do something to Jared? Punish him somehow, or hurt him—" she swallowed "—or you?"

Nick gave her a brief, grateful smile. "Thank you for that, sweet Kate." Then he turned to concentrate on the dark mountain roads. "I know a little bit about Martin DeVoe." He threw Kate a swift shrewd glance. "You don't have to ask how, do you?"

Kate replied promptly, "No. I don't want to know."

A smile flickered across his full lips. "Right. Well, I don't know a whole helluva lot, to tell you the truth. But I do know he's not a murderer—he doesn't have the power or the nerve. He's just a small-time operator, really; small potatoes compared with most. He probably works for some big businessman who wears Savile Row suits and looks like he wouldn't be caught dead doing anything that even smells illegal. There are hundreds of Martin DeVoes in the city, and the last thing any of them wants is to get caught doing something foolish."

"How can you be so sure?" Kate asked in a small voice.

He reached over in the darkness and patted her hand. "Trust me. He's not a killer."

"There are other things that could happen to you besides getting killed."

Nick sighed. "I know. I know." He pulled the truck around a sharp, sudden corner and onto a dirt road. "But we've got to deal with one problem at a time, and right now our problem is whether Dan Avon will give us that book."

"Why do you and Avon have such a bad relationship?"

"I don't know," he answered truthfully. "I've been coming up here ever since Nina married Bob Tate, and Avon and I have rubbed each other the wrong way from the moment we met. Nothing ever happened between us or anything. It's just that he's so morally righteous, and I seem to represent everything he left New York to get away from." He chuckled dryly. "He probably really does think I'm some scummy drug dealer—which is pretty ironic, when you think about the reason for this little visit."

Kate chose not to think about it. "You were watching him yesterday as if he were your mortal enemy."

Nick thought for a moment. "I think," he said slowly, "that sometimes I just suddenly get fed up—with myself, mostly. It really had nothing to do with Avon—" he looked at her "—or with you."

Kate accepted this statement thoughtfully, and they were quiet the rest of the way. Now that they were no longer in the cozy comfort of the sitting room at the Stonecroft Inn, she was beginning to wonder if she hadn't perhaps suffered from a momentary aberration. Was she really about to go barging into some hostile stranger's home demanding to get a mysterious book from a secret drawer in an antique desk? The darkness seemed to press into the cab of the truck, and Nick's preoccupied silence made him seem distant and cold. Once again she felt like Alice in some crazed Wonderland, watching strange and beautiful creatures do things that were utterly alien to her reality. But I'm here, too, she reminded herself. I'm doing strange things, too. She felt like pinching herself to see if it wasn't really all a dream, but she was afraid Nick would see her. Anyway, even if it was a dream, she wasn't sure she wanted to wake up. If the man beside her was a figment of her imagination, or even if he was just leading her on, she didn't want to know about it just yet.

"I have one more question," she said at last.

"What's that?"

In the dark, he couldn't see her eyes twinkling. "Did Ben Franklin's grandson ever really use the cherry desk?"

He looked sharply at her, then smiled. "Well, sweet Kate, what do you think?"

She smiled back unevenly. "I think you have a very vivid imagination."

He laughed outright, the sound reverberating in the small, closed cab. "Hoo! That, my dear Kate, is the understatement of the century. Sometimes I think my entire life is one gigantic hallucination."

Kate laughed with him, although she wasn't sure why. Then she realized he had stopped. "I do have a vivid imagination," he said soberly. "But about some things, I am perfectly clear." He looked at her sideways, and she could tell what he was thinking. "Some things I know are real."

Even in the semidarkness, a current of electricity seemed to vibrate between them, causing Kate's heart to throb erratically. She understood that she was very real to him, that she had somehow made a strong impact on his life in a very short time. And although she would have been at a loss to explain the reason for this effect, she knew that he had had an equally powerful impact on her. Although the night had all the makings of a Gothic melodrama, she knew that Nick was right: some things *were* real. The way she felt about him, and the way he made her feel about herself—vibrant and alive for the first time in years—could not be denied.

Nick turned into a stony driveway and pulled the truck to an abrupt halt. "This is it," he announced.

Kate peered out the window at a wall of trees. "But there's nothing there!" she exclaimed.

"Right," he replied dryly. "Avon's idea of rustic is hiking a quarter mile to his house through the woods." He jangled his car keys and switched on the tiny flashlight. "Looks like this little gizmo is putting in some overtime these days, huh?"

He pointed the tiny beam at the ground and led the way through the woods. Kate could not help remembering the afternoon, and she was sure Nick was remembering, too. He was humming something under his breath, and she leaned forward to catch it, hoping to recognize some romantic love ballad.

He was singing "Whistle a Happy Tune" from *The King and I*—a song she hadn't heard in perhaps twenty years.

Hah! she thought to herself wryly. So much for romanticism.

Finally the outlines of a sprawling frame house appeared against the backdrop of black. Kate could barely make out the tall gabled windows, the drooping wrap-around porch and the double front door, but the effect was suitably Gothic. Firelight flickered in one of the windows, but the rest of the house was in darkness. She let her breath out slowly, hoping to control her hammering heart.

"Looks like something right out of Mary Shelley, or Robert Louis Stevenson, huh?" Nick said cheerfully. "Right down to Mr. Hyde lurking in the parlor, ready to attack luscious young maidens."

He growled and nuzzled her neck. Kate shot him a baleful glance. "Nick!" she reprimanded him. "Stop it! You're scaring me."

But she found that she was not as scared as she thought she'd be. She looked back at the house. "It's so huge. How'd they ever build it up here on this godforsaken mountaintop?"

"Beats me. Slave labor, I guess." He took her hand. "Well, come on, partner. Let's go beard the lion in his den."

"I wish you wouldn't say that," she muttered, and Nick chuckled as they walked up to the front porch.

There was no doorbell, but Nick knocked loudly, and presently they saw a flickering light moving toward them through the frosted glass of the doors. "You're kidding!" he exclaimed softly. "Can it be that Mountain Man Avon eschews electricity?" He shook his head. "How does he listen to his favorite punk music, I wonder?"

The door swung inward with an appropriate creak, and Daniel Avon held his lantern aloft with an unwelcoming scowl. "Who's..." He recognized Nick. "What the hell are you doing here?" he snarled.

"Hey, Dan, good to see you, too!" Nick chirped. "Katie and I were just in the neighborhood, and we thought we'd drop by for a little chat."

This speech was so unexpected that Avon could not reply, so Nick was able to sail through the door right under his astonished nose. Kate followed more meekly, aware of the rank odor of unwashed wool and wood smoke.

Avon recovered when they were halfway across the entry hall. "Wait!" he thundered. Both stopped immediately. "Just what do you think you're doing in my house, Capstein?" he demanded.

Nick spun around. "To tell you the truth, Avon, we need a favor."

"Hah!"

"We do, really. I mean, I know you and I haven't always been the best of friends, but this is an emergency. And after all, we are neighbors of a sort, aren't we?" He was being his most charming, but Kate could tell it was having no effect on Avon.

"Hmmph," was all he would say.

Nick tried a new tack. "Look, Dan, we need something out of that desk you bought yesterday."

"What?" Avon asked suspiciously.

Nick shook his head. "It's something that couldn't possibly be of any interest or value to you. But it's kind of important that we get it back."

"What'd you do, Capstein, leave your drug stash in the secret drawer?"

Nick and Kate exchanged glances. "I told you," he whispered to her, sotto voce. Then he turned back to Avon. "Come on, Dan," he said placatingly. "You don't seriously believe I'm into that, do you?" Avon grunted incoherently. "Of course you don't. So if you'll just let us get what we came for..."

"It belongs to me now," Avon said.

"I know the desk is yours, but..."

"No, I mean whatever's in it belongs to me. God knows, I paid enough for it, didn't I, Capstein?" His small eyes glittered in the lantern light.

Nick let out his breath slowly, making an effort to control his temper. "Technically you're right, Dan," he said patiently. "But we really do need that book."

"What book?" Avon asked suspiciously.

"Oh, what the hell does it matter!" Nick exploded impatiently.

"If it doesn't matter, then why bother coming after it?" he persisted.

"Because it's important to me! Not to you, to me!"

Avon crossed his arms smugly over his barrel chest. "Well, I guess that's for me to decide, isn't it?"

The two men seemed to have arrived at a standoff. Both stood glaring at each other in the dim entryway while the lantern light cast grotesque shadows. Despite her fear, Kate was suddenly exasperated by their stubbornness. They would be there all night, neither budging an inch, if she didn't do something.

"Mr. Avon," she said sweetly. Both men turned to her, surprised. "I know you were having some trouble finding the secret compartments, weren't you?"

Dan Avon hesitated. "Well, yes," he conceded, "but . . ."

"Have you managed to figure them out yet?"

"Not yet," he muttered grudgingly.

"Then maybe I could show you how they operate—in return for letting Nick get that book he needs out of the secret compartment." She smiled at him. "Do you think that would be fair?"

Avon narrowed his beady eyes and gaped at her. Kate could feel Nick's astonished gaze on her as well, but she forced herself to hold Avon's stare without faltering.

"Well, Mr. Avon, what do you say?" She sounded so cheerful that she surprised herself.

Without a word, Avon uncrossed his arms and began walking into the parlor, leaving the lantern behind. Kate stood where she was until she felt Nick prodding her in the ribs. "Don't just stand there," he hissed, "follow him!" He dropped a swift kiss on her ear. "I'll be right behind you, keeping my big mouth shut."

They entered a huge parlor through massive oak double doors. The firelight cast dancing shadows on the walls, but both Kate and Nick stopped in surprise at the threshold. Not only were there several tasteful electric-light fixtures placed around the room, but there was a huge console along the side wall that seemed to contain every electronic device known to man. Two televisions, a complicated-looking stereo-component system and a computer were arranged on polished mahogany shelves along with several telephones, a VCR and an impressive array of videotapes.

Having expected only the most primitive setting, both were taken aback by this display of high-tech living. Dan watched them take it all in with an impassive eye, arms crossed heavily over his chest.

Nick recovered first. "Really roughing it, aren't you, Avon?"

"Shut up, Capstein," he growled, then added reluctantly, "Much as I dislike it, I've got to keep track of things back in the city. I've got…business interests, you know. It isn't cheap to live up here."

"Not like this, it isn't," Nick agreed. "This is quite a spread. Quite an impressive spread." He looked around and nodded approvingly.

Kate had to agree. The entertainment center was only part of the surprise. With her practiced eye, she noticed that the room was filled with high-quality furniture that emphasized opulent comfort. In addition to a massive leather couch and several deep reclining chairs done in dark gray suede, there were a number of very good antiques—too heavy for her taste, but valuable nevertheless. Nick was right. Dan Avon may have avowed disdain for the sophisticated trappings of city life when he moved up to this country manse, but he had not denied himself the comforts of home. And he had spent a great deal of money to get them. Whatever it was that he had done—or still did—in the city, he'd been very successful at it.

Nevertheless, even in this impressive setting, Kate's eyes were drawn to the cherry desk. It seemed to gleam among the dark furniture that surrounded it.

She forced herself to wait until Avon had gone over to the desk. "Show me," he said gruffly. "Show me how it works."

Kate noticed that his fingers, which lingered lovingly on the polished surface, were surprisingly well manicured and delicate for such a large man. She had expected him to have soiled and stubby farmer's hands, although she reminded herself that he was not really a farmer, even though he liked to be perceived as one. And it was clear from the way he stroked and caressed it that he loved the pretty little desk. She cast him a genuinely warm smile.

"It's lovely, isn't it?" she said gently.

He looked at her, and his eyes softened minutely. "Yes. It is nice." He looked around the room. "Doesn't really belong in here, though. I'll have to move it somewhere else." He cast a bitter glance at Nick, who stood silently in the middle of the room. "After *he* leaves."

Kate bent down and surveyed the cherry desk. It looked exactly as she remembered it—exactly as her mind's eye had photographed it when she first saw it. She ran her hands over the familiar planes and grooves. The question was, would she be able to figure out the third secret-drawer opening? It was one thing to draw the little grooves and another to manipulate them. She hoped that Nina had put the book in one of the other two drawers. Those were easy to figure out; Nick had pointed them out to her, and their mechanisms were much simpler.

Nick and Dan Avon were both waiting impatiently, so she pressed the first wooden knob. It gave way beneath her touch at once. "See?" she explained to Avon. "Here's the first one, right here. You just press down . . . like that, and . . ." She sat back on her heels as it swung open. It was empty. She looked up at Nick and shook her head slightly. He rocked back on his heels and tried to keep still.

"That looks easy enough," Avon allowed.

"It is. Now why don't you try it with the other one?" She gave him an encouraging smile. "It works the same way."

Avon bent beside her with a great creaking of limbs. She noticed again that his hands were soft and supple, and he handled the wood with great care. After a few tries, he got the drawer open, and he actually smiled at Kate. "That's easy enough."

"I told you. You just have to be shown the first time." She did not bother telling him that she had not needed such instruction. She also had to force herself not to peer too eagerly into its interior. She was keenly aware of Nick's tension—he seemed to be exhibiting an anxiety all out of proportion to the situation. After all, they were here, they had the desk in front of them; it was just a matter of time and care before they got what they'd come for. But then what? she asked herself, and had to take a deep breath to calm down her jangling nerves.

A quick glance into the drawer proved that it, too, was empty. She did not dare look at Nick.

"Right," Avon was saying. "That's all. Just a little common courtesy." He glowered at Nick. "So, Capstein, where's your precious book?"

"Try the third drawer," Nick said in a strangled voice.

Kate ran her hands over the front of the desk. It was here somewhere. She remembered drawing the tiny little groove that must have hidden the catch. Her fingers probed, but nothing seemed to be happening. Behind her, Avon and Nick were breathing heavily, each for his own reason. Kate knew that her fingers were trembling, and she willed them to be still.

Suddenly something clicked, and a hidden panel swiveled out. It really was a marvel of engineering, the way it appeared with such perfect grace seemingly from out of nowhere. She felt Avon catch his breath beside her as she pulled out the tiny knob that the hidden piece of wood had revealed. Nick, she knew, was no longer breathing at all.

And there it was, a little book with a beveled leather cover, just as Jared had described it. Kate lifted it out of the drawer and automatically leafed through the pages. Only a few were written on, and they contained a jumble of numbers that made no sense to her. For some reason, it seemed extremely anticlimactic. Nevertheless, her photographic eye automatically registered what she saw before she turned to Nick.

"I think this is what you wanted," she said as calmly as she could.

Nick moved to take the book from her hands, but before he could, Avon grabbed it away. He inspected it thoroughly, peering at the cryptic entries with his brow furrowed and his mouth slightly ajar. Kate noticed that his hands were trembling. What had he expected? she wondered.

"See?" she said. "There's nothing in it that could possibly be important to you."

"No drugs, as you can see," Nick pointed out calmly, although Kate knew he was eager to get his hands on the book and put it safely away.

Avon looked for a minute more and then slowly closed the book and handed it back to Kate. "Doesn't make much sense to me," he told her.

"Of course not. It's just...just some bookkeeping that we need." Kate put the tiny ledger in her pocket and glanced warningly at Nick, who seemed ready to take it away from her. She didn't want him to do anything that might make Avon more suspicious than he already was, and he was certainly less suspicious of her than he was of Nick. "Well," she said brightly, "did you understand how the drawer worked? This is the tricky one."

Avon regarded her quietly for a moment. "I think so," he said at last. "Let me try it." He bent down, closed the drawer and managed to open it again himself. "Incredible," he said to himself. "What workmanship." He bent closer and manipulated the groove again.

"We'll leave you now, Avon," Nick announced, his voice sounding unnaturally loud in the room. "I think we both have what we want."

Avon looked up, but it was to Kate that he spoke. "Yes, I believe we do. Thanks," he murmured gruffly. "Thanks for the lesson."

Kate nodded and smiled. "And thank you," she said graciously. She had decided that he was not such a bad man at all.

But Nick was getting impatient. "Don't bother to get up," he said to Avon, who clearly wasn't. "We'll find our own way out." He hustled Kate to the door, but she insisted on turning around and calling out.

"Goodbye, Mr. Avon. Thank you again."

There was no reply, just the hunched shadow of Avon's back as he bent over his new possession.

After the warm house, the air outside was sharp enough to make them both gasp. Nick tucked Kate's shoulder under his arm and hurried them across the small clearing toward the bank of trees beyond which stood the truck.

"That was incredible," he said, his breath appearing in little plumes of frost on the air. "Truly incredible."

"What was so incredible?"

"You! The way you handled him! As if you two were in some polished Regency drawing room exchanging pleasantries." He looked down at her, his eyes wide and shining. "I mean, you were just unbelievable."

"It really didn't take much," she retorted. "I was just being polite, that's all. And really, he was rather nice, once he realized we weren't there to harass him."

Nick chuckled. "My God, Kate, I knew I had found a gem in you, but I never dreamed you had such hidden resources." They had almost reached the trees when he stopped suddenly and swung her around to face him, pressing his cold lips against hers. "You," he murmured next to her ear, "may be the first right thing I've done in I don't know how long."

As she kissed him, gasping from the cold night and the heat of passion, Kate was aware of a surge of triumph coursing through her being. She had done it! He was proud of her! Carl had never said anything like that to her; as a matter of fact, no one had—not in a very long time. Even more important, she felt it was true. Joyously she opened her mouth to receive his.

They stood there, arms wrapped around each other, until both were shivering. The night had grown much, much colder. "I don't think I could manage another alfresco session, do you?" Nick asked at last, his teeth chattering against hers.

Kate shivered. "Definitely not."

"Let's hurry home and crawl into a warm bed together, okay?" Right then, his eyes were the only warm thing about him. "I can't wait to see all of you, to feel and taste all of you."

Kate's knees and loins turned to jelly at the image this conjured. "Let's go," she breathed.

She turned to move on, but Nick held her back. "Wait."

"What?"

"The book. I want to look at that damn book first."

"Nick, wait till we get into the car at least!"

He shook his head. "Come on, let me see it, for God's sake. That little thing has caused more trouble than its weight in plutonium. I can't wait another second to see what all the fuss has been about."

Kate took it from her pocket and handed it over. Then, from behind her, she felt a sudden whoosh of air. Something brushed against her down coat with a sibilant rush, and before she knew what was happening, she was pushed very hard onto the frozen ground. At first she thought it was an animal, but then Nick cursed loudly and she heard the unmistakable thud of flesh striking flesh. Her stomach surged queasily, and she tried to sit up to see what was going on. But everything was black motion above her and she could only make out the awful sounds of two men grunting in combat.

She tried to call out for them to stop but found that her voice was not working. Then, suddenly, there was a moment of deadly quiet. Her heart, which had been pounding mercilessly against her ribs, lurched into her throat.

"N-nick? Are you—"

Before she could say any more, she felt a sharp, stinging blow across her face. And then, nothing.

Chapter Nine

It was raining—a dull, cold, morning rain that washed away the last remnants of snow and left the country looking gray and sodden. Kate stared through the window of the bus, trying to make herself memorize road signs, advertisements—anything to occupy her mind in some safe activity. But twenty-four hours of madness and a sleepless night conspired against her; for the first time in her memory, she could not make her photographic eye do its trick.

There was only one picture emblazoned on her brain, and nothing could make it go away. It was the sight of Nick, lying pale and still on the frozen ground outside Dan Avon's house, a trickle of blood coursing down his forehead and across the bridge of his nose. The events that followed this ghastly image were clear, too, but none carried the weight of that one picture. More than anything else, it embodied the reality of the mess she had gotten herself involved in.

She had never really lost consciousness last night. The shock of the blow had merely paralyzed her for a moment or two. But by the time she'd recovered enough to move, the unseen assailant had vanished into the night. And Nick lay there, deathly still....

For one horrifying instant, she really thought he was dead. She screamed out his name with such force that the sound seemed to hang frozen in the bitter air. But then he stirred and moaned, although he didn't open his eyes.

Galvanized into action, she flew back to Dan Avon's front door, and was relieved when he opened it almost at once to her hysterical pounding.

"What the devil...?" he growled, holding up his hurricane lantern and looking around nervously.

"Oh, please, there's been an accident. Nick's hurt. Come quickly!"

Without waiting to see if he followed her, she rushed back to the spot where Nick lay and bent over his inert body.

"What the hell happened?" Avon asked, hurrying up behind her. He knelt beside Nick and began to feel for a pulse.

"I...I don't really know. Suddenly there was this...this sound, and then I heard Nick, and...it sounded like he was fighting, but it was too dark to tell." She paused, trying to collect her thoughts. "I thought it was an animal at first."

"No animal did this," Avon muttered, then looked sharply up at her. "You okay?"

"I think so. Yes, I'm all right. Is he...?"

"He's had a bad bang on the head, but he'll live." He sounded less than pleased about this, but he tucked his strong arms under Nick's back and heaved. "Come on. Help me get him inside."

Tugging ineffectually at Nick's legs, Kate trailed after Avon, who carried his burden as if it were weightless. Once inside, they took him into the parlor and laid him out on the long leather couch that stood in front of the fire. By firelight, Nick looked a bit better, but only marginally so.

"Why isn't he . . . awake?" she asked, trying to make her teeth stop chattering.

"Got knocked out," Avon told her. "He'll come around." He lifted one of Nick's eyelids and was rewarded with another moan. "How about you—you sure you're all right? You look kinda green yourself."

Kate shook her head. "I'm fine," she insisted, but her chattering lips gave her away. "Just a little cold, but I'll be okay."

Avon got up and went over to a corner cupboard. "No, you won't. You're in shock." He returned and thrust out a small glass filled with whiskey. "Drink this."

Kate obeyed, noticing irrelevantly that the glass was real crystal. The whiskey made her shudder, but its warmth spread quickly through her body, dulling the cold, sharp edge of hysteria.

Avon waited until she finished the shot before returning to Nick's prostrate figure. He knelt and felt for the pulse in Nick's wrist again, and Kate realized that he was really very competent, despite his gruff, taciturn demeanor. "So what happened?" he asked. "Somebody follow you up here?"

"No, of course not," she replied quickly. "Why should they?"

"I have no idea," Avon snapped. "Obviously your friend is in some kind of trouble. Hidden books, attackers..."

"The book!" Kate bent over Nick and searched through his jacket pockets, but it was nowhere to be found. "Did you see it—the book, I mean?" she asked Avon.

He shook his head and regarded her curiously. "No, I didn't. It wasn't on the ground when I picked him up, either."

"Oh, Lord...." Kate moaned. She knew now why they'd been accosted. Somebody had wanted the book. And they had gotten it.

Avon watched her shrewdly, his eyes narrowed. "Listen. Do you know what this whole mess is about, young lady? Do you know what was in that book?"

For one wild moment Kate thought about confiding in Avon, telling him everything that had happened. He seemed so big, so solid and reassuring. Surely he'd be able to help. But then she realized this was not realistic. Avon wouldn't begin to understand the story. She herself didn't understand it. And after what had just happened, she didn't want to.

"I have no idea," she said miserably.

"You looked at it, though," he pointed out sharply. "Didn't you know what those numbers meant?"

For a moment the image of the book appeared clearly in Kate's mind, every mark, right down to the ink spots and the dog-eared corner that marked the place. But Avon couldn't possibly know about her photographic memory. And somehow, she didn't want to let him know. She shook her head. "I don't even remember what I saw," she told him. The truth was, she wished she *didn't* remember.

"I didn't think so. A girl like you..." He shook his head. "My advice to you is to stay away from the Capsteins and all their sleazy friends. They're nothing but trouble." He glared at Nick with undisguised distaste. "You don't want to get involved in his kind of messes, do you?"

"No," Kate said meekly. "I... suppose not." Then, feeling as if she had betrayed the silent figure on the couch, she added, "But I do want to get help for him. A doctor." She looked around the room. "Where's the telephone? I'll call for a doctor."

Avon snorted dryly. "The telephone isn't working. Line goes down all the time up here. You'll have to go down the mountain to get help."

"Oh, no," she wailed in a panic. "That's so far away!"

"Don't worry. He'll live. I'll see to it, though I can't see what purpose it'd serve."

For one awful moment Kate wondered if it had been Avon himself who'd attacked them. How could she leave Nick alone up here with a—a mad mountain man? Then she dismissed her fancies as ridiculous, although she was still reluctant to leave.

"I... I don't know the way," she faltered.

"Don't be silly. There's only one road."

"But once I get to town, where do I go?"

Avon spoke impatiently, as to a child. "Go right to the police station in the center of town. Chief Lahey is usually on duty at night. Just tell him what happened. He'll get Doc Larner up here to take care of everything."

But Kate barely heard him. She was staring out the windows at the night. "Don't be afraid out there," Avon added in a gentler voice. "Whoever it was got what he was looking for. He won't bother you." He waved his arm at her and relapsed into his usual gruffness. "Now get out of here. Go on, do it!"

If Avon had not ordered her out, Kate might never have gotten up the courage to move. A dreadful inertia had set in, an aftereffect of shock. She stood indecisively for a few minutes more, taking one last, long look at Nick, whose breathing was loud but regular. Then, because she simply couldn't think of anything else to do or say, she obeyed Avon's instructions and left the house.

She took Nick's keys, started the truck and headed down the mountain to town, driving with elaborate care, as if she were in control of the situation. Actually, she was an automaton, making the required moves without thinking. When she got to Putnam Falls she did exactly as she had been told. Chief Lahey listened to her disjointed story, looked at her shrewdly and told her to go home, take a stiff drink and get into bed. Then he went to rouse the doctor for the trip to Avon's house.

Kate drove herself back to the Stonecroft Inn and went through her story again for Nina and Jared. Jared wanted to press her harder for details, and he seemed annoyed at Kate's remote responses to his questions. He told Nina that it must have been Martin DeVoe himself who had hit Nick and taken the book, and this seemed to relieve him tremendously. But Nina, wild with fear for her brother, wanted only to rush up the mountain to be with him. Kate had ceased to exist for her, and she didn't even bother to speak with her as she dragged the reluctant Jared out the door.

Kate, still numb and weary now beyond belief, dragged herself up to her room and sank down on the saggy bed. She would not allow herself to think, because she knew that beneath her thoughts was a terrifying tidal wave of emotions just waiting to be released. She had to keep the dam shut tight against it, so she just sat and waited, her mind a blank.

Several hours passed and still Nick did not return. Kate told herself she was relieved. Seeing him again would be even worse than thinking about him. She would once again be drawn into his life, into the incandescent circle of attraction that radiated from him like a beacon. Suddenly, everything that had seemed magical and enticing felt foreign and dangerous....

Gradually Kate realized what she had to do. She had to get away from Putnam Falls, quickly, before the Capsteins and Jared came back. She had simply been overwhelmed by the force of Nick's sensual power, she told herself, charmed into thinking that she was someone other than herself—but she couldn't keep up the pretense any longer. She would have to extricate herself from the dream world she had entered, return to her own clear, cool reality.

Kate's face crumpled, and she burst into tears as she lay on her little bed. She was lying to herself. She wasn't leaving because of what had happened—she wasn't leaving because she was in danger of losing herself in someone else's mistaken image of her. She was running away... because in spite of it all, she had fallen in love with Nick Capstein. Unsuitably, probably unrequitedly, but hopelessly in love.

It was this that made her afraid—much more afraid than the thought that she had gotten involved in Nick's unsavory problems. Even since her affair with Carl, she had been reluctant to get involved. She recognized in herself a potential for passion, and she knew that even in the short time she had known him, Nick had been able to draw from her more feeling—and a greater capacity for living—than Carl or anyone else she had ever met. If she stayed with Nick, she was afraid of the person she might become. She could get lost in a man like him, and that really frightened her.

She also knew that their relationship could not go on as it was. Nick's appetite for adventure and excitement—for rushing headlong into the unknown—was insatiable...and exhausting. Given enough time with her, she was sure, Nick would soon grow restless, looking for more excitement than she could ever offer.

She might never have known this—certainly not so soon—if things had not happened the way they did. But they had, and she was afraid of that, too. In her world, people didn't steal from drug dealers, or get attacked by them. She could not deny that the night's events had been as terrifying to her as they were stimulating to Nick. Unlike Nick and his sister, she saw no charm in danger.

All these fears and uncertainties conspired to convince her of the unreality of her attraction to Nick Capstein and his world. It would never work—*they* would never work. This made leaving seem inevitable, and Kate held tightly to it as she got off the bed, her face set in lines of grim resolution. She felt a kind of numbness wash over her as she packed her belongings. The only time she felt a wrench was when she picked up the sketch she had made of Nick and the cherry desk. Her fingers trembled as she held it up to the light, and tears threatened again. Although the picture was flawed, just looking at it reminded her of his magic. She thought about leaving it behind—after all, she had agreed to give it to him in exchange for their dinner together—but she could not bring herself to do it. She tucked it into the back of her sketchbook and slammed the cover down to shut him out.

Although it was only midnight, she went to the police station and waited there until the general store/bus station opened at six. Fortunately, there was a New York-bound bus coming through at seven—Kate didn't think she could have borne the wait much longer. At any moment she expected Nick to come bursting through the door. She sat huddled on a bench with her back to the door and jumped every time it opened or shut. Once or twice she even thought she heard his voice, cheerfully imperious, asking why the hell she had left him stranded there with Mountain Man Avon, then demanding that she stay. But he never showed up, and at 7:00 a.m. she left Putnam Falls—and Nick Capstein—behind her....

Now, as she gazed sightlessly out the grimy Grey-hound window, Kate mused that the only thing she had to worry about was explaining to Albert Pietro why she had not finished her assignment. That kind of problem was finite, manageable—she could think about it without caving in inside. But somehow she could not get her brain to concentrate on that, either. She kept hearing the smile in Nick's voice as he told her, "You'll think of something. I just know you will." She kept seeing his full lips curve into a sensuous smile as he moved above her on a cold mountain ledge.

Anguished, she closed her eyes against the image. But it was no good. Her photographic memory was a curse, not a blessing. She longed now for blindness, longed for a return to the tranquillity of life before Nick Capstein—before fear and pain, before...love.

No! she corrected herself sternly. Not love. She had been mistaken to think she loved him—and foolish to believe he could love her—it had all been just a whirlwind infatuation, and the sooner she got herself away from it—away from *him*—the better off she would be. So she'd made a mistake—mistakes could be corrected. With rigorous self-discipline and attention to detail, they could all be corrected. Perhaps she would be alone again, but she'd already gotten used to that. Better to be alone than to have her life obscured by a tumultuous, unrequited love. Better to get away now before she fell even more deeply into the dangerous dream that she could have a life with him.

Kate set her mouth in a firm line and repeated these sentiments over and over again in rhythm with the drone of the Greyhound's engine. Mistakes could be corrected. With rigorous self-discipline and attention to detail, they could all be corrected.

Why, then, was the view out the window misted with tears?

Chapter Ten

It was easier to be home, at first. Although it was hard to believe that New York City was more peaceful than rural Vermont, the serenity of those first few hours lulled Kate into thinking that she was glad to be there, far away from the chaotic cloud that seemed to hang over the Stonecroft Inn and its inhabitants. Her apartment welcomed her with its clean, compact simplicity, and she settled herself among her familiar belongings—the frayed Bokhara rug, the Andrew Wyeth and Edward Hopper prints, the ancient calico cat that had adorned her pillow since childhood—with a palpable sense of relief. Perhaps she had not escaped with her heart, but her body and mind were her own again. Her heart, she hoped, would eventually heal.

And for a little while it seemed as if it really would. Kate drew comfort from the predictability of the next day's routine, which made it so easy to forget that she had ever been gone. Even going to work was a comfort, although she had several uneasy moments trying to explain to Albert Pietro why she had not completed her assigned tasks in Putnam Falls. Fortunately, the pieces were being shipped to Simmond's local warehouse, so Kate was off the hook.

She retreated to her small cubicle in the art department and spent her day quietly sketching a collection of antique miniatures, concentrating on the tiniest details with characteristic patience.

She had been most worried about what would happen at night when, alone in her bed, she had nothing to think of but Nick. But the rhythm of the day had soothed her into a grateful fatigue, so that as soon as she got into bed, she fell into a deep, dreamless sleep, undisturbed by the painful thoughts and memories.

But the relief did not last long. After the first few hours at work the next day, Kate found she could not concentrate for very long. She would begin working on a minute mahogany chiffonier and then suddenly find her pencil wandering out of line, meandering off onto the blank page like a wayward toddler. It happened several times before she began to get worried, and even then she did not attribute it to anything more serious than a temporary lapse in attention. She forced herself to focus more closely on the work, zeroing in on the smallest details to make her brain work properly.

It was no use. The images of the miniature furniture standing before her seemed to fade and sway, and Kate found herself making mistakes even though the pieces were right there for her to see. Closing her eyes and relying on her photographic memory was even worse, because then she began to see things completely unrelated to her work. She saw woods and snowy trees and sometimes, when she was trying hardest not to, a smiling face with serious blue eyes bearing gently down on her from above.

By midafternoon, she could no longer pretend that everything was fine. Everything was *not* fine—it was terrible, awful, painful. Her love for Nick had come back to haunt her with a vengeance. A kind of hopeless panic gripped her as she sat in her stifling little office. There was no escaping the images, the memory of his laugh and touch.

She had been a fool, she realized, to think that she could. Nick had been larger than life, a tidal wave across the placid surface of her existence. She could not pretend such an upheaval had not occurred, even though it was over. She knew now that the landscape of her life was forever altered. She was still hopelessly in love, and having run away from the source of her love, there was nothing she could do about it now. She had been trapped by her own emotions, and now they had betrayed her.

The worst part was the way this knowledge snowballed, infecting everything around her. Despite her perfect vision, Kate felt as if she'd been wearing scales over her eyes for most of her life. Without knowing— and perhaps without even caring—Nick Capstein had somehow caused those scales to fall away. For the first time, her life was revealed as it truly was—lonely and bereft of meaning without love. Her work, which had seemed like such a comfort, was now a millstone around her neck. How dreary to spend her days cooped up in a windowless office, copying other people's handiwork like a computerized drawing machine! And after work, how joyless to spend her free waking hours in dogged pursuit of her minimal personal needs. Even the image

of her apartment seemed confining to her, with its
Spartan orderliness, its self-consciously collegiate style.

Nick had said it to her, but she hadn't realized until
now how right he had been. What was wrong with her?
Why couldn't she break out, give voice to the creative
urges that were rightfully hers? Why did she imprison
herself in security, in predictability? More to the point,
why couldn't she admit to herself, and to Nick, that she
was in love with him? Why didn't she just go back to
Putnam Falls and let him know how she felt? Damn her
job, damn her pride, damn her peace of mind. She
wanted Nick Capstein!

But somehow she knew she wouldn't do anything
about it. She had left Nick in Putnam Falls, and she
couldn't go back and pretend that the reasons she had
run away did not exist. Not even now, when she wanted
nothing more than to be back in his arms. So she sat
uselessly at her desk, staring at the work before her, not
even attempting to unravel the hopeless tangle of emotions that bound her. The only thing she could do was
hold a silent conversation with the ghost of Nick Capstein—a Nick Capstein who was glib and eternally
charming, and who filled the tiny room with his electric
presence. "Why did you do this to me?" she demanded
fretfully of the apparition she created in her mind's eye.
"My life was perfectly acceptable to me before you came
along. Why did you have to change it, with your hap-
hazard vision, your careless demands on my heart? Why
did you make me fall in love with you?"

She knew there were no answers, that Nick probably
had no idea of the upheaval he had caused. "What are
you talking about?" her imaginary Nick would reply to
her plea, shrugging his shoulders with an eloquent grace.
"I didn't do anything to you; you didn't do anything to

me. We just had some fun, a little adventure—nothing to get this upset about.''

Yet she knew this was unfair of her, to assume that Nick cared so little for her. After all, he had not left *her* with a huge lump on the head. And then she heard the voice of another Nick, who was kind and funny and wise. ''Don't worry about me, I'm fine,'' he said. ''It's yourself you should be worrying about. There's more to your life than what you've got, Kate. You deserve more; why don't you give yourself a chance? Don't be afraid, Katepalmer—the worst thing in life is to be afraid.''

In a way, this was even worse than the glib, light-hearted Nick—because this one spoke the truth. But it didn't matter, Kate told herself bleakly. Both Nicks were nothing more than figments of her imagination. And they were as close as she would ever again get to the real thing. She had made the mistake of not recognizing her love, of not acting on it. Now she would have to pay the price.

Then, just when she thought she could no longer stand the chaste monotony of her tiny cubicle at Simmond's, all hell broke loose. She heard a commotion out in the hall and listened in, more out of boredom than interest.

''You can't just barge in here!'' someone was protesting. ''This is an office—there are people working in here!''

The voice reached a high pitch of irritation, and then Kate heard something else—the sound of someone humming. At first she couldn't make out the tune, but as the sound drew nearer she realized the song was a jaunty version of an old favorite of hers: ''As Time Goes By.''

She also recognized the singer and froze at her draft-ing table, gripping her pencil in both hands until it snapped in two.

"Hey, little lady," said Nick softly, peering around the corner of her doorway. "No wonder I had such a tough time finding you. They've got you tucked away in a steamer trunk back here."

Kate gaped. There he was, effervescent, eyes twin-kling, grinning at her like a Cheshire cat—and real. She was sure her dreams had finally overtaken reality, and she dared not shatter the illusion by speaking. Nick waited a moment and then, shrugging lightly, stepped into the tiny room.

"Can't draw with a broken pencil, can you?" Gently he took the two pieces out of her hands, shaking his head and making a clicking sound with his tongue. He placed the pieces carefully on the desk, then put his arm around her neck and drew her against his chest. He made no at-tempt to kiss her, but Kate felt the urgency in his grip and in his voice.

"Hey," he said again, "I've missed you, you know that? You were really missed." He pulled away to look into her eyes. "Why the disappearing act?" he asked in a vain attempt at lightness. "Was it something I said?"

Kate looked at him, not daring to blink. He was real; he was actually standing in front of her. She could smell his crisp after-shave and see the faint blue shadow of stubble in the creases of his dimples. And his eyes—there was no mistaking those eyes, or the pain that hid be-hind the smile.

"I...I'm sorry," she muttered, wondering what she was apologizing for. "I...should have waited to make sure you were all right."

"Wrong answer. Wrong apology." He tipped her chin up, looked at her more closely, trying to read her face. Then he took his hand away. "No apology at all, as a matter of fact," he said brightly. "I've found you, despite the pinstripe tigers who guard this cave. So that's that."

"That's what?" Oh, why had he come? What did he *want* from her? Already she felt the familiar blurring of reality and fantasy she always experienced with him. She was never sure what he really meant when he talked to her, never really sure what she was saying to him. She took a breath and began again. "Nick, I . . ."

He put his fingers over her lips. "Silence is golden," he sang in a lilting falsetto. A mocking blue light filled his eyes.

"Stop it!" His relentless cheerfulness rang false and made Kate suddenly angry. "Why do you always do that?" she added truculently.

"Do what?" he asked innocently.

"Sing. Instead of talk." Kate wanted to kick him—or herself. After longing for him with all her heart, all she could do was argue about something inane. But she couldn't seem to stop herself. "It's—it's irritating."

"I'm sorry," he said, then rolled his eyes and grinned sheepishly. "Must be genetic or something. I do it all the time, I know."

There was a strained silence between them. Kate closed her eyes, suddenly exhausted. She had wanted him to be here so badly, and here he was, and once again she felt herself drowning in confusion, incapable of understanding her feelings—or his. She felt awkward and hollow, ashamed that he should find her in her dreary little cubby, staring at four blank walls. "How . . . how is your head?" she asked, looking at him at last.

"A lot thicker than I thought, apparently," he said, raising his fingers to touch his temple gingerly. "The doctor said it was just a slight concussion, no permanent damage." He laughed hollowly. "Which is nice, since I need all the brain cells I've got."

"I—I hope everything worked out all right with Martin . . . with the book."

Nick shrugged. "As far as I know it did. He's obviously gotten his book back, and Jared hasn't heard from him since." He grimaced, then added, "He's still up at the inn with Nina. Probably too afraid to return to the city.

"But to tell you the truth, I don't especially care about any of it. I did my best to get that book back to Jared, and now it's his problem." Nick took a few steps toward her. "I have my own problems now." He came closer still.

Kate swallowed hard, painfully aware of his nearness. "Why did you come here, Nick?" she whispered.

"To find you, of course," he told her, but by the exaggerated innocence of his expression she knew this was not the whole answer.

"No. There's some other reason." He had not come just because he wanted to be with her. Somehow she was sure of it. "What is it? Is it Jared's mess? You say you're through with all that, but I don't believe you could walk away so easily from all that excitement, all that intrigue. You're still involved, aren't you, and you want to use me again somehow."

His eyes narrowed. "What makes you say that?"

She shook her head slowly. "I don't know. I do know you did not come here just because of me."

"That's not true!" His eyes blazed with anger for a moment. Then he dropped them, and Kate's heart dropped with them. "You have to understand, Kate. *Of course* I came here to get you. It's just that—" he held out his hand to her "—look, I don't want to beat around the bush anymore. I need you, to..."

"Why do you need me, Nick? What for?" Tell me, she prayed. Tell me it's because you can't live without me.

He took a deep breath. "Because I need your help. I need *you*. I...I don't know, I can't seem to think clearly about anything without you. I'm trying to make some changes in my life right now, and...I just don't think I can see it through without you." He raised his arms helplessly. "Do you understand what I'm trying to say? Am I making any sense?"

So she'd been right. He hadn't come to rescue her. He hadn't come because he *loved* her. Despite his denial, he was all but admitting that he had come because he *needed* something from her.

Something in Kate's brain snapped with a blinding twinge, and she was suddenly in a towering rage. All the undeclared anguish of leaving Nick in Vermont, the pain of the past few days, became encapsulated in a hard ball of anger. "How dare you?" she hissed. "How *dare* you ask me to understand? You take my life and twist it up like a wet dishrag and then you expect me to *understand*? To help you crawl out from under your rock?"

Nick's mouth opened in astonishment. Obviously he had not expected this instant, shocking rage from her. Her whole body was taut with it, and her slender hands were clenched and white-knuckled. Her soft voice was constricted into a venomous whisper.

"How dare you?" she said again, and then, before he could stop her, she flew past him and out of the room.

She could think only of escape. She looked at the elevators, hoping one of them would be waiting to receive her, but both were closed. She considered the stairs, then decided she couldn't even manage the three floors down to street level. Already the anger was draining away, and the urge to weep was overpowering. She needed to hide somewhere out of sight, and quickly.

The ladies' room at Simmond's was a holdover from a more genteel era. It contained a small settee in the outer room to accommodate whatever unspecified ailments women of that time were thought to suffer from. Although Kate had never given the little couch much thought, she fell on it gratefully now, and just in time: the last shreds of anger dissolved into a paroxysm of tears.

It was not the fact that Nick had come to ask her for help that made her weep. It wasn't that he hadn't even bothered to woo her with soft words before asking his favor.

No, what made her weep so uncontrollably was the complete and inescapable knowledge that, despite all this, she was more in love than ever with Nick Capstein. Now that she had seen him again she realized how deeply and irrevocably she loved him. She cried for what she had found and lost without ever really having had it, and her tears were all the more bitter for that.

Kate stayed facedown on the couch for a long time. She was so wrapped up in her misery that she didn't hear the door open about twenty minutes later or notice the slight depression in the cushion as someone sat beside her on the couch. But when she heard a familiar voice, she froze.

"Kate, you've got to listen."

"Nick!" She raised a pale, shocked face. "For God's sake, what are you doing in here?"

He looked surprised. "Talking to you, of course."

"But this is the ladies' room."

"I told the ladies to use the gents' for a few minutes," he explained, and then, seeing her expression of disbelief, managed a brief smile as he brushed a strand of hair off her damp cheek. "You didn't give me any choice, did you?" he asked her softly.

"But..."

"No buts." He frowned, all business now. "Why did you run away from me?"

"Because I...because I couldn't listen to it anymore." Kate sniffled. "I couldn't bear it."

"Couldn't bear what, for God's sake?"

She didn't want to admit to him that she couldn't bear the burden of her love for him. She drew a quavering breath. "Look, Nick. You came down here because you needed something from me."

"Not need. Want." He paused to reconsider. "Well, yes, need, I guess."

Kate waved her hand dismissively. "What's the difference? I just felt...I feel...used."

He sat back, truly horrified. "You think I'm using you, Kate?"

"Well, yes. I do."

"What on earth *for*?"

The blunt honesty of this statement rankled Kate, and her eyes flashed. "*I* don't know! To help you get your life in order so you can go on to other things, I guess." Looking at his stricken expression, Kate began to wonder if perhaps she hadn't been mistaken. "You told me that you needed something from me..." she concluded lamely.

"And you thought I meant a favor, or some help to get out of a jam?" He actually laughed. "Sweet Kate, I said I needed help from you, yes. But you didn't let me finish. You didn't let me tell you why."

She stared at him, her soft eyes still glistening with tears. "Why, then?"

He stroked her cheek. "For your sanity. Your clarity. Your seeing eye." His eyes traveled across her face and body. "Among other things," he added fondly.

By now, Kate was feeling so confused and so bad about herself, that this statement only made things worse. "But you're wrong, Nick!" she cried. "I don't have any of those things." The tears were threatening again. "I'm not what you seem to think I am."

"Oh, Kate, if only you knew." He sighed poignantly. "None of us are, honey. Besides, how do you know you're not what I think you are? You sure had me fooled this weekend, and I don't fool easily."

Kate would not allow herself to think back on those few days. It was too painful. "I just...I just know, that's all. The weekend was a—a mistake."

Nick looked at her steadily for a few moments and then half rose. "A mistake?" he said softly. "It was all a mistake? Well, then, I guess I'd better leave. I didn't realize you felt that way. I thought you... But if I'm wrong, then I guess I'm wrong. I'll just go back to—"

"No!" She reached out blindly for his hand, and he sat down at once.

"Just joking, of course," he said, his voice perfectly normal.

"Don't joke." Kate was trying very hard to keep from breaking down in his arms. "Don't make light of this, Nick. Please."

"God, Kate, that's the last thing I'm doing. Do you think I'd have come all this way just for the fun of it?"

"I don't know why you came," she said miserably.

He tipped her chin up so that he could look into her eyes. "You're serious, aren't you? You still don't know what's going on, do you?"

Kate could not trust herself to speak and only shook her head, eyes shut tight.

"I thought that might be the case, but I never really thought—" Nick tapped her cheek lightly with one finger. "Kate. Look at me. Why do you think I came, really? The truth now."

She snuffled again, feeling like a sullen child forced to meet an adult's stern gaze. "You came because you have this crazy idea that I could help you out with something."

"Help me with what?"

"I don't know! That's just the point. With Jared, with your business...with your life." Her shoulders collapsed. "Nick, I can barely manage my own life. I can't be responsible for yours." She fell back onto the couch, her head buried in her arms.

"Can't? Or don't want to?"

"Oh, what does it matter?"

"It matters. We seem to have had a major misunderstanding here, and it matters very much. Tell me."

Her voice was muffled, and she ignored the pressure of his hands on her shoulders. "It's not that I don't want to," she admitted. "It's just that...I'm afraid."

"Afraid of what?"

"Of my feelings," she whispered. "And...and yours."

Nick looked as if he were about to laugh and cry at the same time. Just then the door opened and a young woman came in. She stopped short, opened her mouth in a small oval of surprise, then backed quickly out again. Nick ignored her.

"Kate. You have to listen to me, and you have to look at me. Now sit up and let me talk."

She sat up and made a dismal attempt to repair her face. "Never mind that," he said, and took both her hands in his. "Listen, you seem to have missed the point out there in your little cubby. You seem to have missed it altogether, as a matter of fact. Or maybe I was the one who missed it, I don't know. But somewhere along the line I got the impression that we understood each other. Was I totally off the wall, or what?"

Kate started to open her mouth and deny this self-accusation, but Nick did not give her a chance. "Wait a minute. Hear me out. It just occurred to me that you really don't know—that you left Vermont because you didn't know, and you're still under the impression that I...that—" his voice exploded "—my God, Kate, how could you not have known?"

"Known what?" She was aware that her heart was beating very fast. A timid knock at the door startled her, but Nick growled, "Go away!" and the knocking stopped at once.

She opened her mouth to say something.

"Don't talk. Just listen," Nick admonished her. He looked stern, and then his face collapsed into a rueful grimace. "God, Kate, don't you think I know how hard it's been to adjust to all this? I mean, God knows I wasn't looking for this to happen, either. To tell you the truth, after you left the other day, I nearly gave up myself. I figured I was better off rid of you, if you were so dense, so uptight, that you couldn't recognize what was going on when it hit you over the head. All the way down here, I tried to argue myself into turning back. And when you ran out of that little rathole you work in back there, I even left, too, intending to go back to Vermont. But after about ten feet I realized I was being as much of an idiot as you were. *I* was the one with my head in the sand, *I* was the one running away! We were both running away, and it was up to me to stop it."

"Running from what?" Kate demanded. But she was beginning to understand what Nick was trying to tell her, and she felt curiously light-headed. She drew in an unsteady breath and faced him, forgetting about her red eyes and streaked face.

But Nick was too busy with his own train of thought to notice her dawning comprehension and joy. "I thought it was perfectly obvious, but now I can see that I might not have made myself clear. I mean, God knows, how *could* you know what was going on with a crazy person like me? Someone like you, who lives such a sheltered life, how could you know where I was coming from?"

"I'm not a nun, Nick," she pointed out dryly, but he continued to ignore her, caught up in his own confessional frenzy.

"But now I see! Now I understand." His eyes were glazed with self-absorbed fervor. "Of course I need you, you silly goose! I need you more than I've ever needed anything or anyone in my life. And I want you more than I've ever wanted anyone before! But to think that it's only because I need you to help me out of some ridiculous—" He broke off in amazement.

"I made a mistake," Kate admitted, lowering her eyes. When she raised them, they were glittering with mischief. "Haven't you ever made a mistake, Nick? Done something you've regretted?"

He glared at her for a second, then grinned. "Touché. You, me, Jared—we all make mistakes." He lifted her hand and kissed it. "I made one with you, too, didn't I? All this time I've been giving you these mixed messages, telling you to strike out on your own, to not be afraid of trying to express yourself, and then telling you how wonderful and sweet and dependable you are—how much I need you to stay the way you are. And you thought—" he looked at her in mock horror "—you really thought I only needed you to help me out of a jam, didn't you? You didn't realize how I really felt about you!" He shook his head again.

Looking at him sitting on the incongruously petite chaise longue, eyes blazing and holding her hand earnestly in his, Kate realized that she had been wrong. Nick *had* come for the right reasons after all, and she simply had not let him explain them to her. She'd been so afraid of hearing the wrong thing that she thought she'd heard him say it anyway, even though he hadn't. And now he was so wrapped up in trying to put things right that he hadn't yet realized she understood. Now it was up to her to tell him.

"I need you to save my soul, not my skin!" He exclaimed. "I didn't come down here because I needed any *assistance* from you—God knows, I can take care of myself." He looked at her reproachfully. "I just need you, Kate. Plain and simple. I need you and I love you."

"I love you, too, Nick," she murmured softly. But Nick didn't seem to hear. He was getting excited all over again.

"I can't believe," he was saying, "that you didn't realize how much I loved you. Kate, I know you're innocent and all, but how could you really think that I—I mean, for God's sake, I've been taking care of myself since I was thirteen. I know I told you I was at loose ends, but I only said that because...because—" He broke off and looked at her as if seeing her for the first time. "What did you just say?"

Kate smiled. "I said I love you."

He seemed to have trouble understanding her words, but her beatific expression, as she nodded and smiled encouragingly at him, was impossible to mistake. He reached up and tenderly touched the corner of her eye, running one finger along the track of a dried tear. His eyes were full of wonder.

Slowly, a matching smile spread across his features. "Do you mean to tell me," he said at last, "that I've just been shooting off my mouth like a babbling idiot when I didn't have to say a word?"

She nodded solemnly. "Uh-huh."

The smile broadened on both their faces. "Well," Nick announced, "it won't be the first time I've done that, and I'm sure it won't be the last."

"Probably not," Kate agreed. She was suffused with a placid glow that made her inexpressibly beautiful, and Nick moved his palm to stroke her soft cheek.

"I'll tell you one thing," he murmured, looking at her with a rapt expression. "It won't be the last time I tell you how much I love you. I plan to say it every twenty minutes, whether you need it or not."

"I'm glad."

"As a matter of fact..." At that moment the door opened and a woman stepped in. She seemed to expect the scene that confronted her. "Excuse me!" she said loudly, glaring down at Kate and Nick.

Kate pulled away from Nick, flustered and embarrassed. She recognized Mrs. Curtin, the executive vice-president in charge of acquisitions, who was known informally around the office as the Dragon Lady. Her perfectly coiffed silver hair was trembling slightly with ill-concealed outrage. "Excuse me!" she exclaimed again.

"Mrs. Curtin!" Kate suddenly felt weak-kneed, but Nick seemed to take it all in stride.

"Of course you're excused," he said smoothly.

Mrs. Curtin was livid. "And just what do you think you're doing in here, young man?" She peered sharply at Kate, who knew it was only a matter of moments before she placed her as "that quiet young woman from the art department." She was mortified.

Nick rose and helped Kate to her feet. "We were smooching," he informed her. "But as a matter of fact, we're just leaving." He looked down at Kate, his eyes warm and filled with sensual promise. "We have some private business to take care of," he said softly.

"This is a ladies' room!" Mrs. Curtin shrieked, losing control at last.

Nick made a courtly bow and indicated the rest-room stalls with a flourish. "Oh, I know. Please, don't let us keep you from anything."

And while Mrs. Curtin watched in frustrated astonishment, he led Kate past her and out the door. A few other staffers had assembled in the hallway to listen to the confrontation, and they stepped back in amazement as Nick sashayed down the hall, Kate in tow.

"How nice of Mrs. Curtin," he said loudly, "to give you the afternoon off, don't you agree, Kate?"

Kate finally recovered enough to hiss, "The afternoon? I'll probably get the rest of my life off!"

But as the elevator doors closed behind them, she realized that she didn't care.

* * *

Nick took her to his apartment and made good on his promise. He had a huge one-room studio in SoHo, and Kate stopped as soon as he opened the door, intrigued by the way the light splashed across the wooden floors. She wasn't sure what she'd expected to find in Nick's home, but she was surprised by the minimalist good taste that confronted her. There was a large bed, two narrow couches, a refectory table and several high, cane-back chairs. The windows were covered in a gauzy material that let the light in, and there were three or four well-framed modernist prints on the walls.

"I'll bet you expected black lights and rock-and-roll posters, huh?" Nick asked her, watching her face light up.

"Of course not," she assured him, and then admitted, "But I didn't expect anything so...lovely."

"Thank you, sweet Kate." He took her coat and threw it on the chair beside him, then gathered her into his arms. "Lovely is as lovely sees," he murmured against her hair. "Now, where were we?"

Kate snuggled deep into his arms with a little shiver of delight. "I'm not sure. But right here is fine."

"Mmm, it sure is." He kissed the top of her head. "Jeez, I wonder how long it's been since we were back there in that nice ladies' room."

"Why?"

"Because it must be time to tell you again."

"Nick," she said, half laughing, "tell me what?"

"Tell you how much, of course. How much I love you."

She shook her head. "You don't have to. I already know."

He shook his head. "Oh, but I *do* have to say it. It's important that I do. I'm never going to take that for granted again. No more mistakes, Kate, I promise you. From now on, everything gets said, straight out." He put his hands along her cheeks and cradled her heart-shaped face. "Katepalmer, I am hopelessly, foolishly, idiotically, deeply in love with you. Have been since the minute I laid eyes on you, though God knows why."

"What do you mean, God knows why?"

He smiled. "I mean, God knows how I recognized how right you are for me. Probably the first right thing I've done since I taught Nina how to cook." He kissed her softly on her mouth. "Now, you tell me. I'm new to this true-love business, and I want to hear those magic words again. And don't stint. I'd rather hear too much than too little."

"Nick Capstein," she murmured, smiling languidly, "I am hopelessly, foolishly, deeply in love with you."

"You forgot idiotic," he whispered as he closed in for another kiss.

"There's nothing idiotic about it," she told him.

"You're right." His lips pressed softly against hers. "I'm the idiot."

"My idiot," Kate breathed, and then her mouth opened to receive his hungry kiss.

Nick gathered her more closely into his arms, and together they waltzed slowly across the room until they stood next to the bed. His kisses blazed a trail of fire down her throat and neck, across her shoulders, and Kate threw back her head and abandoned herself to the magic of his touch.

Nick slipped to his knees and pressed his face into the warmth of her small breasts and belly, murmuring words of love against the fabric of her clothing. His hands, stroking up and down her stockinged legs beneath her dress, sent shock waves of desire through her.

Kate felt weak and energized at the same time. Her body trembled at his touch, full of anticipation. She slipped down upon the bed and tried to pull Nick with her, although he seemed reluctant to tear his lips away from her body. At last he disengaged himself and, raising up on one elbow beside her, reached out to stroke the hair back from her high forehead. His eyes were smoldering with desire. "And if the words aren't enough," he murmured, "let my body tell you exactly how I feel."

They looked at each other for a long, silent moment, savoring the shared anticipation. Then, with a soft moan, his mouth fell across hers once again, and he pulled her on top of him so that their bodies could touch at every conceivable point. Both breathed in together from the emotional impact of that physical contact, as if they knew that at last there would be no interruptions, no mistakes. Then it seemed as if neither of them took another breath for hours. Oxygen became inessential. The only thing they needed to sustain life was each other, and they breathed, ate and drank from the deep pool of their love like starving pilgrims who had found their oasis at last.

They shed their clothes with the slow-motion, sensual luxury of people who are warm and secure and feel they have a lifetime to discover mutual passion and joy. As Kate removed her shirtwaist, stopping constantly to drop kisses on whichever part of Nick's body was available to her, she felt as if she were shedding her old existence, stripping the shackles of shyness and insecurity that had bound her for so long. In the cold air up on the mountain, it had been impossible to give herself fully to her newly awakened passion. But now, basking in the warmth of Nick's adoration, she blossomed at last into the exotic flower of her imagination, pale and elegant and attenuated, hypersensitive to his every touch. She even thought she detected a faintly exotic perfume rising from her skin as it heated beneath Nick's ardent ministrations; it mixed with his pungent scent to create an opiate of desire that did not numb, but rather heightened all their senses.

Then he pulled her astride him once again, and time telescoped. They no longer had eternity—they had to have each other now. Arching against his loins, opening her body to him and welcoming him to the heart of her being, Kate knew that she had been reclaimed by a passionate will to live, to affirm, to excel. It was Nick who had opened her to it, but the spirit was Kate's as well, and her release was as much a self-affirmation as a physical unleashing of joy.

Afterward, they lay silently together—or rather Kate lay silently while Nick whistled a medley of his favorite love songs, occasionally interrupting himself with a deep chuckle of amazed delight.

"You don't mind, do you?" he asked, stroking her upper ribs with the backs of his fingers so that her nipples grew instantly alert.

She sighed. "I don't mind anything anymore," she told him contentedly.

"I feel the same way." He lifted himself up on one elbow so he could see her face. "I feel like I've been saved, Katie; like my life is so...so full of promise. Know what I mean?"

She smiled. "Exactly what you mean."

"I feel like I could start over, hit my stride, really take on the world—with you around to keep me sane."

"Don't count on it."

His brow furrowed anxiously. "Don't count on what?"

"On me keeping you sane." She reached up and traced the line of his left dimple with her fingertip. "I plan on doing some breaking out of my own, you know."

The dimple deepened beneath her touch. "Oh, really? Like what?"

"Oh, I don't know. Like maybe—" she grinned, suddenly shy "—like maybe trying my hand at some free-lance sketching. A few landscapes, maybe a portrait or two...whatever."

He grabbed her finger and turned his lips to meet it. "Maybe even in color?" he asked, nibbling gently.

She smiled. "Who knows?" She paused and thought a moment. "Who cares?" They looked at each other and laughed. This was a new side of Kate, for both of them.

"That's what I like to hear," he declared. "Get a little outrageous." He leaned over and kissed her chin. "But not too outrageous."

Just then the phone rang. Nick stopped with his mouth just over hers and cursed. "I'm going to pretend I didn't hear that," he murmured, and returned to his kissing.

But the phone continued to ring insistently. "Nick," Kate said, "maybe you'd better answer it."

"I don't want to answer it," he mumbled against her mouth.

"I know, but..." She pulled away.

"But what?"

She looked at the phone near the bed. "It might be something important."

Their eyes met for a moment. Neither wanted to voice the fear that, once again, their happiness together was about to be jeopardized. At last, Nick grumbled and rolled away from her to pick up the phone.

"Yeah," he said curtly. When she heard his heavy sigh, Kate knew who it was.

"What is it, Nina?"

Kate sat up and drew the satin bed quilt around her while she listened. "What?" She could tell by the way his face darkened that Nick was not getting good news. "Yeah, yeah. Okay, Nin, don't get hysterical.... Yeah, I'll come back." He scowled into the phone. "I don't *know* what I'll do! But I'll be there.... Yeah, okay. Just sit tight and tell Jared not to do anything stupid. Or stupider. G'bye."

He slammed the phone down on the receiver and looked at Kate. "Well, sweet Kate, looks like we're in for it this time."

"What do you mean?" Her voice was tight with trepidation.

"As you probably gathered already, that was Nina. It appears Jared just received a call from Martin DeVoe...demanding his book back *now*—or else."

Kate stared at him blankly. "What do you mean? Wasn't it Martin DeVoe who hit you on the head outside of Dan Avon's house?"

Nick shook his head and made a rueful face. "Apparently not. At least, that's what DeVoe says."

Kate was confused. "Then who...?"

"Who attacked us the other night? Good question."

"I...I don't understand."

Nick shrugged. "Neither do I. All I know is what Nina told me. That DeVoe said he knew Jared had the book, and that he was coming up for it—himself—to-night."

"He's going up to *Putnam Falls*?"

Nick nodded. "Apparently he has some business to conduct up there, although I can't imagine what. I don't know, maybe he's going up to score. Anyway, that's not the point. The point is that Jared, the idiot, told him he had the book."

"He told him he had it? But I—"

"Right. You thought DeVoe had the book. So did we. But if Jared had admitted that we didn't have the damned book anymore—that in fact we thought De-Voe'd already *taken* it—we'd all have been in hot water. So he told DeVoe to come to the inn at midnight, that he'd have his book for him then. Do you believe it?"

"But when DeVoe gets there, there won't be any book," she protested.

"Right you are. And Jared—along with my sister—will be up the creek without a paddle." He reached for his shirt. "That's why I have to get my butt up there."

"But what can you do?"

He snapped his shirt through the air in irritation. "Hell, I don't know! I just—" he bent down to retrieve it, then knelt by the bed, taking her hand "—I just have to be there, Kate. Do you understand?"

She managed a wan smile. "Of course I do, Nick. Do you want me to—"

He pulled back. "Come with me? Absolutely not! I don't want you involved in this mess. You've already had more than your share of trouble with that abortive little escapade at Avon's place. I almost lost you because of it, and I'm not going to risk that again."

She shook her head. "You don't have to worry about that."

He sighed and took her hand again. "I know, I know. But I've got plenty else to think about without feeling that I have to worry about you." He put on the shirt and started buttoning it pensively. "Who knows? Maybe I'll think of something brilliant on the way up, and it won't be such a mess after all. But it'll have to be a miracle."

He crossed the room to pull on his shoes and sweater, and Kate watched. Something had just occurred to her—an idea—but she wasn't sure how to broach it.

"Nick?"

"Hmm?" He was distracted.

"I think I know a way to work a miracle."

He stopped. "What are you talking about?"

"I mean, I think I know a way you can get that book for Martin DeVoe."

"But we don't even know where the damn thing is!"

She looked at him steadily. "We could get a copy, though," she said. "A perfect facsimile. A photographic reproduction."

Her meaning dawned on him slowly. "Do you mean...?"

She nodded. "I saw the book. I looked through it, that night at Dan Avon's. It's a common-enough-style notebook, we could get one just like it at any stationery store. And I could reproduce what DeVoe wrote in it exactly, I know I could!" She was getting more excited as she spoke.

He gaped at her for a moment before shaking his head. "No way. It would never work. He'd never buy it."

"Why not? I've fooled experts before, doing repros of Old Master etchings for the Simmond's catalog. This is a simple job, just numbers, and DeVoe's handwriting would be a cinch for me."

Nick was still shaking his head. "Absolutely not," he said, but she could tell he was thinking about her offer as he spoke.

"Nick, it's your only chance. DeVoe doesn't know somebody took the book from us, so why should he suspect a forgery? He'll just look at it and recognize it and that'll be that. And even if he figures it out later, we'll have bought some time to figure out what really did happen to the original." She sat forward eagerly. "Come on, Nick, what have we got to lose?"

He approached the bed again slowly, deep in thought. "We might be able to do it," he said, speaking more to himself than to her. "If we keep the lights low, he might not bother looking too closely. We can always deny it, anyway, and what's he gonna do? Yes, it might work...it just might...." His eyes snapped back to Kate, and he thought a minute before speaking. "Okay, Miss Photographic Eye. You've got yourself a job." He bent down and kissed her swiftly. "Boy, you sure are full of surprises, aren't you?"

Kate chuckled. "I think I'm surprising myself as much as you."

"I doubt it." His eyes moved longingly across her bared breasts. "When was the last time I told you I love you? More to the point, when was the last time I *showed* you I love you? I think it's been more than twenty minutes."

He reached for her, but she wriggled away. "It was less than twenty minutes ago, and anyway we have no time for that now." She jumped out of bed to dress, eager to get on with her task. "I'll go to Brentano's and pick up a notebook and come back here to work."

Nick shrugged. "Okay, okay. Business before pleasure, I guess. I'll call Nina and let her know what's going on.'' In spite of himself, Nick was getting caught up in the plan. ''And I think I'll place a call to my old friend Chief Lahey and put him on the alert for tonight. He owes me a favor, and he's discreet enough to handle this without getting all high and mighty about what's legal and what's not. I'd like to have him on hand just in case.''

''What for?''

He looked at her darkly. ''Just in case,'' he repeated. ''I mean, I know you're a genius, Kate, but it doesn't hurt to have a little insurance.''

Kate had dressed and was standing by the door. She felt a surge of confidence, partly because she was secure in Nick's love and partly because she was already beginning to discover her own untapped talents. If only Carl could see me now, she thought with an inward giggle. There was just one thing. ''Uh, Nick?''

He was sitting on the bed dialing. ''What is it, sweetheart?''

''One thing. I'm coming back to Putnam Falls with you.''

He stopped with the phone poised in midair. ''Oh, no, you're not.''

She smiled sweetly. ''Yes, I am.''

He slammed down the phone, his jaw tightening stubbornly. ''Kate, I thought we'd been through this already. I don't want you up there. I'm not calling Mike Lahey to be polite. I want him there on the off chance that things get ugly—which is exactly why I want you far away!''

''Nick...'' Her voice was soft and cajoling, and it surprised her to hear that it sounded a lot like Nina's had that first night she saw her outside the Stonecroft Inn.

"What?" He looked exasperated, just as he had that night. Kate felt a surge of triumph. This wasn't so hard after all!

"If I can't come, you don't get the book."

His mouth dropped open in surprise. "Kate Palmer," he breathed, "are you blackmailing me?"

She nodded happily. "You bet." In spite of all the pressure, she realized she was actually having fun.

He shook his head, but a tiny smile played around the corners of his mouth as he waved her out the door. "Okay, okay, you're on!"

As she walked out the door, she could hear him muttering to himself, "My God, what have I wrought?"

Chapter Eleven

It was eleven-thirty at night. Once again, they were all sitting in the front parlor at the Stonecroft Inn. Once again, Nick and Kate sat side by side on the couch while Jared and Nina occupied the two wing chairs. Once again there was a palpable tension in the air as the four of them faced each other, their features illuminated by the firelight that glowed on the fieldstone hearth.

Yet it was all very different. The night air outside was still frigid, but in the two days since Kate had left, the promise of spring had touched Putnam Falls. Driving north, she had noticed that much of the snow was already melting, and as they walked up the flagstone path she'd even spotted the tiny green points of a few early crocuses poking their heads through the thin crust that remained.

Thinking of those proud little shoots, she turned her head and looked out the window at the black night. Little white pinpoints of frost glittered off the bare bushes along the path, and Kate smiled at the image of the fragile crocuses shivering bravely in the still-hard earth. How foolhardy of them to appear so early in the season, when one late snowstorm could so easily wipe them out!

But she saw their presence as a metaphor for her own new frame of mind. She, too, was lifting her head bravely through the chilled ground of her former existence, daring to try the untried and risk the unknown. Instead of wanting to disappear from the room as she had before, she now felt a flutter of anticipation. She was taking a risk—they were all taking risks—but that was okay. Taking risks was part of her new approach to life.

She could tell the others felt the difference, too. The tension in the room was not negative, merely imbued with a suppressed excitement. Nick's return seemed to have convinced his sister and Jared that all would be well, although they did not yet know about the forged account notebook. Even Kate's presence had not dampened their obvious relief, and Nina had gone so far as to kiss her on both cheeks and smile brilliantly when she'd come in. It was a clear signal that while she might not be aware of the extent of her brother's involvement with this tall, quiet woman, Nina at least recognized Kate's existence.

Now she and Jared sat forward in their chairs eagerly, Jared's elegant fingers toying nervously with a gold key chain, as they waited to hear how Nick planned to save them from Martin DeVoe's wrath. Kate's eyes glittered; she couldn't wait to see how they took the news.

"Well," said Nick, exchanging a complicitous smile with Kate, "I think we've come up with a pretty good solution to our little problem here." He reached into his breast pocket and pulled out the leather notebook. Kate held her breath. "Will this do the trick, do you think?"

"The book!" Jared and Nina shouted together. Jared lunged forward and grabbed it from Nick's outstretched hand. "How the hell did you get your hands on it?" he demanded.

"Oh, a little of this, a little of that." Nick grinned broadly and winked at Kate.

Nina looked curiously at her brother, but Jared was too engrossed in examining the notebook to bother. "It doesn't matter how, I guess," he muttered. "As long as we have it, everything's copacetic." He looked up, his eyes shining. "Now we can just give it back to DeVoe and be done with it."

"Yeah," said Nina, "and we better just hope and pray he feels the same way."

"Oh, he will, he will." Now that he had the book, Jared seemed utterly confident that everything would turn out all right. Kate marveled at his blind confidence, but she was glad of it just then.

"Look at it again, Jared," Nick said.

"What for? It's all here, isn't it? No pages missing, or anything...."

"Just look at it," Nick commanded.

Nina was getting suspicious. "Why should he? What's—"

"Shut up, Nin," Nick said amiably, then turned back to Jared. "Are you sure, Jared?" he inquired.

Jared looked confused. "Sure of what?"

"Sure everything's okay. You've seen that book before, haven't you?"

"Of course I have. When I first sto— When I first got it, I practically memorized it, trying to figure out what the hell these numbers meant."

Nick pointed at the object in Jared's hands. "And it looks all right to you, doesn't it? Just the way it looked when you stole it?"

"I didn't—"

"Well, does it?"

Jared turned the book over in his hands. "Of course it does! Why shouldn't it?"

Kate felt relief flood through her. It had worked!

Nick bounced up and down and chortled in triumph before leaning over to kiss Kate on the lips. "Ah, sweet Kate, your brilliance is exceeded only by your beauty— and your terrific body." Kate blushed and returned the kiss.

"Nicky!" Nina erupted. "Do you mind telling us what on earth you're talking about?"

Nick disengaged himself and shot her an innocent look. "I'm talking about Kate, of course."

"The book, Nicholas." Nina put her hands on her hips. "Tell me about the book."

"There's nothing to tell." He shrugged. "It's just that it's a fake, that's all."

"A—what?" Jared dropped the book as if it had bitten him. "What do you mean, a fake?"

"Let me see that!" Nina bent down and retrieved the notebook. She leafed through it carefully and then looked up, not at Nick, but at Kate. "You had something to do with this, didn't you?" she demanded.

"I'm afraid I did," Kate confessed, and told them about the forgery.

"I don't believe it," Jared breathed when she had finished and leaned back into the warm circle of Nick's arm.

"You better believe, buddy," Nick told him. "It's right there in front of your eyes."

"I know, but..." He looked from Kate to the book and back again with new respect. "I see it, but I don't believe it."

"I'm glad I convinced you," Kate told him. "But of course that doesn't mean it'll convince Martin DeVoe."

"You're right." Nina sighed. "Jared may have looked at the book, but he didn't write the damn thing. What makes you think DeVoe won't recognize it as a fake?"

"He won't," said Nick firmly, but Kate shook her head.

"We just have to hope he doesn't. If we keep the lights low like this, maybe he'll just assume it's his, like Jared did." She looked at Nick. "And just in case, Nick has alerted Chief Lahey to come by and make sure Mr. DeVoe doesn't start any trouble."

"Oh, he won't," Jared said confidently. "I think once he sees the book and the chief, he'll be happy to go away and forget the whole thing. After all, it's not as though he can press charges against us for stealing, can he?"

All three of them turned to gape at him. "Us?" Nina repeated.

Jared had the grace to look chagrined. "Well, me."

"Anyway," Nick announced with a cheerful grin, "let's just hope Jared is right—for once." He turned at the sound of a car pulling into the driveway. "Maybe," he added in a tight voice, "*pray* would be a better word."

Then they all turned toward the door and waited with their hearts in their throats.

* * *

Martin DeVoe looked so much like what Kate expected a drug dealer to look like that she almost smiled when he came into the room. He was small and thin, with a shiny, bald pate and black, ferrety eyes. He was dressed in an expensively cut suit and a full-length leather overcoat, and he even had a diamond ring on his pinkie. Kate wondered how he could possibly expect to escape recognition in an outfit that practically parodied his chosen occupation.

But although she had expected to be scared out of her wits by the sight of this man, she found herself curiously relieved by his presence. She understood why Nick had not been worried about the threat of physical violence. For one thing, DeVoe didn't look like a man out for vengeance; on the contrary, he appeared to be even more nervous about this than she knew Jared and Nina to be—glancing around furtively, starting at the slightest country sound. For another thing, he simply did not look like a man who was accustomed to using force.

Watching him, Kate was relieved, although she could not imagine why he should be so worried. At the very least, it meant that he might not be too careful about examining his book. And the thought that Chief Lahey would be nearby, ready to come to their aid if necessary, made her feel practically at ease.

Practically, but not quite. Her smile was tight and her hand shaking when Nick, acting as if the visit were purely social, made the introductions. DeVoe nodded tersely at her and at Nina, but his eyes were on Jared and Jared alone. To his credit, Jared seemed calm and collected, although Kate detected a greenish pallor beneath his tan. But the hand he held out to DeVoe was steady, and he rose a few notches in her estimation because of that.

Nick, of course, was in control. In fact, he seemed to be enjoying himself immensely as he led DeVoe to the seat he had vacated on the couch. DeVoe sat down and stared glumly into the fire. Then, with a nervous shake of his head, he stood up again almost at once.

"I'm not here to chitchat," he said, licking his lips as if they were parched with anxiety. "Where's my book?"

"Sit down, Mr. Devoe, sit down." Gently but firmly, Nick pressed him back onto the couch. "You see, before we give you your book, we just want to make sure that this little meeting will be the last on the subject. I'm sure you understand." He sat down beside DeVoe so that the three of them were scrunched together on the couch. Despite her composure, Kate was glad to have Nick between herself and DeVoe. "This *will* be the end of it, won't it?" Nick pressed, still smiling genially at the man.

DeVoe gave a little snort of impatience. "You guys still owe me money, you know," he pointed out caustically.

"Yeah, yeah, we know about that. But I'm talking about the book. The way things stand right now, we've got it and you don't. We don't want it, and you do. Am I right so far, Martin?"

Kate held her breath. She hadn't expected Nick to be so audacious, making it seem as if they had the upper hand when it was clear they did not.

Still, DeVoe seemed too harried to care. He simply gave Nick a swift, shrewd glance and nodded his head. "Right," he said shortly. "Give me the book and we'll forget this mess ever happened." He glowered at Jared, who appeared to be holding his breath, but did not say anything more.

Nick smiled, and Kate could hear Jared let his breath out at last. "Good," said Nick. "I'm glad we agree on that."

"Just give it to me now," DeVoe said, standing up again. "I want to get out of here."

"Jared," said Nick without missing a beat, "give the man his book."

Now it was Kate's turn to hold her breath. Jared pulled the book out from beneath his seat cushion and held it out to Martin. His hands were steady, but the green pallor had increased. Kate was grateful for the flickering firelight, which not only softened the details of the notebook, but also made Jared look a lot healthier than he probably felt.

The room was perfectly silent except for the crackling of the fire and the thudding of Kate's heart. DeVoe took the book from Jared's hands and opened it up to the first page. He scanned it closely for one long moment, then looked up sharply at Jared.

"You have any idea what this is?" he asked.

Jared shook his head. Kate could see him swallow before he replied, but his voice was clear. "Nope. Haven't got a clue." Beside her, Kate could feel Nick's tension, and across from her she could see the frightened glitter in Nina's eyes. "Just a bunch of numbers as far as I'm concerned," Jared went on, and then added with a convincingly light little laugh, "Whatever they mean is your business. I don't even want to know."

Martin was silent. He continued to stare appraisingly at Jared, who somehow managed to maintain his composure even though Kate knew he must be panicked. The moment of truth was at hand. DeVoe looked back at the book and turned the page. Nobody in the room breathed.

Suddenly he snapped the book shut and slipped it into his pocket. "I gotta go," he said, and started across the room.

Kate tried to let her breath out soundlessly, and she knew her three companions were doing the same. They had gotten away with it! The blood was throbbing through her temples, and the firelight seemed to waver before her for a moment. She didn't dare meet anyone's gaze, least of all Nick's, but she could feel the tension seep out of his body.

But they had relaxed too soon. Just as DeVoe reached the door to the hall, they all heard the front door open. Everybody froze. DeVoe gasped, and his hand went to his pocket as if to protect its contents. He turned back into the room as if to flee, and Kate was shocked by the terror on his face...until she realized whom he had seen. A burly man in a police uniform entered the room—obviously Chief Lahey.

"Mike!" Nick fairly shouted with relief. "Hey, man, thanks for stopping by, but...uh...there's no need." He held up his hand. "Everything's all right."

He looked briefly at Kate as he spoke, and she knew he was both surprised and upset by Chief Lahey's unscheduled appearance. According to their agreement, the chief was supposed to wait outside and come in only if signaled by Nick. His presence seemed to throw DeVoe into a panic, and Kate prayed he wouldn't do anything foolish. Or violent.

But it wasn't Chief Lahey who had panicked DeVoe. He had seen someone else coming in behind him, and now, as the chief stepped aside, the second man entered the room.

It was Daniel Avon.

"Ah, Martin," he said smoothly into the shocked silence. "I thought I might find you here. I believe I have something you're looking for." And he put his hand in his pocket and held it out for everyone to see.

It was the stolen memo book.

There was a moment of sheer confusion as everyone in the room tried to figure out what was happening. Kate looked frantically at Nick, whose gaze swept back and forth from Avon to Mike Lahey with dawning comprehension and horror. Jared clutched Nina against him, and she buried her head against his chest. DeVoe suddenly tried to bolt out the front door, but was detained by Chief Lahey, who simply held out one massive arm and stopped him in his tracks.

"No, you don't," he said in a deep monotone. "You're not through here yet, friend."

"Friend?" Nick's voice was oddly subdued, but his eyes flashed blue fire as he regarded the chief. "Who's calling who friend, Mike?"

"It's just a manner of speaking," said Chief Lahey mildly, but he could not maintain his composure beneath the harsh glare of Nick's gaze. "Sorry, Nick," he muttered. "Sometimes things just don't turn out the way you plan, know what I mean?"

Nick's reply was hardly more than a growl, but Nina turned to him, confused. "But Nicky, I don't understand. I thought you said—"

"I said Chief Lahey had agreed to give us a hand," Nick replied, eyes still on the law officer. "Of course, I didn't think that the hand had already been greased by somebody else." He laughed mirthlessly. "I guess I should have known better... Seems to me now I remember hearing something down at the tavern about you taking bribes." His expression was so full of scorn that Lahey looked away uneasily. "I think I even defended you—boy, they must still be hooting over that one, huh, Mike?"

When Lahey did not answer, Nick turned to Dan Avon. "And as long as we're talking about two-faced scum, it appears Mr. Avon is a real pro."

"I wouldn't put it quite that way, Capstein," said Avon, coming into the room and stationing himself alongside the hearth, one arm resting easily along the mantel. It seemed to Kate that his entire manner had changed since she'd seen him last. Gone was the gruff veneer, the heavy, awkward manner. He was still a big man and he still wore the rugged, heavy clothes and thick lumberjack boots of a north-country "back-to-the-lander," but he was different somehow—at ease, definite in his movements and in command. And he seemed to be enjoying himself immensely. "I am a professional, though, and I do what has to be done—just like the chief, here."

"There's no such thing as a professional scum dealer," Nick sneered.

"Shut up!" Avon roared so loudly that they all jumped. He recovered himself quickly, though, and turned to DeVoe, who was staring at the book Avon held as if it were a living nightmare. "Sorry if I've startled you, Martin," Avon said amiably. "You were a little late for your meeting, so I decided to come to you."

"Look, Mr. Avon, I can explain...." Helplessly, he looked from the book he held to its twin in Avon's hand.

"Can you?" Avon smiled sweetly. "Can you explain the contents of this little book here? Or the one that Mr. Cooper was trying to pawn off on you, for that matter?"

DeVoe flashed Jared a hateful glance. "How'd you get this fake, Cooper? I ought to—"

"Oh, no, no, no," admonished Avon. "You're in no position to make threats, Martin. After all, I've got your real account book here, not the doctored version you've been showing me these past few months. Where or how Mr. Cooper got his fake is not important." The false heartiness disappeared from his voice, which became cold and hard. "You've got some serious talking to do."

"Somebody better do some talking," remarked Jared querulously, with the blind fearlessness of the self-absorbed. He turned to Avon. "What are *you* doing here?"

"Good question, don't you think, Martin? You want to explain it to Mr. Cooper, or shall I?" DeVoe looked far too miserable to speak. "Very well, I'll do the talking." Avon settled himself more comfortably against the mantel, although Kate could tell his powerful body was poised for attack at the slightest suspicious movement.

"As you may know, I had a very successful career in New York as a stockbroker. I also have a second career—equally successful, although not quite as well-known."

"You're a pusher," Nick snorted.

Avon's eyebrows drew together, but his voice remained level. "I prefer to think of myself as a supplier. A conduit, if you will. It was my job to see to it that the right goods got to the right place—although I never saw the stuff, much less touched it. Mr. DeVoe here was one of my trusted employees." He emphasized the last two words mockingly, and DeVoe seemed to shrink even further into himself.

"About six months ago I decided I'd had enough of the New York rat race—the stockbroker race, that is. I had already bought my land and house up here, and decided to move permanently. Of course, I had no intention of giving up my second career, since that was what had made it possible for me to retire in the first place. As a matter of fact, it seemed to be an even better headquarters from which to operate than Manhattan had been. I had a network of people with whom I was in constant contact, I was safely out of the public eye and I had some cooperative officials to make it even easier for me to conduct business." Mike Lahey had the grace to look extremely pained at this last remark. Avon glanced at him as if he were a fond possession, and Kate heard Nick curse softly to himself under his breath.

"But it seems that Martin here had some other plans. Obviously, once I absented myself from New York, it became a temptation for him to begin skimming a little of the profits off the top." He shrugged his heavy shoulders. "Now, I don't mind a little skimming. I even expect it. But Martin got a little greedy, didn't you, Martin?"

Martin opened his mouth to reply, but nothing came out. Avon didn't seem to notice, however—he was too caught up in his own narrative. "In fact, he became so greedy that he began keeping two sets of books. One to show me when we met every few months, and one to keep track of the real profits, which were considerably larger than I realized."

"Jared's book," Nick muttered.

"Exactly. The book that Mr. Cooper so foolishly lifted from Martin's desk—and then hid in *your* desk, which I happened to purchase at auction last week." He laughed. "Funny how fate plays these little tricks on you, isn't it? I suspected Martin, but I was never sure—until a few days ago, that is, when his doctored account literally fell into my hands. Thanks, of course, to the efforts of Mr. Capstein and his pretty little friend."

He turned to Kate, and she felt her insides lurch and ripple in fear. His eyes were small and black and piercing, and he regarded her impassively for nearly a full minute while she returned his gaze, not daring to breathe. "Too bad about you," he murmured at last. "I mean, I expected these jokers—" he indicated Nick, Nina and Jared with a dismissive wave "—to be involved in some kind of stupidity or other. The kind of lives they live invites trouble, and they'll get what they deserve. But not you. You just seemed so...so innocent—" he shook his head as if disappointed "—it's a shame you had to get involved in this mess, too."

Nick made a harsh sound of disgust. "Why, you despicable hypocrite! Who the hell do you think you are, passing judgment on everybody, when you're the slimiest thing to crawl out from under a rock in years?"

Avon tensed and straightened, and Nick shot up off the couch as if he'd been expecting this. "Come on, Danny boy. You want to show everybody what a big man you are?" He held up his hands, palms inward, and wriggled his fingers invitingly. "Come on. Come after me. Give me the pleasure of sending your ugly face through the floor."

Kate gasped, and Nina shrieked. It was insanity for Nick to be threatening Avon. Not only was Avon larger and heavier, but he clearly had the upper hand in this particular situation. Kate didn't doubt, however, that Nick would give him a run for his money, if it came to that. She just prayed that it *wouldn't* come to that.

Apparently Dan Avon felt the same way. He looked at Nick, poised in the center of the room, vibrating with anticipation. He laughed shortly. "Forget it, Capstein.

I'm not ready to deal with you just yet." His eyes, cold and deadly, flicked across the room to DeVoe. "I've got other, more important business to take care of first." He looked back at Nick, and his gaze narrowed angrily. "But if you'll just be patient, it'll give me pleasure to make you wish you'd never been born—you and your downtown party playmates."

DeVoe made a last, desperate attempt at pacification. "Look, Mr. Avon, I can explain everything if you'll just give me a chance."

Avon raised his eyebrows. "Can you?" He straightened up and took a few steps across the room, ignoring Nick beside him. "I'd be glad to listen, Martin."

It was excruciatingly clear to everyone, except perhaps DeVoe himself, that Avon was simply toying with him, like a beast of prey with a trapped victim. Kate felt a surge of revulsion and suddenly understood Nick's impulse to smash Avon and strike him down.

But DeVoe, dry-mouthed and feverish, didn't notice. Like a drowning man flailing about in panic and thus destroying himself, he began to dither. "I didn't mean for it to get like this, Dan, really I didn't. I just wanted... It seemed like you were getting plenty, and you know how expensive things can be in the city... and then you were so far away, and I hardly even heard from you... and things began to go wrong...I had expenses..."

As Avon advanced on DeVoe, Kate saw him reach into his jacket pocket and pull something out—something small and hard and very, very lethal. It glittered in the light of the fire. She knew that Nick saw it, too, and wondered now why he didn't move to stop the slaughter that was sure to come. But Nick seemed to be mesmerized by something else; he was staring at Avon's hand, but his head was cocked as if he were listening to something far away.

Kate closed her eyes and fought the urge to run. She knew her passage would be stopped by Lahey, who leaned laconically against the door with his arms crossed over his chest; and she understood that in any case nothing she did would stop Avon's inevitable attack. And after he was done with Martin DeVoe...

Suddenly everything seemed to happen at once. Kate opened her eyes and saw Avon pulling back to strike DeVoe across the face with the barrel of his gun. At the same time, she heard a commotion in the front hall. And she heard Nick, who had not turned around, bellow, "Get the cop! He took your instruments!"

Then all hell broke loose. Startled, Avon turned around, gun in hand, and received the full force of Nick's fist in his face. The thirty-two flew across the room and straight into the fireplace. From the doorway there was an awful roar, and four men in black leather jackets and long hair fell on Chief Lahey, who had not even had time to unhook his arms. Jared, in a burst of foresight, lunged forward and grabbed DeVoe before he could take advantage of the chaos to escape, and Nina, with a wild howl, jumped on Avon's back, making him an even better target for Nick's torrent of blows.

Kate scarcely knew what propelled her across the room or what had made her realize what needed to be done. But she did it just in time, reaching the chief's side just as he freed one hand to reach for his holster.

"Don't bother," she snapped, and was amazed at the way her quiet voice carried through the pandemonium. Everyone stopped what they were doing to look at her. She stood beside Lahey, her face puckered in a frown of concentration and her eyes trained fiercely on her hands as though willing them to be still. White-knuckled and trembling slightly, they were clasped together around the chief's revolver, which she held pointed at Dan Avon.

"Nobody move," she said into the shocked silence, and then, looking up at last, she stared at Nick. "I can't believe I just said that," she added.

Nick started to smile and pulled Nina, who seemed stunned, out of range of the pistol. "Couldn't have said it better myself, pardner," he drawled.

Beside her, Lahey made a move, but he was held in check by Avon, who hissed, "Don't, you idiot!" Then, more quietly, he added, "She'd use it."

Lahey subsided into the hands of the four Ravening Beasts, one of whom turned to Nick. "What's this all about, man?"

Nick shrugged. "It's a little hard to explain. I'm just glad you guys showed up when you did."

"This dude got our axes?" The musician gestured threateningly toward the chief.

Nick grimaced. "Actually, that was a bit of a lie. It was the only thing I could think of off the top of my head that was sure to get you guys into action, no questions asked."

"Oh, man, are you kidding?" All four Beasts backed away. "You mean we attacked a cop for no good reason?"

"Oh, there was a good reason all right." As he spoke, Nick grabbed Avon and shoved him onto the couch. "And he's not a cop." He grabbed Lahey and pushed him down next to Avon. DeVoe was already there, and the three men sat immobile under the steady influence of Kate's gun.

But the band members did not look convinced. "Hey, man," said one of them, "I don't know what you've got going on here, but we don't want any part of it. This is definitely not our style." He swallowed nervously. "We can't afford any trouble—know what I mean?"

Nick grinned disarmingly. "Yeah, yeah, I understand. Look, how about this? You guys clear out now, and I'll...I'll forget about your bill." He ignored Nina's protest with an impatient wave of the hand. "That be all right?"

The band leader thought a moment. "Bar bill, too?"

Nick sighed and nodded. "Bar bill, too. Now, why don't you make yourselves scarce for a while? We're about to call in the cops—the real cops, that is—and you might not want to wait around."

He was right. The Ravening Beasts backed out the door as swiftly as they had arrived, and in a moment Kate heard their van roar off into the night.

Nick turned to Nina. "Call the state police, Nin. I believe we can press some charges here—breaking and entering, assault and battery—enough to keep our friends out of trouble until we can get hold of some harder evidence."

"You'll never find that, Capstein," Avon sneered. "I'm too careful for that."

"Oh, yeah? Well, if I was you, I'd have been a little more careful about picking my associates, because I believe yours are about ready to do some real singing—in harmony."

They all looked at DeVoe, who gulped and nodded. Nick glared at Lahey.

"You can't prove anything about any of us," the chief pointed out sullenly.

"Actually," Nick said, "I can." He walked over to the bookcase and opened the door to reveal a tape deck sitting on one of the shelves. The reel was still spinning. "I planted this here on the off chance that Mr. DeVoe would recognize that our book was a forgery. I figured if we could record our conversation, we might have a little bargaining power in case he got nasty." He tapped the tape deck cheerily. "Of course, I never expected we'd find ourselves with a lifetime supply of *True Confessions*."

"Won't hold up in court," Avon muttered.

"No, but it'll make some people very curious about you, won't it, Avon? And you, too, Chief." He shook his head sadly. "Pity about your badge, isn't it, Mike?" Head bent in misery, Lahey didn't reply.

"My God, Nicky," breathed Nina, gazing at the three captives in fascination. "Do you realize these guys would have attacked us if those musician friends of yours hadn't come along?"

"They're not exactly my friends, but yes, I get your drift."

"How did you know they'd be coming?" Jared asked.

Nick shrugged. "I didn't. But I heard the van, although nobody else seemed to be paying much attention. And I figured it couldn't be anybody else at this ungodly hour. So I just thought of the one thing that would be guaranteed to raise the roof." He chuckled. "You tell four musicians that someone has taken their instruments, and they won't care if it's Attila the Hun— they'll attack first and ask questions later." He drew a deep breath. "But I gotta tell you, my heart was in my mouth for a minute there."

Nina grinned adoringly at her brother and shook her head. "Boy, talk about your lucky breaks..."

"Nick always seems to get lucky breaks," Jared pointed out truculently.

"As far as I'm concerned, there's only been one lucky break in my life," said Nick, putting both arms across Kate's shoulders and drawing her close. "And she's standing right here."

Nina frowned. "Nicky—"

"Call the police, Nina. I'm busy." He smiled into Kate's eyes, and she returned the loving look, even though she still held the gun trained carefully on the couch.

Nina left the room to call the police, and Jared moved around to survey the three men. "What are we going to do with these guys until the police get here, Nick?" he asked.

In reply, Nick took the gun out of Kate's grip, gently prying her fingers apart when she could not seem to do it herself. Then he put it into Jared's surprised grasp, closing his fingers over the handle with the same deliberate care. "I am going to leave them in your capable hands, Jared old buddy."

"Mine? But..."

"No buts," Nick said sternly. "You got us into this mess—it's the least you can do."

Jared looked at the gun, at Nick and at the three men. He seemed to deliberate for a few moments before squaring his shoulders and his jaw. "Okay," he said firmly. "I'll watch them. As a matter of fact, it'll be my pleasure." DeVoe and Lahey squirmed at the eagerness with which Jared trained the pistol on them, but Avon sat mute and still, apparently deep in thought.

"What are you going to do, Nick?" Jared asked over his shoulder.

Nick turned to Kate and tipped her face up to his before replying, "I'm going upstairs with Annie Oakley here," he said with a loving smile, "and let her know how much I love her. It's been a lot more than twenty minutes since I last told her. We're way overdue."

Chapter Twelve

The sun pounded mercilessly on the soft white sand, turning it into an opalescent swath that separated the green trees from the turquoise sea. But a crisp breeze animated the air, and it wasn't nearly as hot as it looked. The jacaranda leaves rustled brightly, showing their silver undersides against a jade backdrop, and the wind was scented orange. From where Kate sat on the shaded stone veranda, gazing out at the view, it looked more like a stage set than a real place. Nothing could be that beautiful, that perfectly arranged by nature's whimsy.

But then everything about Formentera was impossibly perfect, including the fact that she was there at all. The cerulean sky, the lush emerald countryside dotted with whitewashed villages and red tile roofs—it was hard to believe that Nick had not created this reality for her personal pleasure.

In a way, she thought, maybe he had. Certainly he was responsible for her being in this Eden, and responsible for the artist's dream of a vista that stretched before her now. It was a landscape begging to be painted, and that was what she was trying to do. She sat with a sketch pad on her knees, a brand-new box of expensive watercolors on a wrought-iron table by her side—another gift from Nick's magic bag of tricks....

"This is for you," Nick said the morning after their arrival on the little island off the coast of Spain. He seemed almost shy as he handed her the package. "I expect you to use it to become the next Van Gogh—or whoever you want to be." He smiled, causing his dimples to deepen and his eyes to crinkle deliciously. "The new Kate Palmer would be good enough for me."

"Oh, Nick! They're gorgeous!" Kate's eyes shone as she ran her fingers tenderly over the rainbow of colors, smooth and dry and begging to be used. He had included six sable brushes and a pad of extra-thick vellum drawing paper as well. "Brushes and everything—all exactly what I wanted!" She looked up at him and smiled beatifically. "How did you know?"

He twirled an imaginary mustache and spoke in a thick accent. "Ah, vee haf our sources, you zee."

"But supplies of this quality cost a great deal of money, Nick!"

He shrugged lightly. "We have our sources for that, too. Jared's finally begun to pay me back some of the company's money he 'borrowed' over the years, so I'm feeling rich. I was gonna buy you a mink, but—" his eyes twinkled "—somehow I saw you in Prussian blue and alizarin crimson instead."

Kate shook her head indulgently. "You're crazy, you know that?"

"Yep."

She put down the package and patted it. "You shouldn't have done this—" she kissed him "—but I'm glad you did."

"Why shouldn't I? It's what we came for, isn't it? For you to paint? Well, go ahead—paint away!" He stepped back and thrust his hands deep in the pockets of his white pants, as if he expected her to dive into the paint box then and there.

But although she looked longingly at the watercolors, Kate was reluctant to admit her eagerness. For one thing, she didn't want to do anything that would separate her from Nick, even for a little while. "What are you going to do while I paint, though?"

He smiled and chucked her under the chin. "I'll watch you," he replied. "And try to keep my hands off you."

"I'm not so sure I wouldn't enjoy that more," she murmured....

So, for a while, the paints had been forgotten. But eventually they had lured her; by the third day in the little villa that Nick had rented from the friend of a friend in New York, she was eager to explore the contents of the metal box.

And of course Nick, being Nick, was not able to just sit and watch. As soon as he saw her set up on the crumbly whitewashed veranda with her materials, he busied himself with a thousand and one tasks. He had already become friendly with several of the inhabitants of the minuscule village and had managed to find sources for everything from fresh poultry to the delicious red wine they consumed with every meal. Right now he was out swimming; by squinting her eyes beneath her wide-brimmed straw hat, Kate could just about make out his figure moving vigorously through the water. Beyond him, hazy in the distance, lay the larger island of Ibiza. And all around was the Mediterranean sea, an impossible shade of blue green that she had been trying all morning to capture on paper.

She looked down at her work, studying it critically. She did not have to look up again to see that she had gotten all the details of the landscape correctly. Details were not what she was aiming for—not now, anyway. She wanted to loosen up her style, to expand it to include sensation as well as reality. Already, signs of her new freedom were beginning to show. She was not exactly a free-form abstractionist yet, but there was definitely a more relaxed feeling to her work. In the painting she had just done, for instance, she had tried to blur the edges of the horizon so that the blues and greens melted together in a tantalizing mist of color. It was not quite what she wanted, but it was a pretty good start.

She closed her eyes for a moment and took a deep breath. Yes, that was what the horizon felt like: a misty blur of beauty that defied precision and delineation. She could see it shimmering in her mind's eye; now, if she could just get that shimmery quality on paper! She let her head fall back against the cushion of her chair and smiled at the beauty of her inner vision.

"You look like an angel," Nick said, dropping a generous kiss on her upturned lips.

Startled, she sat up. He was standing there, dripping wet, a towel thrown around his neck. His hair was slicked back, and his body was already bronzed after only a few days in the sun. She felt her loins shift with familiar desire.

"And you look like a Greek god," she said, reaching up and running her fingers down his bare chest.

"A Spanish god." He struck an exaggerated body-builder's pose. *"¿Yo soy un dios español, no?"*

Kate laughed and clapped her hands. "Oh, *sí, sí!*" she cried.

Nick bowed low. *"Muchas gracias, Señorita Palmer."* He perched on the edge of her chair. "Now, let's see what you've done this morning."

Kate showed him her work, leafing back through the pages to the first one, a charcoal study of the elderly Spanish woman who had come to the door to deliver fresh cheese and olives. Nick studied it with grave concentration, as he always did.

"It looks just like her," he commented approvingly. "You really captured the way she stands, all gnarled, but so strong. And this, this is a great view of the house. We should send this to Mike Gold—he'll love it."

"We should give him some kind of thank-you for renting us the villa," Kate agreed.

"Thank-you? Hah! I'm paying him an arm and a leg for this place, and he knows damn well it's off-season." He flicked through the rest of the sketchbook and stopped at the last page. "Hey, this is really good, Katie! I think you've got something very special here."

"Something good enough to sell, do you think?" She tried to keep her voice offhand.

"Sure!" He looked at her shrewdly. "You're not thinking of going into the picture-painting business, by any chance, are you?"

Kate shrugged. "Well, I was thinking that when we got back I might try going to a few of the galleries with the stuff I do here. Not that it'll lead to anything, but..."

"Of course it'll lead to something! You just have to believe that it will. You're good, Kate, very good." He was really excited.

Kate pressed her fingertips against her mouth and looked critically at her work. "Maybe," she murmured. "Not yet, but maybe..."

Nick knelt down impulsively. "Kate. I think you should quit."

"What?"

"Quit Simmond's. Tell them you're never coming back. Quit and start painting on your own full-time."

Her eyes opened very wide. "Just like that?"

Nick waved his arms impatiently. "Hell, yes, just like that! What other way is there to do it?" He leaned forward and put his hands on her bare, slightly sunburned knees. "Look, Katie. You've got talent. You've got connections. You've got the time, if you'll only give it to yourself. Why, you've even got me!"

She laughed, but he shook his head. "No, I'm serious. What else have we learned from each other over the past few months except that we have to do what's right, when it's right? We have to seize the moment, make the most of it, live up to our dreams, don't we? What else can we really count on—besides each other?"

She leaned forward and kissed him gently on the tip of his nose. "And what about you, Nick?" she asked softly, evading the question. "What are you going to do with your new life?"

Nick sat back on his heels and gazed thoughtfully out to sea. "I'm not sure yet," he mused. "Not that I haven't thought about it, but I just haven't made up my mind."

He glanced up at her and grinned crookedly. "I've convinced Jared that we'd both be better off if we dissolved our production company—not that it'll take much to do that now that Jared's business shenanigans are a matter of public record."

"He won't be prosecuted, will he?"

"You mean for dealing with Martin DeVoe?" Nick squinted off into the light. "No, I think he'll probably get off with a slap on the wrist and a reminder never to do it again." He laughed. "Which I don't think Jared'll need, after what happened up at the inn."

Kate shuddered at the memory. "I certainly wouldn't."

"Me either." They were silent for a moment, recalling the terror of that night. Both knew how lucky they had been, but neither wanted to test their luck that way ever again. "Anyway," Nick resumed after a pause, "we've dissolved the business, and Jared's on his way to returning my share of the investment—which didn't really amount to much. But at least I'm on my own now. Fortunately, I've been doing some investing with Mike Gold all along, so I'm not worried about cash for the time being. And Jared's already got plans to go into the video business with Nina, so I know they're all set."

"But what will you do?" Kate pressed gently. She knew the question had been on his mind for several days, or she never would have asked. "Something else in the music business?"

He hesitated thoughtfully. "I'm not so sure I really want to stay in music at all. I've done a lot of thinking about why I wanted out with Jared, and I realized it wasn't so much that particular business as the way of life in general. I mean, all that pushing and shoving and hustling for position...all that time wasted..." He shook his head and took a deep breath. "No, it's not for me. Not anymore, anyway."

Kate was not altogether surprised to hear this. Nick had been hinting at a change ever since he first told her about his life. "You'll find something else," she said. "I have faith in you."

He took her hand and dropped a kiss on the palm. "I know you do. Thank God, you do." He kissed her several more times and then looked up. "Listen, Kate," he said suddenly, "I've been thinking. What would you say to coming back up to Putnam Falls with me? You could paint, and I would run the inn. It wouldn't be forever— just until I got some money together from my investments and decided what I really wanted to do with the rest of my life." He squeezed her hand. "Besides spend it with you, I mean."

"Is that why you want me to quit my job?" she asked carefully.

"Well, yes. I mean, I think you should anyway, on general principles. You've outgrown them, and you know it. It's high time you went out on your own. But I have to admit to a selfish motive. Or partly selfish, at least. I think it would be a good experience for both of us. I mean this. . . ." He indicated the breathtaking view with a sweep of his arm. "This is heaven, but it's not the real world. If we ran the inn for a little while, that would give us time to decompress." He wriggled his brows impishly. "It would give you a chance to decide if you really did want to spend the rest of your life with a wacko like me."

Kate made an effort to resist a smile. "And if I didn't want to go up there with a wacko like you?"

He shrugged. "I wouldn't go, of course. I'd just make my decision sooner and get busy in Nueva York, I suppose. Mike's been begging me to go in with him on a few schemes, and a couple of other people I know have asked me to join their businesses. Of course, I could always start something of my own, but—" he stopped and gestured eloquently with one hand "—to tell you the truth, Katie, I've got a lot of options, but nothing's really beckoning to me, you know what I mean? That's why the idea of going back to the inn for a few months appeals to me. It'll give me time to whittle down my choices, decide which is the best." He cocked his head to one side meditatively. "You know, this is the first time in my life I'm not rushing into some scheme head over teakettle. And I think it's important that I go slow. I'm not like you, with all my talents telescoped into one clear vision, all neat and clean. I seem to be...all over the place."

Kate started to protest, but he stopped her. "No, no. I know I've got something—I'm just not sure what it is yet, and I don't want to risk making the same mistakes again by doing something I don't really love to do." He smiled ruefully. "The only thing I'm really sure about is you, sweet Kate. Thank God for you." He reached up and stroked her cheek. "If you want to stay in New York, then New York it is. As long as we're together, I won't mind."

Still smiling at him, Kate fumbled in her sheaf of papers and produced a page of onionskin. "Read this," she instructed him, holding it out.

"What is it?"

"Read it. It's a copy of a letter I wrote the day after we got here."

"'Dear Sirs,'" Nick read. "'I am writing to advise you of my resignation from Simmond's art department, effective thirty days from today. Personal and professional commitments require that I leave the city, and I do not expect to return in the foreseeable future. Should you be interested in my services on a free-lance basis, I'd be happy to discuss such an arrangement on my return. Yours, Katherine Palmer.'" He looked from Kate to the letter and back again. "Why, you devil!" he said at last, shaking the thin page in her face. "You've known all along what we were going to do, haven't you?"

Kate shrugged. "It seemed the only thing that made sense for both of us. I don't want to be in New York any more than you." She patted her drawing pad. "At least, not until I'm ready for it."

Nick was shaking his head. "And you let me rave on and on like some disgruntled college kid, while you already had the whole thing figured out, didn't you?"

"That's about the size of it. Simmond's already wrote back telling me they'd love to have me work on a freelance basis. They even have someone in their accounting department who's dying to sublet my apartment for as long as she can get it."

Nick got up on his knees and put both hands on the arms of Kate's chair. "And what did you tell her, O Wise Sorceress?"

She grinned. "I told her she could have it for as long as it takes."

Nick ducked his head onto her lap, kissing her hands as they lay on top of her sketch pad. "And how long will that be, Divine One?"

"Oh, I don't know," Kate replied, thrusting her fingers into his thick hair. "Maybe forever."

Humming a song that she couldn't identify at first, Nick took the sketch pad out of her lap and laid it on the floor beside him. Then he reached up and began unbuttoning the front of Kate's sundress. He opened the lapels to reveal her breasts and kissed them both tenderly. The nipples thrust out into the sun, which shed its warmth over them like melted butter. Suddenly she recognized the song Nick was humming—"The Wedding Waltz," a schmaltzy tune she never thought she'd love so much.

Kate lay back in her chair and sighed deliciously. Nick's lips and hands worked busily to whip her sun-drenched body into a hot froth of desire. He did not stop humming, although his tempo was growing erratic, as was her breathing. She'd thought she would eventually grow accustomed to the feeling of instant arousal his touch engendered, but each time was so different that she was constantly caught unawares. Now, as his lips moved lower and deeper, she tried to protest, but her voice was already weak with desire.

"Nick, no, not right out here!"

"Why not?" His voice was muffled between her silky thighs.

"People could . . . they can see us . . . oh . . ."

"Who cares if they see? What's wrong with two people in love and showing it?" Nick stood up at last, his eyes shining and deep with desire. Without taking them off her face, he slipped out of his trunks. Then he held out his hand. "Come," he murmured. "Don't be afraid."

"I'm not afraid," she said, rising and letting her dress slip down around her ankles. Her knees were weak, but she didn't want to step into his arms just yet. Nick's nudity, bronzed by the sunlight, was so beautiful that she wanted to cry. Instead, she laughed softly. "I just think there has to be a middle ground between prudery and exhibitionism."

"There is," he said, reaching out to stroke her flanks as she stood before him. "We'll just have to look for it some other time."

It didn't take much to be convinced. With a soft little moan, Kate stepped forward and let him sweep her into his arms and down onto the thick chaise longue on the other side of the veranda. The sun was hot here, but she didn't care—her body had already been stoked to the melting point by Nick's caresses.

As they moved together on the cotton matting, their bodies welded in perfect unison, Kate abandoned all thoughts of a middle ground. Their life together stretched before them like the Mediterranean—a rainbow mist with the horizon blurred by possibilities. There would be plenty of time to get used to the realities of being Kate and Nick together. Right now, to dance at the end of the universe in Nick's arms was all she wanted. He was right: there would be time to find the middle ground later.

* * * * *

Silhouette Special Edition

COMING NEXT MONTH

#403 SANTIAGO HEAT—Linda Shaw
When Deidre Miles crash-landed in steamy Santiago, powerful Francis MacIntire saved her from the clutches of a treacherous military. But what could save her from Francis himself, his tumultuous life and flaming desire?

#404 SOMETIMES A MIRACLE—Jennifer West
Bodyguard Cassandra Burke wistfully dreamed of shining knights on white chargers. Cynical ex-rodeo star Alex Montana had long since turned in his steed. As they braved murder and mayhem together, just who would protect whom?

#405 CONQUER THE MEMORIES—Sandra Dewar
For social worker Carla Foster it was time to face the music. In an adoption dispute, Drake Lanning recognized her for the singer she used to be, and he vowed to learn why she hid her talent . . . and her heart.

#406 INTO THE SUNSET—Jessica Barkley
Lindsay Jordan wasn't just another city slicker playing cowgirl, no matter what ornery stable manager Nick Leighton said. And despite his sensual persuasion, she wasn't greenhorn enough to think of riding off into the sunset with him!

#407 LONELY AT THE TOP—Bevlyn Marshall
Corporate climber Keely LaRoux wasn't about to let maverick photographer Chuck Dickens impede her progress up the ladder. But traveling together on assignment, the unlikely pair found that business could fast become a dangerously addictive pleasure.

#408 A FAMILY OF TWO—Jude O'Neill
Hotshot producer Gable McCrea wanted newcomer Annabel Porter to direct his latest movie. But what inner demons prompted him to sabotage her work . . . and her growing love for him?

AVAILABLE THIS MONTH:

ATTRACTIVE, SPACE SAVING BOOK RACK

Display your most prized novels on this handsome and sturdy book rack. The hand-rubbed walnut finish will blend into your library decor with quiet elegance, providing a practical organizer for your favorite hard-or soft-covered books.

Only $9.95

Approximately 16" x 8" when assembled

Assembles in seconds!

To order, rush your name, address and zip code, along with a check or money order for $10.70* ($9.95 plus 75¢ postage and handling) payable to *Silhouette Books.*

Silhouette Books
Book Rack Offer
901 Fuhrmann Blvd.
P.O. Box 1396
Buffalo, NY 14269-1396

Offer not available in Canada.

BKR-2A

*New York and Iowa residents add appropriate sales tax.

**Available
August 1987**

ONE TOUGH HOMBRE

Visit with characters introduced
in the acclaimed Desire trilogy
by Joan Hohl!

The *Hombre* is back!
J. B. Barnet—first introduced in *Texas Gold*—
has returned and make no mistake,
J.B. *is* one tough hombre... but
Nicole Vanzant finds the gentle,
tender side of the former
Texas Ranger.

Don't miss *One Tough Hombre*—
J.B. and Nicole's story.
And coming soon from Desire is
Falcon's Flight—the story of Flint Falcon
and Leslie Fairfield.

D372–1R